BRIXTON HILL

Lottie Moggach

corsair

CORSAIR

First published in the UK in 2020 by Corsair
This paperback edition published in 2021

1 3 5 7 9 10 8 6 4 2

A CIP catalogue record for this book
is available from the British Library.

ISBN: 978-1-4721-5538-2

Printed and bound in Great Britain by Clays Ltd, Elcograf S.p.A.

Papers used by Corsair are from well-managed forests
and other responsible sources.

Corsair
An imprint of
Little, Brown Book Group
Carmelite House
50 Victoria Embankment
London EC4Y 0DZ

An Hachette UK Company
www.hachette.co.uk

www.littlebrown.co.uk

Lottie ⸺⸺⸺⸺⸺⸺⸺ ⸺ich was
shortlis⸺⸺⸺⸺⸺⸺⸺⸺⸺⸺⸺, won the
Portsmou⸺ First Fiction award, and is published in seventeen
countries. It was also adapted into a six-part Channel 4 series.
Her second novel is *Under the Sun*. She lives in London with
her partner and son.

Also by Lottie Moggach

Kiss Me First
Under The Sun

For Kit, again.

1

Rob

The first time a high-risk prisoner is allowed out on day release, they're escorted by a plainclothes officer, to make sure they remember the rules of the road and don't punch the first person who crosses their path. My screw, Hasan, was unusually cheerful; I think he was more pleased than I was to escape prison for a morning stroll. As we emerged from the gate and started down the hill, me stumbling on the uneven pavement after seven years of smooth floors, he told me that Brixton Hill is part of an old Roman road, a straight run into London. Like a tour guide, he pointed out the city in the distance, and I squinted at a huddle of skyscrapers, pooled together in a gap between the nearer buildings. Some of their shapes I recognised from before, some were new to me. When the sun hit them they sparkled, like a Disneyland logo.

That was two weeks ago. Now I'm out on my own, I keep my head down. I've got used to being outside, but it's still more comfortable to focus on the near distance. The walk to work takes sixteen minutes door to door, but I think of it in stages. Two minutes to the posh café, where young men with beards and women in shapeless tops sit under bare lightbulbs, silver laptop screens in front of them like menus. Three to the secondhand furniture place, which is more of a junkyard, with baggy leather sofas and cheap filing cabinets colonising the pavement like the contents of a minicab office has been fly-tipped overnight. This bloke, I presume the owner, is usually planted on one of the sofas with a fag and a cuppa, looking dodgy as hell, giving people the eye as they pass.

Another two minutes to the Londis. If there's a dog tied up outside, I dart over to offer it my hand. Then it's the Job Centre, where by 8.50 a.m. people are already hanging around outside, scrolling through their phones, looking simultaneously agitated and defeated.

At the bottom of the hill, there's traffic lights and then, opposite, a huge KFC. At that point, everyone else crosses the street and disappears into the entrance to the tube. But not me. My place is just a few doors down, on the high street.

This morning, when I start off on my journey down the hill, it really feels like spring finally. For the past fortnight the sky has been white and featureless, but now it's as if that blankness was shielding preparations for the grand production, and the curtain has just been lifted. The sky is the blue of the current Arsenal away kit, and clean; not even a plane trail. Right now, before the day has properly got going, it feels like the season is winning out over the city, the air so fiercely fresh it overpowers the traffic fumes. If I closed my eyes and ears I could almost be walking through a field rather than beside an inner-city A road. The pavement has been swept overnight and is as clean as it'll ever be, the day's crisp packets and chicken boxes yet to settle. Passing by a horse chestnut, I hear the *chink-chink-chink* of blackbirds shielded by its leaves, and I think of the Reader's Digest *Book of British Birds* on my shelf in the cell, and how soon I'll be able to go birding for real, out on a marsh or a beach or a forest. Or maybe I won't care less about birds once I'm out. Who knows?

Around me, people continue streaming down the hill to work, more joining the throng from residential side roads. There's barely anyone walking up – the pavement might as well be one way. Most briskly overtake me. During my first few times out I couldn't bring myself to look properly at the women; it was too much. I can manage it now. Because they're moving past, I don't always get a good look at their faces but that doesn't matter. Without their coats on, in these flimsy, bright clothes, they feel oddly intimate, as if instead of being strangers on a big, busy road, they've just stepped out of their bedrooms, as fresh as the day. I clock bra straps on bare shoulders; knicker lines under skirts; hair still damp from the shower. Wafts of shampoo, deodorant and perfume in sweet feminine scents: almond, mint, strawberry. Music leaks from headphones; I catch snatches of conversation from phone calls. 'Yeah, I know I said that but . . .' 'I miss you too, for god's sake . . .' 'Why don't we speak after work and see how we feel . . .'

And I'm not just clocking the conventionally attractive women. It's not only about sex. Young, middle-aged, big, tiny, black, white, brown – they all look great to me. In my glances I notice details about each of them, the little things they probably see as flaws and would be embarrassed if they knew I'd noticed, but to me are marks of their gorgeous realness. The little red spots on their upper arms; the tough skin on their heels; chipped nail varnish; strands of grey hair; bumps of acne; bulges under tight vests. As I walk amongst them I

3

notice everything, sensitive to the beauty and uniqueness in all of them.

There are men too, of course, but I don't pay attention to them. Right now, I'm in the midst of a female army on the march, and I think how good it is to be alive in a world full of women, in all their glorious and varied forms.

As I pass the furniture place, one weaves in front of me. She has blonde hair, curled carefully at the ends so it sits springy on her shoulders. A red, fitted, short-sleeved dress – I notice the zip hasn't been pulled right up to the top. Thin, very tanned arms and legs. She's walking expertly on high heels. A smart professional woman, heading for an office somewhere in that glowing city.

Then, suddenly, this faceless woman lurches to one side and drops to the pavement in front of me.

I stop. I have to – she's right there, in my path, on her knees. Her handbag is on the ground, surrounded by its contents. An orange wallet, make-up, a phone. A set of keys.

Everyone's streaming around her, as if she was a fallen horse at the races. I should probably say something.

'You all right?'

She glances up and gives an embarrassed smile as she shovels her stuff back into her bag. Then she does something I'm not expecting – holds out her arm for me to help her up. I stare at her hand, at her pale, glossy nails and the gold watch on her wrist, and then take it, but it's so small and tender it slips from my grasp. I grab again, tighter, and pull her to her feet, but misjudge the force and yank her too hard. She cries, 'Whoooah!' and almost topples over. I release her and then stuff my hands back into my pockets, my fingers squeezed tight, as if trying to hold onto the sensation of that little hand.

As she straightens up I glimpse a narrow, pretty face. Not mother old, but not girlfriend young. Early forties, maybe. Then my gaze is drawn to the top of her dress, which has a slit down the front. It's not actually revealing at all, but there's something about that slit that does it for me. Carol, who does the weather on BBC Breakfast, wears these sorts of dresses a lot. This woman is slighter than Carol but still, it works. What I thought were bare legs are actually very thin tights; there's a ladder down her left leg, which she's now examining.

'Sorry,' she says, head down. 'I'm an idiot.'

I can't quite place the accent – south London or north Essex. Then she looks up and meets my gaze properly for the first time, and I'm taken aback, because her eyes are a knockout – bright, golden brown. A colour I associate with wolves, not humans. Her brows are thick and straight and sit unusually low, giving a strength to her face that cuts against the dollishness of the rest of her, and transforms her from attractive into something more rare.

'S'OK,' I say, and then I hear myself say, 'I like your dress.'

But she doesn't seem to hear me, because she's looking down at her phone and frowning.

'Shit.'

She turns it so I can see the smashed screen. It's an old iPhone 4. There's a photo of someone on there, but I can't make out their face behind the web of cracks; it could be a man or woman, adult or child.

'Can I use your phone quickly?' she says. 'I've got to look up an address.'

I'm about to say I don't have one when I see she's clocked the phone in my hand. I've been using it to check the time. I open my fingers to fully reveal it.

5

'It's not a smartphone,' I say.

'Very retro,' she says, peering at it. 'I've been meaning to get one of those. Waste far too much time on mine.'

I can't think what to say to that, and seeing the phone's display serves to snap me out of this weird moment. People are still marching past us, and now they're like sand pouring through an egg timer, reminding me that I'm going to be late. I nod goodbye to the woman and then peg it down the hill, swerving through the crowd, past the Job Centre queue, across the road, not waiting for the lights. The KFC doors are open and as I pass I slow down for a moment, to get a lungful of those fierce aromas, before speeding up again.

I make it to the shop on the dot of nine but of course Carl is standing outside with his lunchbox, as if I've been keeping him waiting. There's absolutely no need for him to wait for me outside, but I guess he wants to remind me that I'm not a proper employee. More an unwanted guest. After a reproachful 'Good morning,' he unlocks the door and escorts me across the shop floor, as if it's Tiffany's. The stockroom at the back, that's my domain – amongst the piles of rubbish not fit to be put out front at a charity shop.

When I was given the job I thought I might be sorting out the donations but apparently that's too important a task for me. Only Carl gets to decide what's worth selling. When people drop off things he acts like he's doing them a favour in accepting them, but as soon as they're out the door he's protecting them like they're a job lot of winning scratchcards. He often goes home with bags himself – I suspect he creams off the good stuff and takes it home to sell on eBay.

Today, like most days, my task is packaging up the rejected

items to give to the recycling guy. There's a lot of it; I'd say at least eighty per cent of the donations are worthless. Broken china ornaments; books that have clearly been dropped in the bath; empty DVD boxes; ancient cassettes with their tape hanging out; still-full hot water bottles; plastic toys encrusted with a baby's years-old dinner. Stained sheets. It's out of order – these people must know their stuff isn't sellable and are just using the shop as an alternative to the dump. They don't think about the consequences of their actions – that someone's going to have to sort through all their shit, and then someone else is going to have to dispose of it.

Some, of course, are OK. The ones who linger as they hand over the bags, saying 'There's some nice things in there', or 'Paid a lot for that', or tell the story of their father dying and having to clear out his house, fondly describing the collection of novelty salt and pepper shakers he built up over fifty years, only to be met by Carl's expressionless features. It must be hard getting your head around the fact that your beloved childhood toy, or a pair of trousers you saved up for, is now worthless, and you're lucky if a grumpy old geezer in a purple jumper will deign to take them off your hands.

Then there's another category of stuff, that hasn't been loved and looked after, and has little value, but which sparks a memory or feeling in me. I had it last week with an old *Beano* annual, because I used to get one in my stocking each year – right up to adulthood, actually. A 2008 calendar of Border collies; twelve photos to remind me of Badger. A beret, like the one my mother wore for a while, until someone told her they were in fashion and she threw it away. A paperback of the book *Bulldog Drummond*, which always used to be on the bedside table in the guest room at my grandparents' place.

An empty Fortnum & Mason's shortbread tin. A filthy white Michael Kors handbag, which when new would have been similar to the one I bought Tania for her nineteenth birthday.

Mondays here are always quiet. Sami, the most regular volunteer, doesn't come in today, so it's just me and Carl. When he's not at the till, Carl tends to station himself in the doorway of the stock room, impeding the view from my domain out onto the shop floor. The door buzzes occasionally throughout the morning and when Carl moves away to the till, I peer out. The customers can broadly be divided into those who genuinely need to shop here, who couldn't afford new – probably some of the same people waiting for the Job Centre to open – and the lonely, mostly elderly ones. For the second group the shop is just part of their circuit, by which they while away their days, to have contact with someone. A fair few of them are mentally ill; I can spot them the moment they walk in. Some make it blindingly obvious – one guy comes in most days, cackling, and pretends to twist off Carl's nose, like Carl is his five-year-old nephew or something. In fairness to Carl, he's quite tolerant of the crazy ones. He reserves his disdain for the sentimental donators – and for me.

When I first started here I tried to make conversation with Carl. Admittedly, my attempts were pretty lame – for instance, I noticed his eyes were streaming and there was a packet of hay fever tablets beside the till, and so I made a comment about how bad the pollen was this time of year – but they were harmless. But he just looked at me as if I'd pissed on his shoe. So now I've given up. He's just the shop manager, so I guess it wasn't his idea for the charity to provide opportunities for offenders, and he doesn't think it's a very good one.

The closest I get to the customers is when someone tries something on in the changing room, which is a curtained-off area just inside the stock room. I can't see them, but I can hear them. If I wanted to, I could reach through the curtain and touch them. Around midday, a woman goes in and I hear her say, 'Jesus, why do these places smell so rank?' At first I think she's addressing me, but she can't have known I was there. Although I'm sitting on a pile of bin bags just a couple of metres away behind that flimsy blue cloth, I'm completely silent and still. She must be talking to herself. I consider replying, telling her the answer – that the donations aren't washed before going up on display. A spray of Febreze and maybe an iron if they're really crumpled; that's it. So that funky smell is a stew of unwashed fabric, dead skin cells, secretions, fag smoke, dusty old cupboards, sweaty plastic bags, ancient dry-cleaning by-products, the traces of dogs, cats, mice – with a dab of odour eliminator to take the edge off.

On my first day here Sami, the volunteer, told me that the smell sorts out the wheat from the chaff. People are put off coming to just browse; only serious bargain hunters are prepared to bypass the odour. She apologised to me about it. But I don't mind it, I'm used to the funk of people. Although, of course, the smell inside is more alive – and also less varied, its source being hundreds of men with a similar washing schedule, using products from the same limited canteen list.

As I bundle up the rags, I wonder what the woman from the hill is doing now. She was clearly a professional of some sort, so I imagine her at a desk, peering at a spreadsheet. She'll have told her colleagues about her fall this morning. Showed them her smashed phone, her ripped tights. Or maybe she bought a new pair of tights on her way to work and changed into them in the toilet. I wonder if she's mentioned me. But why would she? Then I imagine a male colleague leaning heavily against her desk, trying to join in the conversation, asking if she wants to grab some lunch, and her looking up him with those wolf eyes under that lovely low brow, mouth moving as she makes her excuses.

As I'm folding a jacket, I feel something hard in the lining and carefully ease it out. An actual, current pound coin. What luck! I roll it around in my fingers for a bit, tracing its edges, like it's a foreign object, before looking around for a good hiding place. I end up sliding it under a pile of dusty old *Auto Trader*s on a shelf that have clearly not been disturbed for some time.

At 1 p.m., Carl puts his head in and announces I can 'have ten minutes'. The mandatory lunch breaks are half an hour, he knows that and I know that, but I just smile and thank him, while thinking *fuck you*. He hands me a plastic bag. The shop – meaning Carl – provides lunch for me; always cheese sandwiches. He must make them days in advance, as the cheddar under the bread is three shades lighter than the stuff at the edges, pale and clammy as a corpse. They're as bad as the ones we get inside.

When I first started here, I felt I should go outside at lunchtime, but I soon stopped that. The high street is too hectic – within a minute of stepping onto the pavement my head feels as if it's in a tightening clamp. I can deal with the crowds in the morning on the hill, when people are moving one way, on one mission, but down here at lunchtime they're milling about like drunken ants. People thrusting clipboards and magazines at me; beggars grabbing my ankles; junkies shrieking in my face; office workers shouldering past with their gym kits; horns and sirens; mad men bellowing about God outside the tube; clouds of vape smoke. And the shops are full of things I can't buy. So now I prefer to just skulk back here, in my hole.

The afternoon drags, as afternoons do. Eventually, it's home time. I find I move faster going up the hill than down, now outpacing the workers as they trudge home, loaded with Sainsbury's bags, hair and clothes rumpled, plugged into their earphones. There's a dog tied up outside Londis, a sweet black terrier. I go over to say hello but it freezes in alarm, so I move on. As I pass by the spot where the woman fell down, I think again of that surprising slender hand in mine.

I arrive back at the gate with two minutes to spare. Bates is on reception. Wilko clocks in just after me and gives me a happy nudge in the ribs. Bates hardly ever searches; he's too lazy. Today, he barely looks up from his *Mirror* as he nods us through. It doesn't make any difference to me if I'm searched, but it's good news for Wilko, who's usually carrying something. Today, as most days, his face looks mottled, and his pupils are dilated and shining. His official job is working in his cousin's wholesale company but really he spends his days snorting coke and taking topless selfies for his Instagram and Tinder profiles. He claims he's getting a sponsorship deal from some energy drink manufacturer.

After handing my phone in to reception, I'm taken back upstairs. As I push open the door, Deller is crouched over the kettle, but he jumps up as I step inside, far more responsive than that dog outside Londis. The cell reeks of onion powder.

'Mate, I'm making you a curry,' he says, 'and in return I want to hear every last detail of your most delectable customers. That lithe little hippy chick with unshaven armpits and incense fumes in her hair, bending over to rifle through the remainders bin . . .'

Deller has these elaborate fantasies, which still make me laugh, however many times I hear variations of them.

'. . . moistening her finger to turn the pages of a stained old cookery book, digging her hand into her tight jeans pocket to search for her loose change . . .'

'Mate, I told you, I don't see anyone,' I say, as I do every time, in my role as the straight man. 'I'm stuck in the back room, with the warped shoes and stained duvets.'

'Oh, pull your neck out.'

Deller is disappointed in me because I haven't scored in the whole two weeks I've been at the shop. This is his second stint inside – he did two years for dealing a decade ago – and so he's been through the whole day-release process, and I've heard extensively about the action he had. That he had a pint within half an hour of leaving the prison building, and a shag within the day. As I've pointed out several times, that attitude might be a clue as to why he's now back in here again, watching *Bargain Hunt*, many years away from the outside world.

'You'd clean up,' he says. 'You look dench. You're clever and funny – sometimes. And you don't even have to lie about what you're in for.'

The perceived wisdom is that, amongst the women who accept advances from cons, convictions involving drugs, fraud, armed robbery and manslaughter are OK. GBH and burglary don't go down so well.

'Maybe you should use the website,' he adds. 'Or just go on Tinder like everyone else. Jesus, if that had been around . . .'

'*Mate* . . .'

'But you don't have tech, so that's tricky,' he continues, as if musing to himself. 'I can ask Joe for the name of the brass house. The one on the hill. Remember, prisoners get a discount, because we're so quick.'

'Stop it!'

He's saying all this with a tone of genuine concern for my welfare. Even if he could get out, Deller wouldn't need to use a website or a brass. Outside, in his dealing days, he was rougher looking, puffy-faced and sweaty-haired, but he still had amazing girlfriends. I've seen pictures. Now, a year inside has stripped the excess off him, and he's buff and bright-eyed. His wife was on a reality show and is a legend of the visit hall. Even the screws talk about her with reverence. I've never seen her in the flesh, but Deller's got photos of her up on the wall, including a tabloid photo snapped outside the prison visitor centre on her way in for a visit.

Deller swears loyalty to her, but that doesn't stop others from writing to him; these mooney south London girls who loved him when he was the big guy outside, spending a grand a month on trainers, and love him now. It's his birthday tomorrow and he's got twelve envelopes propped up on the windowsill.

It's the same in here: even the toughest female screws aren't immune to his charm. They go all girlish around him, try and amuse him; he's always the first to hear the gossip. One got a warning for being too friendly and offering to bring him in her DVDs of *Breaking Bad*.

13

'Yeah, maybe you don't need to,' says Deller now, as he carefully ladles curry from the kettle into our mugs. 'Now you're so close to the end. Just wait for release. When you've gone without for seven years, what's an extra few months, eh?'

I accept my mug from him and start eating.

'This is your best yet,' I say.

'July fourteenth, isn't it?' he says, between mouthfuls. 'Your release?'

I nod. 'Yeah.'

'It's good at the end, isn't it?' he says, meeting my eye.

I return his smile. He's right. Moreover, it's a kind of good that's hard to explain to anyone else who hasn't been there; who hasn't experienced the realisation that the moment your whole existence has been pinned to, which you've obsessed over and fantasised about, which feels like it'll never actually happen, is finally within sight. It reminds me of taking E, and only wanting to communicate with someone else on it, who understood exactly what I was experiencing. The closest I can get to it is the image of a liner docked at a port, being prepared for sail. The porters are scurrying on with their bags, crowds lining up to wave it off, the foghorns going. Maybe it's something like how women feel when they're counting down to giving birth, waiting for this scheduled life-changing moment.

As we eat, Deller tells me the stories he heard today. Some newcomer on the B Cat wing is causing trouble. Somehow the guy had got the idea that he'd be allowed to go home between conviction and sentencing, to get his stuff together. Instead he was sent down straight after the verdict, still wearing the smart brogues he wore in court. They're the only shoes he has, and every time he walks down the wing with his

14

hard soles, the inmates think it's an officer and flush their gear down the toilet. So now he's been threatened with a beating if he doesn't stop wearing them. Also, some white-collar fraudster down the landing called Mark Ford is delighted, as a guy with the same name has just won *Celebrity Big Brother*; this will push the fraudster right down the Google search results for the name.

After doing the washing up, I climb up onto my bunk and open *A Suitable Boy* but don't start reading.

'Actually, there was this one woman,' I say, after a moment. 'She talked to me. On the street.'

'Mate!' He jumps up so his face is level with mine. 'There you go. You should have nailed it. You know where you go, right? Behind the Londis. There's a car park, no CCTV.'

'I don't have time. I can't be late. And anyway, she wasn't the sort.'

'What was she like?'

'Nice. Smart. Older. Old enough to know better.'

'No such thing,' he says, and then he's off again, telling me when, before he got into dealing and was working on a building site, he shagged a posh single mother who lived next door to the house he was doing up. 'So I've got a bag of cement on my shoulder, pretending I'm not dying under the weight of it, and she opens the door to put the rubbish out, just in her pyjamas. These cosy pink ones. I used to be a right shy one, but when you haven't had any for six months, you find some inner strength, you know? So I say . . .'

I've heard this story before but I let him continue. Deller should annoy me far more than he does. Other people in here repeat themselves because their brains are mush or they don't care whether they've told you before. But with Deller

15

it comes from a sort of guileless enthusiasm. His stories are generally true, too: he's not a blagger. He's not like the scumbags who wallpaper their pads with porn and coerce their girlfriends to play with themselves on FaceTime for the delectation of their mates. And although he's sex mad, there's a respect there. It's like him and women are a mutual appreciation society.

Basically, Deller just acts like I imagine he was on the outside: easy-going and quick to laugh, animated, interested in everything. Also, he doesn't moan about how he was fitted up or only pleaded guilty to save his missus, or whatever. You'd think he was in a Soho bar on a Thursday night rather than at the start of a ten stretch. His attitude is: it was fun while it lasted, and now he's paying the bill.

For sure, there's a slightly crooked streak to him; you can see what got him in here. He likes to game the system; he'll watch it closely and see what he can exploit in order to make life more comfortable for himself. A case in point: he's somehow managed to get into this cell with me on the D Cat wing, when he's actually a C Cat prisoner. But there's a sort of honour to his machinations – it's at the system's expense, not anyone else's.

Basically, he's a pretty decent guy, and those are as rare as unicorns in here. He's the first real mate I've had for ages. I'd had a few friendships back in the closed prisons, Wandsworth and the Scrubs, but none since being in here, before him. The other guys love him, too. So many of them come scratching at our door for him, the paint's coming off the frame. And his popularity has rubbed off on me. When he moved in to the cell, the people who didn't know what to make of me, how to place me, became friendlier.

16

No one's going to come round for him tonight. Chelsea are playing, and every telly in the place is on, except ours. Deller doesn't like football either, and prefers to read in the evenings. Another reason to like him. Sometimes I feel I can almost be myself around him.

We lie on our bunks with our books, hearing the TVs around – on each side, above us, below us – in muted stereo. I rest my book on my chest and close my eyes, remembering the feel of that woman's hand in mine, that brief contact. I make a loose fist, imagining holding her hand, gently squeezing her fingers and her squeezing mine back. There's a joyous roar as a goal is scored – followed by a metallic rumble as two hundred cell doors are kicked in unison.

The next morning, I start out on the hill on my way to work, and as I pass the posh café I glance in, same as I usually do. And there she is. She's sitting at the window counter but unlike those next to her she's not focused down at a screen but gazing straight ahead, onto the street. We spot each other at the same time. I stop, and she gives me a quick smile before glancing away.

I should move on but I don't. It's another lovely day, and the sight of her has had an instantly buoyant effect, propelling me to the top of the seesaw. But more than that, it seems truly extraordinary that I'm seeing her again. That she's there, twenty feet away. That she really exists. My dreams last night had transformed her into an apparition.

I can't let this moment go. I check my watch and see I've got about five minutes to play with, if I leg it the rest of the way. Five minutes. It's a challenge but, more than that, it's a risk. We're right by the prison, and attempting to form relationships with women is a violation of my licence. *Fuck it!* I hear Deller say. *Some risks are worth taking, right?*

In a couple of steps I'm at the door, and in one movement I push it open and stride over towards her. The place is full and I can't see a spare stool nearby. Rather than lose momentum by searching the room, I lean awkwardly against the wall beside where she's sitting.

'Hello again,' I say.

She makes a surprised *hmmm* and smiles again, but this time more cautiously. I see now she does have a laptop in front of her too, but it's closed, so I couldn't spot it from the street. It's a black, old-fashioned Dell, like the one I had a decade ago, and it looks clunky next to her neighbour's sleek silver Mac. She's wearing a sleeveless, silky, white top, showing off those brown arms. Her face is tilted up to me, and her forehead is line free, as shiny as glass.

'You know, I'm very pleased to have bumped into you again,' I say.

'Oh, really?'

'Yeah. I need a woman's advice on something.' I pause and swallow, trying to hold my nerve. 'So, my mate has a problem, right. He's got this new girlfriend, but she's telling him that if he's with her he can't have any contact with any of his exes ever again. Even just as friends. What should he do? Do you think she's being reasonable?'

It's a line that I've had some success with before, a decade ago, but as I speak I see a shadow cross her face. Almost a flinch. I'm thinking about how to change tack when she replies.

'Well, I guess it depends how much he likes this new girlfriend. I mean, it's not reasonable of her, obviously. But people agree to all sorts of crazy shit when they're in love.'

'Yeah,' I say, but the wind has gone out of my sails, and I can't remember how to move on from the pick-up line to the next bit. We're silent for a moment, me feeling like a dick, looming over her. She's looking down now, and I have a good view of the top of her head. Even I can tell that her dye job is expensive; there are about a dozen different shades in there, from chocolate to honey, each strand individually tended to. She's a different species to the women working inside, with their drawn faces and scraped-back hair, growing out bleach jobs that belonged to a more hopeful time in their lives.

I must say something. I look away from her, back down at the counter, where her phone sits.

'So you got another phone. That was quick.'

'Yeah,' she says, touching it. 'They biked one over last night. Good customer service, actually. It's always nice to be pleasantly surprised by something.'

I peer at the phone, for want of something to say. Although I don't have one myself, it's impossible to escape the talk of iPhones inside; an obsession ranking alongside bicep circumference and the lunch menu and which female officer wants it most. It's not a new model, and the casing is worn.

'Went for a used one, then?' I say.

'Er, yes,' she says, shortly. I feel bad, like I've embarrassed her by implying that she can't afford the latest one, when really I'm just trying to think of something to say. Then, after an awkward silence. she looks up at me, finally giving me the full benefit of those eyes. But now I don't feel like I deserve them. I'm cocking this up. I glance around the room, trying to collect myself. The smell of real coffee in here is fierce. In fact, it seems to me like everything has been dialled up; not just the smells but the colours too. The walls are a blinding, flawless white, as if they were painted yesterday. There are pot plants everywhere, their large, glossy leaves a shade of green I haven't seen for a long time; hyper-real, the colour of lime cordial.

A waiter approaches with a plate of food for the guy beside us. Toast with a vast pile of green mush on it, and salad leaves on the side. More freshness on that single plate than I see for a week inside. The waiter, a chunky, bearded ginger guy, purposefully catches my eye as he turns back to the kitchen, so I know he's watching.

'So, you're off to work?' I say to the woman, hating myself for being so lame. I can't for the life of me think of anything witty to say. Chatting up girls used to come easily to me – although I admittedly wasn't so good at following through – so this feels like standing up after a long sleep and realising your legs have become paralysed in the night.

'Yeah,' she says. 'I'm an estate agent, for my sins.' She grimaces, whether at the admission or the cliché it's not clear. 'Actually, I'm starting out on my own, I'm going to be a new kind of estate agent. Honest. Ethical.' She laughs. 'Well, that's the idea. Early days yet. Maybe I'll be like the rest of them soon enough.'

Again, I can't think of anything to say in reply. My gaze rests on her bare arms. So tanned for the end of April. Maybe she's just come back from holiday – skiing or something. Her watch is small and gold and her nails have a neat white strip at the top, the way Tania used to get hers done for special occasions. It's warm again today and the veins on her arms are visible. There's something intimate about seeing them. The pale blue patterns under her skin remind me of tube lines. The one on her left arm looks like the Circle Line;

the right, the southern end of the Northern Line, where it branches at Kennington.

I try to rev myself back up; stop thinking about her veins and try to imagine what she looks like naked. But it's just not coming. She's not accessible, this golden woman. It's only now, as she sits here, still and glinting in the window, that I appreciate quite how far she is out of my league. I was right: she is supernatural. And I'm completely fucking this up.

'Pad,' she says, then.

'What?'

She's looking at me steadily now, under those low, heavy brows.

'My agency. I'm thinking of calling it Pad. What do you think?'

'*Pad?*' I say, and I'm aware of an edge to my voice, which isn't what I intended. I'm just surprised. *The slang for a prison cell?*

Some music has started playing: woozy, meandering jazz. A kind that I haven't heard for years – decades – since my mother went through a brief phase of liking it. I really couldn't stand it – it made me feel sort of alienated, and it never seemed to end. There's a little cactus on the counter, embarrassingly phallic. The water vase has a sprig of mint curled inside; it reminds me of a foetus suspended in a jar. At my brief stint at boarding school, they had a baby crocodile in a jar in the science lab.

Beside her laptop is a menu, printed on brown paper. To mask my awkwardness, I pick it up and inspect it. There are a number of ingredients I don't recognize – *shakshuka, matcha* – and the ones I do know appear to be combined randomly. *Smashed banana on toast. Boiled egg with asparagus.*

21

I move down to the drinks list. A long list of coffee variants. Then I go still. *Cold Brew.* Beer? Is this is a licensed premises? I'm jerked from my trance. Never mind talking to a woman; I could argue that she started talking to me and I was just being friendly. But being in a licensed premises, a clear breach of my licence, just a hundred metres from the prison, when I should be at work? An act of madness.

I resist the urge to peg it straight out, and instead move slowly, making sure my movements and voice don't betray the panic inside.

'God, is that the time,' I say in a monotone. I'm already halfway to the door. 'I'm late. Sorry.'

Without looking back at her, I leave.

Out on the street, as soon as I'm past the window, I pick up speed until I'm swerving around people, bombing past the sofas, the Londis, the Job Centre. My thoughts don't have time to settle. Cross at the lights. KFC. As I approach the shop, I slow down to walking pace.

Carl is waiting, of course.

'Three minutes past,' he says, as I reach him.

'Yeah, sorry, mate. They were late letting me out.'

In reply, he says nothing but raises one of those mad grey eyebrows. The gesture doesn't come naturally to him; I reckon he's been practising this sceptical expression in the mirror, ready for just such an occasion. My adrenalin is still running high, and it acts as fuel to a spark of anger. As he bends to unlock the door, I take a deep breath and follow him across the shop floor, silently counting to ten in time to my steps. Calm down. Remember the consequences.

In the back, Carl hands me a pile of tatty old jigsaws and instructs me to count the pieces, to check they're complete.

He leaves, and I settle down on a fat bin liner of clothes and start on the first, a thousand-piece puzzle. The pieces are tiny and damp in my fingers; barely more substantial than sawdust. I count them into piles of a hundred. The box shows an old-fashioned country scene – a wagon, a hay bale – although it seems a miracle that all these sodden scraps of brown could ever form a coherent, attractive picture. That a thousand bits of nothing can add up to something.

Carl clearly gave me the task as a punishment, but it's actually just the kind of activity I need. Repetitive and mindless. Still, it doesn't stop me going over what just happened. My buoyancy on seeing the woman this morning feels like it belongs to another lifetime; now, I feel extremely low, as heavy and useless and unappealing as the sodden duvet someone dumped on the shop's doorstep last night.

I try to rationalise it. No one has to know about what a dick I was in the café. The only thing that matters is I didn't get caught. The rest of it can fall away. I've had a lot of practice at this: focusing on the end goal, shrugging off stuff that isn't helpful to me. Like a mountaineer shedding belongings on a long climb up a peak. I'm not good at many things, but I'm good at this. It was a decision I made in the van from the Old Bailey to Wandsworth after sentencing, all those years ago, as I sat in my suit, being bumped around on that hard, narrow seat, watching the road through the tiny window, the tinted glass making the world look dark even though it was the middle of the day. This is the attitude I'd take, to get through. And I've stuck to it, mostly. But what happened this morning pierced my armour.

Remember, I tell myself – you're nearly out. You're nearly there.

Back at the prison, it's Bates again on reception. He's engrossed in the TV pages of the paper, and Wilko, who's in front of me, leans over the desk to have a look at what he's reading, so emboldened that he must still be high.

'*Narcos*,' he says with enthusiasm. 'You seen series four?'

Bates shakes his head.

'Aw mate, you got a treat!' Wilko continues, eyes wide, and then starts telling him the plot in ludicrous, rambling detail. Bates listens, nodding, and it doesn't appear to occur to him to wonder how Wilko, who is six years into his sentence, has managed to watch the current series of a show that is only on Netflix.

When I get back to the cell Deller isn't in. Most likely he's playing poker. Good – I can prepare his birthday surprise. I've been planning it for a while, buying the stuff on canteen and hiding it in my locker. A pastry; some peanuts; some matches. I set it all up, ready for him.

His birthday cards are open, propped up on the windowsill, and as I wait for Deller I glance at them. Girlish writing; hearts; a smiley emoji. *Big love, Kika*. An intricately detailed child's drawing of some underwater scene, complete with fantastical fish and octopus and a submarine.

I only read what I can see without picking the cards up. Although I know Deller wouldn't mind if I did, it still feels a violation of his privacy.

As I'm standing there, I hear a noise, and turn to see Deller at the door. I instruct him to turn his back.

'All right,' I say when I'm ready. 'Happy fucking birthday!'

He turns and starts laughing at the sight on the desk: a pastry studded with peanuts. The idea is that the peanuts act as candles, the oil in them keeping them alight, but when I attempt to light them they keep going out. Still, I insist on trying to get all thirty-four of them going at once. It takes an age, but we have the time. Eventually I give up, by which point we're both laughing. Deller carefully cuts the pastry in two, shutting his eyes to make a wish, like a seven year old.

Most people don't celebrate their birthdays inside, me included. Who wants to be reminded of time marching on, another year gone of a life that you've completely fucked up? Birthdays are about being loved and celebrated, and neither of those apply to me. Better to try and ignore the markers of time. But Deller has no truck with that kind of attitude.

'What did you wish for?' I ask.

'Can't say!' he says, and then, with barely a pause, 'OK, well, I wished that one day I'll have a kid.' He pauses, uncharacteristically downcast all of a sudden. 'The missus says she'll wait. Fingers crossed. But maybe I'll be a shit father.'

'Course not,' I say. 'Even if you were stuck in here you'd still be better than most of them. Certainly better than mine, anyway.'

I'm not sure why I said that, as I haven't a clue what my dad is like. I've never met him. I was conceived with a sperm donor, and the one time I ventured to my mother that I might like to try and find him, she was so hurt I never asked again. So who knows: he might be fantastic, the best guy ever. I've never really gone into my father situation before, and I'm not keen to start now. So I'm relieved when Deller changes the subject.

'Anyway, tell me about your day,' he says, cheerful again.

I briefly consider telling him all about the incident in the café, but – trying and failing to chat up a woman in a licensed premises, in spitting distance of the prison? Nothing funny or clever about that. And I worry that going over it again will plunge me back down the well I'm not sure I've fully clambered out of. So instead I tell him a very edited version, leaving out the woman entirely. I say I went into the café, thinking I'd get a cup of coffee, but then saw how expensive it was; then I realised that it was a licensed premises.

'Cold Brew?' he says, kindly. 'Mate, that's some poncey new kind of coffee, I think. Not beer.'

I laugh with him at my mistake, feeling slightly better, and ask him about his day. He tells me about the visit he had from his mum. She bought him all the Bounty bars from the visit hall café as a present, forgetting that inmates aren't allowed to take food back to their cells and everything has to be consumed within the visiting hour. Deller managed to eat four before admitting defeat, and then his mum tried to hand the rest to the neighbouring tables but an officer stopped her.

Then, we talk about our best ever birthdays. His was his twenty-first, when he was dealing and making fifteen grand a month, when he flew ten of his mates out to the opening night parties in Ibiza. I tell him about when I was ten. and woke up to the sound of my mum giggling beside my bed and an unusual sensation at my feet – this soft, warm, writhing thing – and looked under the duvet to find a puppy. Badger.

Later, when I'm lying on my bunk, I think about my truly best birthday. I was nineteen, and hadn't long met Tania and dropped out of university. We had just moved in together, into the flat in Clapham, and I had got a job as a runner in Soho, fetching lunch for people in editing suites. We didn't have any money to go out and so she cooked me steak, for the first time, and afterwards when I licked her face her skin tasted of salt and fat. When we had sex that night, it was on another level entirely. Clamped tight, we looked into each other's eyes and both saw this incredible depth of intimacy. I thought, so this is what people mean by love – but surely, it wasn't possible that other couples felt this strength of connection. If they did, then the world would stop revolving; nothing would ever get done.

Often, when I'm lying in bed, I think of decisions I've made, and go over experiences I've had with people, and create different endings to them. I suppose I'm rewriting the past. There's a lot I wish I'd done differently, but not that night.

2

Steph

They're so easy to spot. I don't mean the obvious ones – the losers even a cat would cross the road to avoid, with gums like tar and tracksuit bottoms shrunk in the prison laundry, limping fast towards the scent of drugs or easy targets. Or the lunks in their V-neck T-shirts walking like they're carrying a carpet under each arm, who spent their time inside consuming old copies of GQ and increasing their reps, and who'll be inside again soon, even though they don't know it, because their need to be The Man overrides any finer judgement.

The ones I'm talking about are desperate not to be noticed, are trying to re-enter the world by a side door. They walk slowly, even if they think they're hurrying, eyes down, keeping their distance. They don't carry much stuff; they have these shitty prison-issue Alcatel phones, or at least they do until they pick up the iPhones they've got stashed somewhere on the outside. Their jeans are clean but years old; the same ones that sat in a holdall hidden behind the dock as the verdict was read out.

Then of course, when you get up close, you notice the pallor, from all that cheap bread. And the eye contact. Even when you just ask them the time or whatever, their eyes bore into you, trying to suss out your agenda.

Sometimes, they come into the café and act weird with the door: pausing in front of it, expecting it to be opened for them, or pushing it too hard, because it's lighter than the ones they're used to. When they pass the tables they pocket a handful of sugar and salt sachets, without even thinking. Prison turns you into a low-level kleptomaniac. If they queue, they do so with exaggerated patience. Apparently, in the lead-up to parole, the prison will observe how men behave in the lunch hall because those who queue-barge and leave litter are statistically far more likely to reoffend.

Some of them who work out get given money for lunch – a five-pound note folded into a small brown envelope – and they'll walk into the café thinking *I'll get a coffee, my first real coffee after three years of Nescafé sachets* and then – *two quid fucking fifty?* A few days ago, this guy came in and asked about the sandwiches, and when the man behind the counter started listing ingredients – sourdough, halloumi – the con slammed the counter in fury, as if the words had been invented to expose him.

I wonder how many of the locals, streaming onto the hill from the residential side roads to go to work, know that there are prisoners in their midst. Murderers, armed robbers, grade one scumbags who've stolen our hard-earned tax for hookers and hot tubs. Not many of them, I bet. Not even the gangs of rude boys who hang around the Londis, their trousers under their arses, trying their best to look like graduates from C Wing themselves. The prison is hardly a secret, but I imagine it's easy to forget about it. Set back from the road, shielded by a block of sixties flats, the place doesn't advertise itself. Modern London has grown up around it like a privet hedge. Besides, you don't expect serving prisoners to be roaming about, do you? People vaguely know about the idea of day release, of course, but still, you don't imagine them to be just walking around, getting the bus, standing behind you in the café queue, serving you, staring at you.

Oh, the homeless guy who stations himself near the prison turnoff – he knows. In fact, I reckon he's a former prisoner himself, because he's aware that the cons who are returning from work can't take any money back in with them, so if they have any small change left from that fiver, he's there to help them out.

I've read up on the prison's history. In Victorian times there used to be a treadmill there; inmates literally had to walk it for eight hours a day. Men and women. Mothers had to feed their babies while they were on it. The authorities may have put a stop to that, but the basic structure of the place hasn't changed. It is notoriously unfit for purpose: two big twenty-first-century criminals crammed in a cell designed for one nineteenth-century pickpocket. And then someone had the great idea to dedicate a wing of it to D Cat prisoners: those coming to the end of their sentences, preparing for release into the world again. The thinking was that it's easier for them to work out in London. But then, there are the temptations of the city, too. There's a good reason why open prisons are usually in remote rural locations, where there are no passers-by and getting to the train station involves a slog across fields and dual carriageways.

The authorities now realise that having an open wing in a London prison is a bad idea. The place is awash with drugs –

not least thanks to people like my brother. They're trying out all sorts of measures to stop them getting in, really coming down hard on drones and corrupt officers, but in the longer term they're also talking about shipping all the D Cats out to one of the purpose-built rural places, and making the wing closed again. Apparently they're then planning to fill the space with sex offenders; the prison receives more money for them. And then eventually they'll move everyone out, and sell the building and land to developers, and all the people in those million-pound terraces in the neighbouring streets can boast that their gamble on the area has paid off.

For now, though, they've got to share the hill.

Before getting married, I briefly lived in a flat on another of London's big roads, even bigger and dirtier than this one. I hated it until someone told me that in the eighteenth century, the road was the route down which animals were shepherded from the country to the market at Smithfield. After that, whenever I went to Morrison's or waited at the bus stop, I'd imagine the ghosts of the road: the cows obediently ambling towards their death; a spirited pig trying to escape down a side street and being whacked back into line.

The ghosts on this road are visible, though; and their families, too, as they come for visits. Women step carefully off the bus in their heels, all dolled up to give their men something to think about in their bunks. Wearing the skirt he asked her to during their last phone call, the one he's planning to stuff his hand up when the screws aren't looking. The kids in tow; baby girls in their best headbands, little boys in their pageboy waistcoats and short back and sides trailing behind, lured by promises of Wotsits and Ribena. I spot them as they get off the bus and I know where they're going, and what's awaiting them when they disappear through that horse-and-carriage width prison gate. The peeling waiting room, air barely stirred by a plastic table fan, the closed-off volunteers at the desk. The lockers that only accept old one-pound coins, and which there aren't enough of. If you can't get one, then tough: there's nowhere to store your stuff, so you can't go in. Never mind if you've come all the way from Doncaster. The final make-up touch-ups. Security checking your mouth for chewing gum, brandishing the tissue you forgot in your pocket. Then another waiting room, furnished by ungrammatical posters showing cons in comas after spice attacks and advertising suicide helplines that are only manned for two hours three times a week. The children playing up or staring open-mouthed at the mute TV in the corner. It's like going through the world's shabbiest and strictest airport, but where you're not allowed to carry even a magazine for amusement.

Then, finally, the visit hall, where each numbered table is the stage for a crappy little tragedy. The men amble in wearing their netball bibs; their kids burst into tears or barely react to their arrival. Mothers spend half their precious hour queuing for food at the café, and then the rest of it silently watching their hulking baby boy wolf down chicken pies and chocolate, the table a moat between them. Kids pull at the hands of their anchored fathers, because while they might just about accept that their dad is confined to this building for a while, they can't compute the absurdity that once seated, he isn't allowed to stand up. Men clumsily feeding their babies, the mother looking nervously on. Toddlers staring at the groping couple at the next table. No phones for distraction. An hour visit is both inadequate and overlong; there's too much and too little to say. Then time's up. The visitors file out. The men remain seated until everyone's left and at that point, apparently, there's this weird, silent, heavy minute, a sort of decompression, before they get to their feet, shuffle out and get absorbed back into the wing, back into their little lives full of inflated grievances and petty dramas and shouting and drill music.

For their friends and family on the outside, though, it's a different story. The best way I can describe it is when someone you're close to is put away, it's as if a crater opens up on the floor of your lounge. You learn to step round it, eventually you stop talking about it all the time, but it's always there, this hole. And that's the case even if, like me, the person inside is just your half-brother, who you haven't lived with for years. Even if you don't have a drop of love left for them.

Obviously for the wives and girlfriends, it can be a proper nightmare – they've got the bills and the kids to worry about on top of it all. Yet the majority of them seem to stick around, even if they'd have no trouble finding another bloke. Roxie is the obvious example. I've read these earnest things online about the psychology of prison wives, trying to understand why they allow the life to be drained out of them as they wait for their dodgy men. But to me it's not worthy of study. What's a love story without separation and hurdles to overcome? Moreover, if your man is in there, you don't have to live with them. Yes, you'll miss his income and sex and snuggling on the sofa in front of *Strictly*, but there's also no watching them eat with their mouth open, or being tight in restaurants, or opening their mail and not bothering to throw away the empty envelope, or being too rough with the kids. In their absence they can be the perfect partner. Both of you can pretend he's someone else.

And when you do have contact they're on their best behaviour, because they're dependent. Now you have the power. They need you: for their probation reports, to bring in the kids, to send them money, to break up the monotony, to give them some status inside, to reassure them that they're not worthless.

And, of course, you know that they're bursting for you. Out in the world, you're one of millions, maybe past your best. In there, sitting across a table, you're a fucking goddess. There are whispered desires across the table, in ten-minute phone calls, in letters. And again, you don't have to contend with the disappointing reality.

Of course, there are those who want to do more than just hold hands with a con glued to his chair in a bib. The bad boy – hardly an unusual fantasy, is it? Apparently there's even a website, for women to hook up with prisoners out on day release. The men say they'll be in Luton town centre or whatever for an hour between this time and that time, at this building site or in this charity shop, and a woman who likes a bit of rough will meet them for a quick shag in a car park or toilet.

These women need to manage their expectations. The buff, pent-up rogue is a far less common breed than the sad paunchy bloke with brown teeth and a bald patch. Saying that, this one, my target, is pretty OK. Whether that'll make my task easier or harder, I don't know.

3

Rob

Passing by the café on Wednesday morning, I slow down to glance over the bent heads, but she's not there. I keep going. It's warm again but there's no zip to the air. Rather, it's got a stagnant, used feeling, like it's already the end of the day. I feel flat, too. Any boost I got from Deller last night has worn off. The road is solid, the buses lined up like bullets in a barrel, cars impatiently revving. Some aggressive techno blasts from a van's window. Today, the women trudging down the hill alongside me don't seem magical. The fragrances from their various products clash, and the music escaping from their headphones seems rude and antisocial. They're just female humans of various shapes and ages, flawed as all people are. And all of them would reject me, like the café woman did.

And today I notice the men, too, with their suits and pointy shoes and shoulder bags containing whatever important papers and expensive gadgets. They look quite young – I guess around my age, late twenties – yet they've clearly built up lives for themselves. I can't imagine what it is they do for a living, but it occurs to me that they're probably off to jobs they've spent years working towards. Getting qualified and trained and performance reviewed. Steadily moving up the pay scale. They've probably got a bunch of other suits in their cupboards, and I think about how much it must have cost for each one, and for the men to get their hair cut every fortnight and their shirts dry-cleaned, and to take girls out for drinks and away for the weekend, as well as paying rent and bills and insurance and all the boring life stuff. I glance up at the city in the distance, through narrowed eyes, as if looking into the sun; the skyscrapers look like fangs.

There's an angry shout from the road, and I turn to see a cyclist gesticulating furiously at a guy weaving through the stationary traffic. The guy keeps crossing to the other side, not reacting at all. His shoulders are hunched, and he's wearing grey tracksuit bottoms. One of ours? I don't recognise him, but maybe. Despite the efforts to prepare us, prisoners do all sorts of stupid shit when they're first let out – get smashed in the first pub they come to, launch themselves on shop assistants, abscond; basically illustrate the absence of self-control and long-term thinking that got them inside in the first place.

I think back again to my first time out, on this hill, accompanied by Hasan. Everything seemed huge. Buildings, distances, horizons. Prison really fucks with your sense of perspective; I'd spent years not seeing more than twenty feet in front of me. Ground level was tricky, as well – I felt ultra-sensitive to unevenness in the pavement. But the change of textures felt good, too, and I found myself purposefully walking over the scrubby patches of grass at the base of trees, and, at crossings, rubbing my soles on the raised bumps on the kerb meant to help blind people. I didn't take any of it for granted. Crossing the road, I realised that there are a hundred decisions involved in it, this simplest of things I'd done tens of thousands of times before. Whether to wait for the green man or cross in a gap between traffic; gauging how fast the traffic was moving; choosing where to walk; avoiding people coming in the opposite direction. At one crossing a car turning left mounted the pavement, and I actually let out a cry of alarm. My sense of personal space was off; I kept bumping into people. People on either side of me were moving at different times, and I didn't know whose example to follow. I was conscious of using too much brain power to make tiny decisions.

I didn't feel panicky, exactly, about re-entry into the outside world. Self-conscious, mostly. Or, more precisely, simultaneously hyper-aware and spaced out, as if my inside wasn't in alignment with my outside. One moment, I couldn't get over the fact that none of these people passing by knew who I was or what I'd done. That I wasn't being judged. I could be one of those worker men with the pointy shoes and the shoulder bags on his day off. I could be living with a girlfriend in a little flat somewhere, in one of these streets off the hill, with a mortgage and a cat and a wine rack. At other times, I felt that everyone who glanced at me knew what I was and where I'd been; I might as well have been wearing shackles.

That evening, as I lay in bed going over it all, it occurred to me: officially, I should now be a different person to who I was when I last walked on a pavement. A reformed character. Getting your D Cat; transferring to open conditions; being cleared for day release: these are the final stages of the rehabilitation process. So, if not a new person, then at the very least I should now be back to who I was before that fateful evening in Farringdon. The old me, with a load of extra self-knowledge, humility and self-control thrown in.

I thought of those thousands of hours staring at the ceilings of various prisons, contemplating my crime. All those hundreds of hours of courses and training and programmes that I had to complete in order to reach this point, being allowed out to work.

So, was I rehabilitated? I'd take their word for it. But it occurred to me then that I'd only really be tested when I was out there on the street for real, rubbing up against society.

Now, I focus back on the pavement, on walking, on the crowd of moving shapes ahead. As I pass the Londis I glance over to look for dogs and, just at that moment, the door opens and a woman comes out.

It's her. She's wearing sunglasses, but it's definitely her. The same style of fitted dress, a decade too old for her. Same handbag. That bouncy hair. She's carrying a leather zip-up folder, the kind that all estate agents have. I immediately turn my face away, and when I glance back, she's already walking on down the hill. I start moving too, keeping her in my sights. I look at those thin, undefined legs, clad in tights that are invisible except to me. She's carrying a bottle of water, and I watch as she unscrews the top and elegantly takes a swig, tipping her head back, without breaking pace. She has a very upright posture, as if she's carrying an orange between her shoulder blades. She walks as if she's being watched – which she is.

Then, without warning, she glances behind her, straight at me. There's no hiding this time. She smiles, and stops.

'Hello,' she says. 'Again.'

In five paces I've caught up with her. As soon as we're level, she sets off again, matching my pace. It's as if the pavement is one of those moving walkways in an airport, compelling us to keep on the move.

'Did your mate decide what to do?' she says.

I look at her.

'About his girlfriend,' she explains. 'Not wanting him to be in touch with his ex?'

'Oh. Yeah. No. He's still not sure.'

She nods, and smiles, and then I smile back, because this is a good sign, I think. She must have known what I said in the café was just a bullshit chat-up line, and her bringing it up again now shows she's prepared to overlook my clumsiness and hasty exit. My mood lifts, like I've been pumped with helium.

'So you live around here, then?' she says.

I pause, before nodding.

'Whereabouts?'

'Just up there.' I indicate up the hill with my head.

'Which street?'

I can't think of a reply; I don't know the names of the streets around here.

'Sorry,' she says. 'None of my business. I'm already in work mode.'

We walk in silence for a bit, but it's companionable, not awkward like it was in the café. Then I say,

'I used to be an estate agent.'

'No way!' she says, turning to me and smiling.

'Well, sort of. I worked in an office for a bit. When I first came to London.'

I fall silent again, turning over what I've just said. On the face of it, it's nothing – just a statement. A dull one at that.

39

What's amazing to me is that, in the past, the fact of my brief spell at Benham and Reeves was embedded in a bad history, and crusted with painful associations and emotions. How it came about after I'd reluctantly given up the Soho runner's job, which I'd loved, because it paid next to nothing. My mother's horror when I told her – dropping out of university was upsetting enough, and now an *estate agent*? How Tania got me the job through her mate James, who worked there, and of course everything that happened after with them. But now, it's almost as if the fact has been lifted from its context and cleaned up, and it's now fit for everyday conversation. I don't have to say any more about it if I don't want to. I don't have to feel any more about it. It's like my past has become palatable. And I'm hit with this tremendous sense of freedom, and relief. Maybe this is what rehabilitation feels like.

'Did you like it?' she says.

'God no.' Worried that might sound rude, I add, 'I was crap at it. Too lazy, probably.'

I'm channelling Deller now; talking myself down, but in a cheerful, disarming way. He told me that he once pulled a girl by telling her he was terrible in bed.

'Lucky escape,' she says. 'What do you do now?'

Now I barely hesitate at all.

'I work in a shop. Clothes and stuff.'

An old geezer in a baggy brown suit is struggling up the hill and as he passes us, he loudly clears his throat and spits onto the pavement, not far from my feet.

'A former customer,' I say, when we're safely past him. 'I wouldn't let him exchange a shirt without a receipt.'

It's not a great joke – not even a good one. Still, she laughs.

'It's just temporary,' I go on. 'Until I decide what to do

next. I'd rather do something worthwhile than just lie in front of the telly all day, you know?'

She nods.

'But don't you just hate having to deal with the public?' she says. 'I mean, I'm not a psychopath. But sometimes I just want to be in a dark little room where no one can talk to me.'

I laugh, too loudly.

'Yeah.'

She tells me about a viewing she did the previous week, where the male house owner insisted on being present – in full drag. In return, I tell her about some of the weird customers who come in the shop; the same stories I've told Deller. She listens, head bent, and laughs at the right moments. It's so much easier now than it was sitting in the café. Walking and talking like this, I feel like we're in a film. I feel the pulse of that old, long-buried feeling, when you know you're getting it right. She keeps glancing over and smiling at me, and I just wish she'd take off her sunglasses and give me those knock-out eyes. Those glasses might as well be her dress; that's how desperate I am for her to take them off.

Then, as we pass the Job Centre and approach the traffic lights at the bottom of the road, she answers my prayers. She takes off her glasses and folds them away into her bag. As we wait for the lights, she meets and holds my gaze and I look back, and feel like I'm in the grip of something huge.

I notice the high colour in her cheeks. The traffic lights are on a short timer, and before we've moved they've turned to red again. We both look away, over to the high street, where people are cramming themselves into the tube entrance as if they're escaping a bomb.

'Suppose I'd better join them,' she says.

We start moving again, crossing through a gap in the traffic, and stop outside the KFC.

'I will wish you farewell outside the biggest KFC in the world,' I say.

'Is it really the biggest?'

I shrug, happily.

'Can't beat a KFC,' she says, and I laugh, as she really doesn't look like the type, and because everything she says is delightful.

She walks quickly over to the tube and I watch her back until she disappears into the throng, and then I turn and peg it to the shop, dodging the pedestrians. I'm two minutes late but fate is working for me today. Rather than Carl, it's Sami waiting at the door. Carl's away on a training course and she's in charge, she informs me, as she solemnly escorts me through the shop.

Alone in the stock room, I sit on my nest of bin bags and close my eyes. The bags feel warm and fat against my back; I could be resting on some hay bales in the sun.

Obviously, it can't go anywhere with her, this golden woman. I might never see her again. But that's not the point. Walking down the hill with her, talking like that, I was using a muscle that had been dormant for years. I felt, for those few minutes, like the pre-prison me. Deller was wrong – I didn't have to tell her that I was inside. I could interest her on my own terms.

It strikes me that she's the first real woman I've chatted up. Sure, Tania was eighteen when I first met her, but she was really a girl. The ones before her were definitely girls.

Sam has yet to give me anything to do, so after a while I get up and wander about, inspecting the piles of random stuff.

The old ripped copy of *The Low Sodium Cookbook*. A pile of paperbacks, which I've already looked through – I heard Carl order Sami not to accept any more books, because they take up space and who reads them, anyway? A box of horse brasses. A trio of empty perfume bottles. I spot a game of Guess Who? and pull out the tattered box. I once badgered my mother to buy me this for my birthday, and she did, but after the first game she threw it away in disgust, declaring it sexist because there were far too few women on the board. Now I prise open the box and see half the cards are missing, but the characters are just the same as when I was a kid.

A couple of years ago, I read this book called *The Museum of Innocence*. It's still on my shelf but I haven't thought about it for ages, until now. It's about a guy who is obsessed with a girl, and collects objects that tell the story of their relationship. A comb, a teacup; a cigarette butt with her lipstick on it. And now, it strikes me that everything in this shop, even the crappiest stuff, has a meaning beyond itself to someone, somewhere. One day, the woman's things – her sunglasses, that dress – might be stuffed in a bag and donated to a place like this, and from then on, no one will know what they meant: what eyes those glasses hid, or the feelings evoked by that neckline.

Through the course of the morning, the doorbell chimes as someone enters the shop. If it's a donor Sami accepts whatever they give her without question and dumps the bags in the back with a sort of reckless bravado. One of them is full of books; old-fashioned ones with leather covers. Carl will be displeased. I have a look: it's a set of volumes of *Les Misérables*. A book as long as it gets. I tried to read it once, a few years ago, but it defeated me. This set looks old, and possibly worth something. I wonder if I should point this out to Carl when he gets back, and earn some brownie points. Mostly, as ever, the donations are just bin bags of old clothes – the bags a similar size to the one I'll soon be clutching as I leave the prison gate for the last time. All the possessions I've amassed over the past seven years, in one single bag. Maybe two, if they've got enough spare.

I hear talking out in the shop and lean forward so I can see around the door. An elderly woman is at the till, shaking a jigsaw box at Sami.

'My husband was very upset,' she's saying. 'It took him a week and a half to finish it and then there was all these gaps . . . He thought it was his fault. When I bought it I specifically asked if all the pieces had been counted.'

Sami makes exaggerated noises of sympathy, as if the woman has confided about a terminal diagnosis, before opening the till to give the two pounds back.

I sit back down in my bin-bag nest. I hear the woman leave, and a moment later Sami peers around the door frame.

'Just to say,' she says, timidly, 'that if you want any help with anything – I mean counting, reading, that sort of thing – I'm happy to assist.'

'Thanks, but I'm OK,' I smile at her. I suppose it's a fair assumption that I'm illiterate; the majority of prisoners are. I could tell her I got accepted into Leeds University to study maths, but there's no need to embarrass her.

I know Sami's type well. Prisons are overrun with middle-aged lady volunteers, running courses, trying to be useful in the final chapter of their lives. Spinsters and widows, or unsatisfyingly married and restless now their children have left home. Most want to mother us, but some get a thrill from young men doing their bidding. You can spot those ones pretty easily; they're gently flirty and slightly pressing at first, and then get angry if you don't respond exactly as they want. But Sami's OK, I think.

She's certainly taking her role as caretaker manager seriously. At 1 p.m. on the dot she comes to the door, holding a plastic box.

'I know Carl usually provides a sandwich,' she says timidly, 'but I thought you might like to try my samosas.'

I accept the box and prise off the lid to reveal a nest of tinfoil. Sam darts forward to unwrap the layers, revealing four neatly arranged pastry peaks. I dig one out and take a bite. It's delicious. A taste sensation, actually: the filling has a depth of flavour I'd forgotten existed. Chewing, I nod my appreciation.

She extends her finger to pat the surface of one of the samosas.

'Oh no, they're stone cold!' she cries. 'I didn't use enough foil!'

'They're great,' I say. 'Anyway, I'm used to cold food.'

She's looking genuinely upset, face all scrunched.

'Food's always cold inside,' I continue. 'That's because during the riot at Strangeways, the prisoners got access to the kitchen and that's why the riot could go on for so long. Because they could feed themselves. So since then, they've put the kitchens in a completely separate building, and the food's cold by the time it reaches us.'

Her eyes widen and she cocks her head, her upset turned to interest. I'm sure she's surprised that I'm telling her this, and I'm quite surprised myself: I usually say the minimum necessary in any situation. But right now I feel chatty and happy, and I want to reward her kindness by throwing her a bone about prison life. I imagine her sitting with her friends later, hands curled around a cup of coffee, them cooing as she shares this titbit from the con.

She leans closer. I can smell the sweet oil on her hair.

'What about . . . the toilet?' she whispers, giggling at her daring. Now I've broken the seal by mentioning life inside, she's grabbing her chance to ask the burning question. 'Do you really have to go in front of someone else? I just *couldn't*.'

'Well, you try and time it so your cellmate is out. But,' I go on, 'it's funny, all these things you think you couldn't do, it turns out you can. You adjust really quickly.' I leave it there. No need to explain that the everyday stuff – the hygiene, the lack of privacy, the food – is no challenge at all, really. If you're of a reasonably sound disposition, it's not hard to divorce yourself from your environment. Even the bigger mental stuff – the loss of freedom and control, the idiots around you, the stultifying boredom – you can live with, although it frequently threatens to do your head in. The big challenge is holding onto your identity, and onto hope.

Later that afternoon, while packaging up some rags, I glimpse the logo of the Stereophonics and unearth a T-shirt. Merchandise from a decade-old tour. They're Deller's favourite band. There's a stain near the hem, but apart from that the shirt looks in fair nick. I glance over to the door – I can hear Sami out front, talking to someone – and then in a flash rip off my sweatshirt and T-shirt, put the Stereophonics one on, replace my sweatshirt and then stuff my old T-shirt in the rag pile. The switch is done in about five seconds. The T-shirt feels clammy and foreign against my skin.

I'm going to give the T-shirt to Deller as a birthday present. You're not meant to change clothes when working out, although it's not the biggest deal if you're caught. It wouldn't affect my release date. But the officer won't notice, I reckon. Anyway, whatever. For Deller it's a risk worth taking.

As it turns out, I am searched that evening. There's a new guy on reception who clearly wants to practise the techniques he's just learned in training: no strip search, but right down to our insoles. Wilko gets done first, and he's relaxed as anything, cracking jokes with the officer, who doesn't respond. Either it's a distraction tactic, or his contraband is already up his nostrils or arse. The officer is paunchy, and old enough to have white eyebrows. My guess is he was made redundant after years with an insurance company or something, and the prison service is the only place that will have him.

When it's my turn, I stare at the ceiling, my arms raised over my head, adrenalin surging with each pat. I've spent seven years on the straight and narrow, and now this is my second dodgy act in a week.

He doesn't spot the T-shirt, which is no real surprise – he's focused on more conventional contraband. Nonetheless, when he waves me on my way, I'm surprised by the rush I feel from getting one over on the system, even in this tiny way.

As I head down the landing towards the cell, I grip onto the bottom of my sweatshirt. My plan is that as soon as I'm inside, I'll stand in front of Deller and rip it off to reveal the T-shirt underneath.

The door's ajar and the TV's up loud, louder than we usually have it. When I push open the door, my first thought is, absurdly, that we've been burgled. The floor is littered with stuff; my belongings, chucked about. My mattress is half off the bunk, the bedding heaped on the floor. The door of my locker is open.

Then I notice that the toilet curtain is drawn, and there's someone sitting behind it, and I can tell from the silhouette that that person is not Deller.

I'm seized by the crazy idea that whoever is behind that curtain has killed my cellmate. I stand motionless and silent, until the toilet is flushed and the curtain pulled back. The guy is wearing grey tracksuit bottoms and nothing on top; his upper body is as hairless and narrow as a teenager's. He doesn't look surprised to see me standing there.

'I thought the point of open conditions was that the crapper is outside,' he says, in a London accent. 'I want my money back.'

'Where's Deller?'

The guy shrugs. He's youngish, around my age, and he has the kind of pinched, sharp features that are so common in here, it's as if prison has its own gene pool.

'Guy next door says he shouldn't have been here in the first place,' he says. 'Taking up my space. Guess he's gone back to the closed wing.'

This is not unlikely, I know – even Deller's luck might run out. Still, I'm not satisfied.

'If he was just moved, then why all the mess? Why did they do a spin?'

'I dunno. You tell me.'

'He didn't have a phone.'

He shrugs. 'Gear, then.'

'He didn't take drugs.'

I push my mattress back onto the bunk and then climb up

there, so he can't see my distress and confusion. Did Deller have a phone? If so, he must have hidden it well, and used it when I was out of the cell. Protecting me, because he knew we'd both get into trouble if it was discovered. I'd have my day release cancelled. It would fuck up my parole.

It strikes me that maybe the cell wasn't spun at all; Deller was moved out, peacefully, and then this new guy came in and ransacked the place. I wouldn't put it past him.

'Well, if they did find his phone, then he must have taken the rap for it,' says the bloke. 'Nice of him.'

'He was nice,' I say.

I stare at the wall, at the blobs of dried toothpaste from where Deller has pulled down his photos. A Pink Floyd poster remains; his birthday cards are still on the windowsill. They must have only given him a few minutes to pack his stuff.

I've been in this position before, of course. Padmates have been transferred; been released; moved to different cells. There's usually some notice of a departure – a few hours between the slip being pushed under the door and the screws arriving – and they usually don't mind if the guy staying put uses that time to sort out a replacement. Saves them the bother. So before when it happened to me, I'd scramble around and find someone at least non-smoking and half-bearable.

Now, though, because I'm out all day, I missed the whole thing. And I've never liked anyone as much as I liked Deller. I honestly thought we'd be together until the end.

'Don't think I would do that, by the way,' says this guy, who's now reclining on Deller's bunk.

'What?'

'Take the rap.'

'You have a phone?'

He doesn't reply, so I repeat myself, louder and more forceful. When there's still no response, I jump down from the bunk and stand in front of him. I'm not going to go down for this cunt when I'm so close to release.

He looks up at me from his reclining position, arms stretched over his head as if he's posing for a painting.

'Nah, mate,' he says, and it's obvious from his smirk that he's trying to antagonise me, so I can't tell whether he's being straight or not. And I know that he knows I have to keep a lid on my anger; I have to keep him sweet. One allegation of bullying or violence or foul play, however groundless, and I'm in trouble. When you're on the way out, you have to be faultless.

Deflated, I change tack, and begin the weary rigmarole required with a new padmate.

'What's your name?'

'Marko.'

'Rob,' I say. Neither of us move to shake hands. 'How long have you got?'

'Seven-month sentence, three left.'

I knew he'd be in for a short stretch. These pricks are a different breed to us long timers. Everything that's manageable for a short sentence is unbearable on a longer one. All they have to do is sit around, eat their Pot Noodles, scratch their balls and watch daytime property shows. Then get released, get up to the same tricks, get caught, and repeat. They have a different mentality; they have little to lose.

'What you in for?' I ask, although I know the answer. He has the ratty look of a thief.

'Theft,' he says, and explains he was nicking designer handbags from Selfridges and reselling them on eBay. This is his fourth stint inside.

'You?' he says.

'Been in seven years, out in two months.'

'What for?'

I pause for effect.

'Manslaughter.'

This should be the point when he acknowledges defeat; I'm so far above him in the pecking order. But his face shows not a flicker of response.

'You got PlayStation?'

'No, mate,' I reply, feeling weary.

By now I'm moving around the cell, putting my stuff in order again. My trainers. My books. My cup. I think there's a can of Coke missing from my canteen shelf, but I decide against bringing it up. I keep my eye out for a note from Deller, but there isn't one. His herbs and spices are still on his shelf; maybe he deliberately left them for me as a parting gift. I put them in my locker and straighten my papers before closing the door with its useless broken lock. I'm still wondering whether Marko might have had a nose around in here, but my instinct is not; he seems too lazy. My Rule 39 legal correspondence file is undisturbed; not even screws are allowed to look at that.

Marko is quiet for a few minutes, and then I hear the rasp of a match.

'No smoking, mate,' I say, over my shoulder.

'I asked for smoking.'

'No smoking,' I say, turning. Anger has edged into my voice. 'And that's my plate.'

Marko looks down at the plate he was using as an ashtray, and then across to the identical plastic plate on the table. He gives a theatrical sigh.

'You long-timer cunts are such a pain in the arse. So fucking uptight.'

'Just keep off my stuff and we'll be sweet.'

I get up onto my bunk and lie on my side. I hear him light his fag again; the smoke drifts up to my bunk. I squeeze my eyes shut. Even if I have him until the end, I tell myself, it's just two months. In the early days I had plenty of nightmare cellmates – guys who ranted, who stank, who snored, who wanked into their socks. One stuffed the loo with food; an OCD Romanian pressed the officer alarm if I dropped a crumb on the floor. There have been several who've been mentally ill, including one who liked to strain his tea through his T-shirt. I can handle this guy.

'Where you been today, then?' Marko says.

'Working out,' I say.

There's the sound of a sudden movement and I open my eyes to find him standing up beside my bunk, his face horribly close to mine. He's giving me a sort of leery grin; I can see the plaque on his teeth.

'What are you bringing in?'

'No, mate,' I say. 'None of that. I'm on the way out.'

'I'm not talking big stuff,' he says, sounding offended. 'Just little fucking stuff. Minor. You know. Are you listening?'

'Nothing, mate,' I say. I wrap my arms around my chest, hugging my hidden Stereophonics T-shirt, and turn away from him to face the wall.

'Don't be a cunt,' he says. 'Come on, mate. Now they're cracking down on drones, we'll make a mint. I'm a Red Band, 'cos of delivering canteen, innit. I can easily get it to the other wings.'

'No, mate,' I say. 'Please don't ask again.'

I hear Marko give a sigh of disgust and then, after a moment, begin to move around the cell.

'*A Suit-able Boy*,' he says, sounding out each syllable. He must be at my bookshelf. '*Mi-ddle-march. Lone-some Dove. A Man in Full*. Why are they all so fucking long? Like fuck you've actually read them.'

I don't reply.

'Wait, any of them first editions?' he goes on, his tone lifted. 'I was watching *Cash in the Attic*, right, and they told us how you can tell if one is. You look at the numbers in the front and stuff . . .'

'No, none of those paperback books from the prison library is a first edition,' I say.

'Well I don't know, do I,' he says, offended again. 'Don't know what a fucking first edition is. Just that you make a mint on them, right?'

I hear him move a few steps.

'Why you got a tube map on your wall?' he says. He's at my noticeboard now. 'Planning your journey home, eh?'

Still no reply from me.

'You were a Listener.'

Now he's looking at my certificate.

'You want to hear my problems, do you?' he continues.

'No, mate, I'm retired. I haven't done that for a while,' I reply. I'm engaging with him now because it's occurred to me where's he looking at, and what he's likely to say next, and I'm desperately keen to distract him. 'Have you ever used them?'

It doesn't work.

'That your bird?'

My eyes are wide open, staring at the sweaty cream bricks

of the wall. He's looking at my photo of Tania. I want to scream at him to fuck off and mind his own business, to never look at her or touch my stuff or talk to me again. To go and hang himself. But instead I say nothing.

'She's OK,' he says. 'Yeah. Bit fat but all right. I'd do that.'

I close my eyes as I silently count to ten, and think of the consequences.

4

Rob

Thursday morning, I start off down the hill in a terrible mood. It turns out that when Marko isn't relaying to me everything he's learned from *Cash in the Attic* and *Bargain Hunt*, he's glued to Russia Today. I shouldn't be surprised. Half the prison population are conspiracy theorists, and the channel is their news source of choice – I suppose because it's anti-establishment and goes on about how shit the country that has locked them up is. So my evening was soundtracked by documentaries about deaths in the NHS and adverts for gold bullion, as well as being subjected to Marko's unsolicited thoughts on chemtrails and how roadworks are a conspiracy to make us use more petrol and fund the new world order.

Then, when at midnight he finally agreed to switch it off, he claimed he couldn't sleep without the radio and so turned on LBC – a torrent of belligerent, uneducated opinions. It was like being in the mess room here. I tried reasoning with him and when that didn't work, I got up and switched it off, but he just turned it back on again, and on it went, him cackling at my annoyance. At 2 a.m. he conceded to change the station to

Magic FM, so what sleep I then managed was laced with love songs, which latched onto memories, conjuring ghosts I don't want to hear from. Not only must I endure Marko during waking hours, but he's intent on invading my subconscious, the only place I have to myself.

I don't like the radio, even during the day. In my first month at Wandsworth I listened to National Prison Radio. It's quite terrible, but then I was feeling like a terrible person, and one of my early strategies was to shut out the outside world and surrender myself to the prison experience. So I listened to programmes designed for offenders' ears only. In-cell guided yoga lessons; request shows in which men sent messages of love to family who couldn't possibly be listening; tips on staying safe inside; book clubs and music all carefully vetted for any lyric or sentiment that might sadden, arouse or enrage us. I didn't give myself the option to change stations or switch off, I just listened to what was provided. I thought I had to get used to taking what I was given. To forgetting that I had tastes; which music and books I liked. I had to become an empty vessel. I even made myself keep listening when they played songs that reminded me of my mother or Tania.

Then after a few months I stopped that, when I realised that I was going about things all wrong. That the only valuable thing I possessed was my brain, and I had to guard and nurture it. If I didn't, it would be stolen by prison, as surely as your kettle will go if you leave your cell door unlocked. So, then I tried Radio 4, but it pained me to hear reviews of films I wasn't going to see. More than that, I was conscious that pretty much everyone I heard on that station – the presenters, the guests – were not only free but lived well-off, enviable lives. After they left the radio studio, they were going to go back outside to the streets, get on the tube or in a car, and go home to their families and drink nice wine in a cosy house, and have interesting conversations, and sex.

So at that point I decided to stick to books and, occasionally, the TV. TV doesn't have the same impact. Radio is like someone who knows you whispering into your ear, and its effects are powerful, like an intravenous injection. TV, you can keep at a distance. Deller understood all this, too.

The one thing on TV I don't like to miss is Carol doing the weather in the mornings. But this morning, when I woke after fractured sleep and put on BBC Breakfast, Marko started being disgusting about what he wanted to do to her. Another one of my precious things tainted.

So I'm walking down the hill quickly, feeling disturbed and distracted, trying to shake off the ghosts who pawed me all night, barely aware of what's going on around me. It's not raining, that much I know. Not looking where I'm going, I stumble over a bike lying felled on the pavement, still tethered to a lamp-post.

Then I become aware of someone walking close to me, closer than they need to be. Just a few feet away, pressing up against my personal space. I look over, and it's her. Wearing the same dress as on the first day, the one with the slit down the front. No sunglasses this time. She's clutching a takeaway cup of coffee. She must have emerged from the café just after I passed it.

Like the other day, we're moving at exactly the same pace, despite the fact she's wearing heels. Then, as I'm looking at her she glances over at me and smiles, but there's no surprise in her face, and it occurs to me that she must have spotted me and deliberately caught me up.

Then, if that wasn't amazing enough, she offers me her coffee cup, as if it's the most natural thing in the world. And, pretending that it is, I accept the cup and put it to my lips as we walk.

The coffee is barely lukewarm – odd, if she's just bought it. Still, the strength of it makes me blink. It's been years since I've had proper coffee. Before, I used to love it, neck espressos throughout the day, but then once inside I quickly adapted to the little Nescafé sachets.

The opening in the lid, the little slit, is slightly tacky. It occurs to me, too, that just a few seconds ago, her lips were also pressed against that thin plastic.

As I sip, I look over at her, at that pale pink, shiny mouth. She's still smiling, showing a row of neat teeth as white as the cup's lid.

My mood is abruptly transformed. Marko vanishes from my thoughts; him and the spirits of the night whisked away like rubbish in the wind. I hand back the coffee cup as we continue walking. We're passing the Londis now.

'OK, so I've got a question for you,' she says. She's copying my phrasing from when I chatted her up in the café, and the teasing way she's looking at me suggests she wants me to know it. 'Should I get rid of all my books? Just have a Kindle?'

Before I can reply, she continues,

'I'd say ninety per cent of the properties I see have no bookshelves. Like they've been discontinued or something. But it's just so nice having books around, isn't it?'

Her tone is cheerful and familiar, as if we're work colleagues chatting at adjoining desks. As we walk, her hair bobs on her shoulders, the curls the size of Coke cans. I nod, still not able to think of anything clever or funny to say. But she doesn't seem to mind.

'But then they always make me late,' she goes on, 'because if I see one, I can't resist picking it up. This morning, I found myself sucked into this one and I was like, Stephanie . . .'

Stephanie. Her name is Stephanie.

'. . . it's 8.20 a.m. – do you really think you should be starting an eight-hundred-page Victorian novel you've read twice before?' She smiles. 'God, listen to me. Must sound like a right square. I do have other interests, too, I promise.'

I should tell her that I've read many novels that long; in fact, that for the past seven years I've exclusively read long novels. I've probably read the one she's talking about. But I don't. I'm not entirely sure why, I suppose because reading, that long-distance immersion I practise, is tied with being in my cell, which I don't want to think about right now. Also, she might ask how I have the time to read such long books, and I don't want to invite questions like that.

'*Our deeds still travel with us from afar, and what we have been makes us what we are.*'

'Sorry?' I say.

'That's a quote I read this morning,' she says. 'In this book. I just remembered it.'

'*Middlemarch?*'

She stops and gawps at me in exaggerated astonishment, and then gives me an amazing smile before carrying on. We walk in happy silence for a bit, still a few feet apart, but I feel conscious of a shift in our centre of gravity. We're passing the furniture place now. There's a full-length mirror propped against one of the filing cabinets, a new addition to the stock, and as we pass I glance at my reflection. It's the first time I've seen myself in a full-length mirror for a long time. I look OK, I think. My face is getting a bit of colour now and my hair is in a neat fade courtesy of Jackson two cells down, who has the only pair of clippers on the wing. Seeing my reflection, looking presentable, emboldens me.

Stephanie. She said her name was Stephanie.

'So – your name's Stephanie?' I ask. She nods. 'Steph to my mates.'

'I like Steph. And Stephanie.'

'And you?'

'Rob.'

'I like Rob,' she says, and we both laugh.

'No one *likes* "Rob",' I say, tingling. She laughs again, and shrugs.

'So I have another question for you,' I go on. 'My turn. Do you always finish the books . . .'

'Aiiiiiiiiiiiii!'

I recognise the screech as the one that bounces off the walls of D Wing and turn to see Tubey loping down the pavement towards me, one hand down his waistband, cradling his nuts.

'Aiiii!'

I ignore him and keep walking, hoping she doesn't notice and that Tubey will take the hint. But of course he doesn't. He continues to screech at me, moving ever closer. Passers-by turn to look, and Stephanie does too.

'Aiiiii!'

I will him to back off. When he's only a few feet away, he registers Stephanie beside me and does a big exaggerated double take, raising his arms in a 'don't shoot!' gesture. I get a whiff of Ice Blue, the prison issue deodorant.

'Who's your mate?' Steph says as we walk on, leaving Tubey in our wake.

'Just some mad bloke,' I say. 'Friend of a friend. You know.'

She nods, seeming to accept this, but I fall quiet, shaken by how close I came to being exposed in front of Stephanie, and how upset I feel about that prospect. We're at the Job Centre now. We cross at the lights and come to a stop outside the KFC, facing each other. God, she's lovely.

'So, hey, listen,' she says, locking me into her tractor-beam gaze. 'So this may sound weird, but if you ever fancy coming back over to the dark side . . . you see, I'm trying to set up this new agency, like I said, and it's so hard to recruit people.'

Her tone is nervous and artificially bright; it appears that she's been building up to this speech. While I was worrying about Tubey just now, she was thinking about this.

'I know you said you didn't like it,' she continues, 'and you've got another job now, but – can I give you my number, anyway? In case you change your mind?' She looks away, a tint to her cheeks, and if I didn't realise what was happening when she began her little speech, I do now.

'Sure,' I say, and get out my phone, trying to appear casual as I scroll through the menu, keeping the screen turned away from her. I don't know where or how to input a contact on this phone. I feel the seconds tick by. Eventually I find the place, and say 'Go ahead,' and she tells me her number. Then, with a last quick, embarrassed smile, she hurries off towards the tube. I watch her get swallowed up into the crowd, before turning and running to work.

My first move when I'm alone in the stock room is to clear her number from my phone. We're not meant to use the phones for personal calls; they're issued so we can contact the prison if need be, and them us, when they do spot checks to make sure we're where we're meant to be. But as my thumb rests on the delete button, I pause, and decide I must write it down first. Just in case. The nearest surface to hand is a jigsaw box; I find a biro and note the number on the inside of the box lid, out of sight, and then scrub the phone.

For the rest of the day I feel like I'm stoned. I don't mind my job. I don't mind Sami coming into the back room, nattering on in exhaustive detail about her children's academic successes. And when I get back to the cell that evening, it doesn't bother me that Marko keeps badgering me to bring stuff in, and uses my tea towel to wipe up a spill on the floor. It's like I've grown an extra skin – been given a protective coating, like the fluoride they paint on our teeth here. Russia Today; the thumping on the door at 2 a.m. as an inconsiderate night officer checks we're locked in; the bellowing from down the landing. I feel insulated from it all.

I'm not deluded. I'm in here, and she's out there. And even if I were out there, she's maybe fifteen years older than me. More to the point, she's totally out of my league. But for that short stretch of time this morning, as we were walking down that hill, those things didn't matter. It was like we were in a sort of an air pocket between the inside and the outside world, where the normal forces don't apply.

5

Steph

I'm late for lunch and when I arrive at the restaurant they're already there, Tony and the other couple. Tony emailed me their names, but I didn't register them. Tony stands up from the table, throwing his arms wide, flashing the electric blue lining of his suit jacket.

'And here she is!'

I smile, apologise and shake the couple's hands as we're introduced and again, their names go straight out of my head.

'She kept me waiting for an hour and a half at the altar,' continues Tony in a mock-confiding tone, his hand on my back as he guides me to the chair beside him. 'I thought she'd come to her senses!'

I smile. The couple make polite demurring noises.

'New dress?' says Tony to me in a quieter voice, as we sit down.

'Lauren lent it to me,' I reply, as casual as I can, pulling my napkin onto my lap. 'You like?'

He cocks his head, as if considering. He hates it, I know. Rob's fantasy dress is Tony's nightmare: mumsy and menopausal.

I had intended to change this morning, when I returned to the flat after meeting Rob on the hill. Instead, I got back to the apartment and, after stashing away my secret phone, I found myself sitting on the sofa, staring out of the window, absorbing everything that's happened, until I realised I'd be late. It was risky keeping it on, this dress I don't usually wear. Tony will recognise it for the act of rebellion it is. But for now, the presence of this couple means he can't react as he'd like.

'It's a great dress,' he says. 'But I like you looking like you, not Lauren.'

'Ahh, that's so sweet!' says the woman, in an Irish accent. 'Dave, why don't you say lovely things like that to me?'

The tease in her voice and the indulgent way her husband smiles at her makes it clear that this complaint is a joke, and he constantly says lovely things to her. She's wearing the kind of outfit that Tony likes and which I usually wear: tight white trousers and a frilly sleeveless top that reveals a good slice of her orangey-brown, grapefruit-sized breasts. Her face is plump and ageless, but from the grainy skin on her chest I'd guess we're around the same age. Her husband is pink and bulky, his shaven head ridged at the back, as if he's got a brick in there.

I pick up the menu, already I know it off by heart. We come to this restaurant every few months; it's where Tony brings his potential new clients, to persuade them to invest in his latest cryptocurrency. The place isn't anything special, or even nice: a soulless basement on a street behind Selfridges, lined with dusty black marble, water features in place of windows, a column of young blank staff and a mess of a menu that aims to please Russians, Chinese and Arabs, as well as the odd south London wideboy. Tony knows the manager and is noted as a VIP on the till system, so he gets the whole *Goodfellas* treatment – 'Welcome back, Mr Winder' – and the best table in the empty room. I'm sure he also gets some sort of discount, but nonetheless this single lunch will cost more than my grocery budget for the month. I'm supposed to focus on the wife, keep her glass topped up and affect interest in her children, holidays in Estepona and beauty salon business idea.

'Well, I think you look very sophisticated,' this one says to me now. 'A smart working lady.'

'Oh, Stephie doesn't have a job,' says Tony, squeezing my shoulders. 'I make the money and she spends it – isn't that how it works?'

Brickhead chuckles his agreement.

'Damn right!' cries the woman.

I smile.

It's clear to me that Tony has already sussed out this couple's dynamic, and is mirroring it: the tough businessman with a soft heart, in thrall to his adorable, demanding wife. My role is to play along with whatever image he's portraying of us, like sticking my face through those cut-out boards you used to get on seaside piers. Last time, the client was a ratty Albanian who came alone and totally ignored me, and so Tony did too – missing out my glass when he was pouring water and only acknowledging my existence at the end of the meal, when he was negotiating. 'I can't go below eight,' he'd said, and then, nodding towards me, added, 'she's expensive, you know.'

At least on that occasion I could shut down, didn't even need to bother smiling. Today's loving display will be harder to endure. And riskier, too: today I feel powered by a dangerous energy and playing bubbly isn't going to help quash it. Wearing the dress is one thing, but I mustn't go further than that. Be careful; don't get demob happy. Chat nonsense with the wife for ninety minutes, that's all you have to do.

A bottle of white wine has appeared on the table, and Tony takes charge of dishing it out. I don't want any, I need to keep my wits about me, but Tony likes me drinking, and so I take a sip. The woman takes a big gulp of hers and gives a loud sigh of relief. Ah: she's one of these cartoonish, uninhibited people, happy to act the fool to make other people feel at ease.

'Well, he's nice, yours, isn't he,' she says, nodding towards Tony. 'Lucky my Dave has so much inner beauty.'

She blows a kiss towards Brickhead, who leans towards us.

'Too right,' he says, amiably. 'Just call me Shrek.'

Tony laughs along, as if he can understand either a man being so free of vanity as to make a joke like that or a couple being that at ease with each other. He puts his arm around my shoulders. I feel wholly detached, as if I'm observing the scene like one of the statue waitresses stationed in the shadows.

'But then, you're really pretty too,' the woman continues. 'A perfect match! Where did you guys meet?'

She leans over to the olive bowl and picks one out, using her nails like chopsticks.

'He was a friend of my brother's,' I reply. 'Is a friend, I mean.'

'Oh, lucky!' she cries. 'I always wanted an older brother, it'd have been so useful.'

'He's younger, actually,' I say. 'And he's only a half-brother. But – yeah.'

'We were all in awe of her,' says Tony. 'Competed for her attention. And for some mad reason, she chose me.'

66

'Aww, stop!' says the woman. 'You're too cute!'

Tony squeezes me against him and, unexpectedly, I feel myself relax against his shoulder, just for a moment. It's not from the heart, but rather like a reflex, a memory flashback to the days when he said nice things to me often, not just in company, and when I still believed that he meant them. When it wasn't hard to please him, and when I wanted to please him, rather than felt I must.

He abruptly releases me and shifts in his seat, angling himself towards Brickhead. Small talk over; down to man matters. I have no idea what's going on with his business – even in the old days, he never talked about it – but from the increasing frequency of these pitches for new investors I assume things aren't going too well. I turn to the woman, who is thickly buttering a piece of bread. She's had her Botox done recently; I can see the tiny freckly bruises around her eyes.

'So, do you understand all this cryptocurrency stuff?' I say.

'God no,' she says loudly. 'I'm only interested in the money that works on Bond Street.' But as she says it, she gives me a wink, and maybe I'm reading too much into it and looking for a connection that isn't there, but it seems to me that she's acknowledging that we're both playing a part. And I feel the sudden urge to confide in this warm, understanding stranger – for us to go off to powder our noses and, while she's peeing with the door open, tell her about what Tony is really like, how things are very much not what they appear, and about Rob and my mornings on the hill, and watch her mouth fall open.

But instead we look at the menu, and comment on its randomness: oysters and sushi, curry and beef sliders. She squeals when she spots beetroot soup, and tells me how her mother used to make it with black pudding, and then moves on to a story about how her eldest son once attempted to make it for her as a surprise, and she came into the kitchen to find the units splattered with red and her son looking sheepish.

'And honest to god, my first thought was that he'd stabbed someone. My son, who's the gentlest, sweetest creature on this earth. Him making me my favourite soup as a surprise is like, five million times more likely than him randomly killing someone, but still that's what came into my head. Funny how your mind works.'

I laugh politely. 'Is he your only one?'

I glance over at Tony. He's turned away, taking Brickhead through his company record, but he's also listening to us. I know, because, under the table, his foot has moved over to the top of my sandal, the polished sole of his shoe resting on my bare toes.

'Oh no, we've got three. All grown up now, thank god. Although no one seems to have told them that. You?'

Tony's foot presses down more firmly on mine, like he's on the brake pedal of a car.

'Yes,' I say. 'Liam. He's seven.'

'Oh, sweet. Just the one?'

Tony's foot is hurting me now. He's worried I'm going to start telling the truth and break down, or go quiet, or say something sharp like, 'Well, just be grateful your son can make you soup.' All of which I'm perfectly capable of, but not today. I let him sweat for a moment, and then just nod.

'Yeah. One's quite enough for me.'

The woman purses her lips, but before she can ask anything more, I say,

'So tell me about yours. Still at home, then?'

Obediently off she goes, detailing the disgusting habits of her young men, their successes, her troubles with their girlfriends. I nod and laugh appropriately. After a minute, the pressure of Tony's shoe eases off, but he leaves his foot resting on mine, just in case. I'm conscious of the bulk of his shoulder a few inches away. We only sit so close at these lunches. There's a sour odour to him, like he's put on aftershave without washing first. I wonder if he has a new someone else. It's been three weeks since he visited me at the apartment – for sex, that is. He comes over every Sunday, to go through the bank statement.

Still smiling and nodding at the wife, I glance over at him. He's telling Brickhead a story, his face and hands animated, eyes twinkly and warm. In Tony's case, his eyes are not the key to his soul; they give the wrong impression entirely. As Brickhead's wife observed, he looks nice.

A phone starts to ring and everyone pauses to work out whose it is. The sound is coming from my handbag, on the floor. Apologising to the table, I reach down to mute it, glancing at the screen as I do. It's the prison number. My heart deflates, as it always does when I get these calls. I silence it, knowing that there'll be a voicemail waiting for me.

A platter of sashimi arrives – I didn't notice anyone ordering it. As we eat, on autopilot, I ask where they live, and Brickhead describes their five-bed detached with pool in Rainham, and then Tony does his PR job on Nine Elms, trying to convince them to join us in being part of the vanguard buying there, trying to convince himself that our apartment was a good investment. The woman starts talking about the problems with their extension and their efforts to sue the builder, and as she continues, starting to rant, I decide that actually I don't like her as much as I thought; I certainly no longer want to drag her off to the bathroom and confide in her. Instead, I take another couple of gulps of wine and chew on a mouthful of salmon and retreat into myself, thinking about the shabby houses and flats I've seen recently, imagining what it would be like to live in one of them, what it would take to make them a home. And then my thoughts drift to Rob. I wonder what he's doing now, in the back room of the charity shop; going about his business, unaware that he is my saviour.

Might be my saviour. I mustn't get ahead of myself. This is nowhere near in the bag.

I think about this morning: about his sharp, watchful expression; the precisely shaved hairline on the back of his neck. The fact that he identified that *Middlemarch* quote, the one I found on Google. Of course, I intended him to recognise it – that was the point – but it only occurs to me now that it's quite impressive of him, carrying a huge book in his head like that. But then, it's not hard to be better read than me. When did I last read a novel?

I wonder how I'd behave if I was inside on a long stretch. Whether, like Rob, I'd use the time productively, or just give up and shut down until it was all over. The latter, I suspect. I can't think how I've ever self-improved. On the outside, yes, of course – that's an everyday job. But not on the inside.

Except I suppose you could call what I'm doing now self-improvement. If it all goes to plan, it'll lead to a better life, and a better me.

In my wooziness I'm aware of a hand on my thigh, and then I wince as it squeezes my flesh painfully hard. Tony has noticed my dreaminess and, while talking to Brickhead, is discreetly bringing me back to the room. The woman is scrolling through her phone. She's given up on me, and I can't blame her. I should talk – I'll be in trouble for not – but I can't think of anything to say.

'I can't accept less than eight,' Tony is saying in a solemn voice. Then, draping his arm around me, he adds, 'Look at her. She's an expensive girl.'

His arm feels like a dead animal draped over my shoulders. I smile and count silently until eventually he slides it off. Thankfully no one wants dessert or coffee, and Tony signals to a waitress, who immediately steps forward with the bill. After a half-hearted tussle about paying, Brickhead and his wife claim their Range Rover is on a meter, and head towards the exit before the waitress has returned with the card machine. Their departure jump-starts me and without thinking it through, just desperate not to be left alone with Tony, I leap up, picking up my bag, kissing him on the cheek, babbling something about having an appointment, heading for the door, all in one continuous movement, as if that means he can't stop me. But he can.

'Darling,' he says, to my back, when I've only advanced a few steps towards the door. I stop and turn round. Still engaged with the waitress, without looking at me, he indicates with his head that I should sit back down. And, of course, I do, watching him dumbly as he folds the receipt into a neat little square and tucks it in his wallet.

'Did you have a nice morning?' he says, glancing at me. His tone is casual, but this isn't a casual question.

'Yes, thanks.' Although I've prepared for this, I feel a clutch of panic, which I try to keep out of my voice. 'Well, as nice a morning as you can have in Brixton.'

I decided it best to bring up Brixton myself. If he's

asking about my morning, it means he knows I wasn't in the apartment – the most likely scenario is that he sprang one of his surprise visits this morning, found the place empty, then tracked my phone and saw I'd left it behind. But there's always a chance that someone he knows saw me in Brixton, and told him. It's even possible that Tony is tracking me by a different method, with a bug in my bag or something; I don't think he's gone that far, but you never know.

'Oh. I thought visits were only at weekends.'

'Oh no – I wasn't at the prison! It's Liam's course.'

He frowns.

'I told you – or at least I think I did.' I'm careful to speak gently, non-accusing. 'That intensive therapy course . . . the ABA thing . . . it's this private therapist, she lives over there.'

'Oh, yeah,' Tony says. Then, 'Remind me how much it's costing?'

Another trap. We both know I'd never have even brought up the idea of Liam having treatment if Tony had been expected to pay for it.

'Nothing,' I reply. 'NHS. They give you a certain number of weeks free.'

He grimaces again and waves his hand – he's heard enough. I think my excuse is relatively safe. Tony's aversion to anything to do with Liam means he's unlikely to investigate. It's the one area of my life he leaves alone. And if he is suspicious and decides to contact Liam's school to check on this supposed absence, the office has a policy of not giving out pupil information to people they don't know, even if that person claims to be the pupil's father.

I change the subject, to the performance review I know is coming.

'Lunch seemed to go OK?'

'Well, yes, in that it looks like Dennis will bite. But what was going on with you? You weren't engaged at all. She was on her phone after about five minutes. And bringing up Liam – I know you can't help yourself, but . . . thank god you didn't go on.'

He squints at me.

'You've got a weird energy about you today.'

'Do I?' I say, with a quizzical laugh. 'That's odd.'

He keeps looking at me, steadily, saying nothing. I know this is done to oblige me to fill the silence, and by now I'm quite good at not giving in.

'Do I need to pay you more attention?' he says, softly. I flinch – I can't help it – and he smiles at my discomfort.

'Well, thanks so much for that!' I say too brightly. 'Delicious lunch. You're so generous.' I kiss him on the cheek. His freshly shaved skin feels as clammy and dead as the sashimi.

'You're most welcome,' he says, mockingly formal. 'See you soon.'

No point in asking when he'll next come to the flat; his policy is to give me no notice.

As I walk towards the door, he calls after me,

'And give Lauren back that dress.'

Leaving the restaurant feels like escaping a kidnap cellar. I hurry down the street, wrapping my arms around the shoulders of my ill-fitting dress. That dress – the dress Rob loves and Tony loathes – right now, it feels like a life jacket.

6

Rob

On Friday, as I step out onto the hill, all I'm thinking about is whether she'll be there. And there she is: standing just up from the café, near the kerb, looking at something on her phone. I've never met her this far up the hill before and I'm so happy, as now we have more time to talk on the way down. A full fifteen minutes.

As I reach her, she glances up, smiles and falls into step beside me, dropping her phone into her bag, all in one smooth movement. She's wearing blue trousers today, with a matching jacket, her hair freshly spun on her shoulders. That zip-up folder is tucked under her arm.

It strikes me that maybe she wondered why I didn't call her, and I wonder if I need to make an excuse, but she starts talking before I have to decide.

'Please tell me you watched *Fatal Attraction* last night. Or that you've seen it already. Because I have a question about it.'

'I didn't,' I say. 'But ask me anything, I've seen it a dozen times.'

I like the image of her curled up on the sofa, watching a film I know so well.

'A dozen?' she says.

'Have you really not seen it before? How can that be?'

She smiles and shrugs, holding her palms up to the sky. There's something about the gesture that makes my chest flutter.

'Well, I may have seen things that you haven't seen,' she says.

'True,' I say. Anything that came out in the past seven years, for a start. I move back to safer ground. 'I confess, I've got a soft spot for Michael Douglas.'

'Oh!' She raises one of those lovely brows.

'I'm not gay! I just like him. As an actor,' I say, adding, 'Fatal Attraction was one of my mother's favourite films. She thought the girlfriend was the hero.'

Steph laughs.

'Wow, your mum sounds cool,' she says. Then, 'I'm not sure mine has ever taken the woman's side.'

We're passing the furniture place, and for once the man on the sofa doesn't stare at us; he's lying back with his eyes closed, face tilted up to the morning sun.

'She just thinks men are the superior race,' she goes on. 'It's what she was taught and what she taught us. It's so obvious to her, there's no discussion to be had. Like, when we were growing up, me and my half-brother, he always got the first bath, and then I had to go after in his cold, dirty water. When I asked if just once it could be the other way round, Mum said, "Don't be so silly!"'

She sighs sweetly and rolls her eyes. I'm not entirely sure what to say, but luckily she continues,

'Do you have brothers and sisters?'

I shake my head.

'I'm jealous,' she says.

We're passing the Londis now, and there's a black dog tied up outside. It's one I've seen there before but for once, I don't feel the need to stop for it. But without a word Steph slips over and gives it a quick stroke. As we continue walking, we start a good-natured argument about the best breed of dog. She likes Dalmatians, and I vote for Border collies. And I think to myself, Steph is just so *agreeable*. Inside, all the blokes are full of these fierce, stupid opinions formed in a vacuum. Unpalatable, like concentrated squash. Whereas Steph is lovely and light and refreshing, diluted by the outside world. It's like she doesn't need to prove anything or constantly remind herself who she is, or who she thinks she is. I hadn't realised how much I missed female company.

We lapse into relaxed silence. Steph's trousers are long enough to conceal her shoes, but I know they're heels from her height and the smart clip-clop she's making. We're keeping pace with another couple, who are dressed in work clothes walking hand in hand, and it occurs to me that anyone glancing at me and Steph might think we're the same. A couple who half an hour ago were doing up each other's zips; making cups of tea in just the way they like; commenting on the news; asking where the keys are.

'Friday, at last, thank god,' she says. 'So, what's your idea of a good weekend?'

I pause to cobble together an answer from what I've gathered people my age get up to.

'Wake up, like, at ten a.m. . . .' Does that make me sound

lazy? 'Or maybe nine a.m. Go for a run. Erm . . . Brunch? Read the papers . . .'

Too late, I realise I've taken the wrong path. My answer is boring and clichéd, and I run out of steam. Steph doesn't speak, and it's obvious she's waiting for me to finish. This is something else I'm not used to: inside, even those rare people with a basic grasp of conversation, who ask the odd question, always leap to talk about themselves at the first pause for breath. And when people do listen, it's usually for their own benefit. They're listening between the lines, sussing you out, looking for weakness to exploit. Steph's interest in me seems honest and uncomplicated.

Her pause gives me strength, and I start again.

'So, when I was a kid, my mum used to get these ideas of things we'd do together, get really enthusiastic about them but then get bored. Like – one day she'd decide that we'd start horse riding at the city farm, but then actually she'd stop lessons after a couple of weeks because she thought the teacher was patronising. Or she'd say we should learn Italian together, but then she'd abandon that because it was too hard. And so one day when I was about ten, she got it into her head that we were going to walk the whole of the Thames footpath. Start at the Thames Barrier and end at Hampton Court, which she told me was this amazing castle. Up there the river was all green and lush and magical, with these little secret islands where people lived. It'd take us two days to walk it, and along the way we'd stop off and find somewhere to camp overnight. Like – camping in central London? She hadn't really thought it through. Anyway, we start walking through these grim estates in east London, you know, with Union Jacks hanging from windows and fighting dogs throwing themselves at us, and it became clear it wasn't quite what she expected it to be. After a few miles she began to get blisters, and started complaining. And when we had only got to the South Bank she decided that we'd give up. We'd only done, like, a fifth of the walk. I was gutted. I really wanted to carry on and get to this green magic land.'

I pause to catch my breath. I haven't talked like this for a very long time.

'Anyway,' I add, finally. 'One weekend, I'd like to finish that walk. Get to Hampton Court. Although it'll probably be an anticlimax now.'

I glance over to Steph. The obvious response to this story would be 'Well, why haven't you done it then?' Or to criticise Mum for cutting the trip short. When I told Tania this story, her reaction was pretty fierce. But instead, Steph says,

'They have one of those penny machines, at Hampton Court. Well they did have, anyway, a few years ago. You know, the ones where you put in a penny and pay a pound and then turn the wheel and the penny is stretched.' She pauses, and when she speaks again, her voice sounds deeper. 'I took my son to it. I thought he would think it was cool – he was only five. But actually, he got really upset when I explained he couldn't actually buy anything with the penny now. He couldn't get his head around the fact that we'd paid to make some money worthless. Or at least, that's what I guessed he was upset about.'

There's a pause. I'm surprised, because she hasn't mentioned a son until now, and I feel that I should ask her more about him, or make it clear that I don't mind she's got a child, but before I can respond, she continues, now back to her normal, bright voice,

'Anyway. I'm sure you can take it – the coin machine, I mean. It won't upset you! You should go. To Hampton Court.'

We've reached the bottom of the hill, at the Job Centre now. We wait for the lights and then cross the road and stop at our spot outside KFC. Neither of us speaks, and then Steph touches the top of my arm.

'Hey. Look. I'm just going to say it.' She pauses, and in that pause I know exactly what she's about to say, because it's the only thing that should be said right now, after the walk we've just had. Except, of course, it should be said by me. 'If you fancy a drink this weekend – or anytime – then, well . . .'

She glances away, and scratches her ear.

'I can't,' I say. 'I'd like to – love to – but, I'm busy.'

She smiles, sadly, still not looking at me.

I want to say something to make her understand this isn't a brush-off, that I would honestly like nothing more in the world than to go out for a drink with her, or to lie on her bed and watch Michael Douglas films, or to sit reading long novels and test each other on our *Middlemarch* quotes. Even go to the playground and push her son on the swings. Anything, as long as it's with her. But there's nothing I can say, and I can feel upset welling up, so I mutter 'Bye' without looking at her and start off towards the shop.

I've gone about five paces when I hear my name. I look round, and she hasn't moved, is still standing there, the one still person amidst the jostling crowd.

We gaze at each other, and I wonder why she isn't walking towards me if she wants to say something else. After a moment, I start towards her. As I get closer, I can see that there's something different in her expression; a sort of exasperation.

'Rob,' she says when I reach her. 'Listen. I know why you can't come for a drink with me.'

My face turns to stone. I stare at her, unblinking.

'I know who you are. I mean – what you are. Where you live.'

She's looking at me with something like amusement. I return her gaze, expressionless, feeling my insides retract. Then she reaches out to touch my arm.

'It's OK!' she says. 'Really.'

And then, she shouts 'Stop!' But I can barely hear it, because I'm already moving away from her, shouldering my way through the crowd.

Twenty seconds later, I'm at the shop. Sami's waiting outside, and I respond to her greeting with a nod. I don't trust myself to speak. She laboriously unlocks the door and, once we're inside, rather than escorting me straight through to the back, she stops in the middle of the shop floor.

'Ooh, I've just had an idea!' she says. She's not a good actress; it's obvious this is not spontaneous. 'I think it's time to rearrange the window display. Could you help me?'

No. I just want to get back into my room, alone, curl up on my nest and die.

'Now?' I say.

'Yes! Best to do it while it's still quiet.'

I dumbly follow her to the window, where we awkwardly squash together in the narrow space in front of the display. The morning sun is hitting the glass and it's already uncomfortably warm. Sami starts fussing around with a dinner set, asking my opinions on the pattern, as if we're a couple in a department store. I'm boxed in by a grubby headless mannequin on one side and Sami on the other, too bulky for the space, bending over to rearrange the plates. In the dusty light, we both look like we're coated with dandruff.

Passers-by are glancing at us. I feel that they all know what's going on, who I am. A lag on display in a fucking charity shop window. A specimen in a tank.

'Two plates propped upright, or four?' she says. 'This cardigan or the yellow one?'

I feel sweat gathering under my T-shirt. Sami's overheating too; moisture is beading on her upper lip and her black hair is shining. My feelings about what just happened with Steph are swilling around dangerously, like a burst pipe under a pavement.

I summon all my strength to go through the motions and do what's required of me, nodding or shaking my head randomly to what she asks. Eventually, Sami declares her work is done and allows me to climb out from the window. But now she's hit her stride, and decides we should rearrange the other displays in the shop, too. She puts the radio on and I stand in the middle of the shop floor as she flits between the shelves and racks, dancing to the music, almost whirling around the place.

She pulls out some purple thing from a rail and holds it against herself, giggling.

'What do you think?'

I don't know what I'm supposed to say – whether it's supposed to be nice or horrible. Her silliness and lack of sensitivity to my mood is winding me up; I'm aware of it, and concentrate on trying to contain it. Now Sami's holding up a little jacket, far too small for her, and looking in the mirror.

'Ooh, I had one just like this once. When I was young and thin.' She glances over at me. 'Bet you can't imagine me young, can you?'

'No,' I snap. 'I can't.'

Her smile drops. Properly plummets, like a child's. Inside, people don't let themselves show such obvious hurt or upset, and I feel simultaneously repulsed and ashamed of myself.

'What I mean is – you're hardly old now, are you?' I add. 'You look young.'

It's a lame attempt to retrieve the situation, and we both know it. Sami turns away, busying herself with putting the jacket back on its hanger. The atmosphere has turned. There'll be repercussions, I know, but at least right now I've found a way of escaping the situation.

'I should go to the back,' I say. 'There's some stuff to package up.'

'The last one was dealing drugs in here,' Sami says, her voice sharp, her back still to me. 'Leaving money in the clothes. His acquaintances would come in, pretend to try the clothes on and leave the drugs for him in the pockets. And shoes. Carl found a pair of brogues stuffed with them.'

'That's terrible,' I reply flatly.

I slip away, back into the stock room, pulling the door almost closed behind me. I don't turn on the light, and I sink down into the nest of bin bags. Alone at last, in the gloom, I prise the lid off what just happened with Steph.

I try and concentrate just on the facts, and bypass the emotional stuff. What was it that gave me away? I scroll back through everything that's happened over the past week, on the hill. Tubey bounding over? It would be a leap for her to guess I'm inside just from that – unless she already had her suspicions. My abrupt exit from the café? But it was after that that she asked me questions about where I lived, and other things that she surely wouldn't have asked if she knew I was inside. In our earlier conversations, were there any giveaways? Did I let slip some slang? No – I was careful. I *am* careful.

Maybe it was something else that I'm unconscious of; something telling in the rhythms of my speech, or the way I walk. Or something ineffable, like an aura that I'll never be able to detach from.

I get to my feet, switch on the light and pull aside the dressing-room curtain. Inside is a half-length mirror. I'm wearing jeans and a navy, unbranded sweatshirt, and I didn't think I looked any different to the other blokes on the street. In fact, in the mirror on the hill the other day, that glimpse when I was walking beside Steph, I'd looked good; worthy of her, almost. But now, under artificial light and framed by blue nylon curtains, the man staring back at me is a horror. Skin the colour of an uncooked pie. My eyes like I've been up for three days. Hair clipped too short. The high, sharp cheekbones of a wing rat. Of course she guessed.

I back away from the mirror. Maybe I should try and distract myself. My task at the moment is bundling up knitting needles. I sit down and get to work, binding them together with so much masking tape they look like tusks. The morning inches by. Sami stays away from the stock room. At some point, I hear the phone ring on the shop floor.

'No, I don't know whether we have a red blouse in a size fourteen,' I hear her say, in a furious voice. 'You'll have to come in and look for yourself.'

At lunchtime she comes to the door and shoves a Tupperware box towards me, without meeting my eye, before retreating.

It's clear I'll need to work hard for any rapprochement. I take a bite of samosa, but today it's like soil in my mouth. I spit it out and hide the rest in the bin, take a deep breath, and go out onto the shop floor to return the lunch box to Sami. The weight of her fury and hurt is too much to take on top of my misery about Steph, and I need to make it stop. So, summoning all my energy and will, I tell her how delicious the samosas were and how grateful I am for her kindness to me, and how she must forgive me if I sometimes speak roughly or out of turn: a consequence of the stresses of incarceration and the company I keep. I'm on autopilot, but she seems to buy it. She visibly thaws, cocking her head in sympathy at my plight.

'I'm here if you need me,' she says, hand on my arm.

I slink back to my bags, and stay there for the rest of the day. Some people come into the shop during the afternoon; I don't bother to look around the door at them. I feel stuck in a time loop, forensically revisiting all those walks on the hill. Reliving it all, especially the lovely, innocent moments, is painful, but I can't stop doing it. My usual habit is to create alternative endings to past scenarios, imagining different decisions at crucial junctures, but now, with Steph, it's not a useful exercise, because I don't know where exactly I went wrong.

Finally it's time to go. Sami gives me an unwelcome hug before releasing me. Out on the street I walk fast, averting my gaze as I pass the spot where I left Steph this morning. As I wait at the crossing, the traffic noise feels uncommonly loud; the fumes burn my throat. It occurs to me, for the first time since I started coming out, that instead of crossing the road and heading up the hill, I could turn right. Or left. Or turn back, down the high street and head down into the tube. Jump the barrier, pile into a carriage, get off at – East Finchley. Willesden Junction. Wherever. And from that wherever, go somewhere.

When Mum and I lived in the cottage in Scotland, I used to get a thrill seeing the signs on the motorway: *The North*. It sounded so open and mysterious; not just another part of the country but another realm. I could head to *The North*.

But. No. Almost everyone who absconds gets caught soon enough. The friends and family who are helping them run out of money, or get spooked by the severity of the penalties for harbouring and abetting. And if you don't have money or people to help, you won't last a week. Absconders I've met over the years say that they were glad to be caught, as the fear and paranoia sapped their escape of any pleasure. And once you're back inside, you're looking at another pile of years on top of your sentence.

And what would I do, anyway, in *The North*?

So I press the button on the crossing, although someone has already done it, and obediently wait for the green man before crossing. The truth is, I may have the illusion of freedom, but my path through the outside world is as restricted as a racecourse. Down the hill, and back up again, on a timer.

I'm passing the Job Centre when, a little way off, I hear someone call my name.

Not someone. Her.

I hesitate, just for a second, then keep walking, not looking round.

'Rob!'

Her voice is much louder and now here she is beside me, trotting to match my pace. I still don't look properly at her, but glance at her from the corner of my eye. My cheek twitches.

'I tried to find your shop,' she says, short of breath. 'I went in every clothes shop on the high street.'

I still don't speak, but now I do look over at her. She's looking crumpled, by her standards. Her hair has lost its bounce; her shirt is creased around the armpits; that frosty lip stuff has worn off. I wonder if she's really been hanging around here all day.

I keep ploughing on up the hill. Beside me, Steph keeps slowing down to a more manageable pace, hoping I'll follow suit, but I don't oblige.

'I'm sorry,' she says, beside me, short of breath now. 'I handled that so badly. I just wanted you to know that – well, that it's OK. I don't mind.'

We're passing by the furniture shop now. The guy on the sofa is watching us.

I halt abruptly. It takes her a moment to catch on and stop too.

'When did you realise?' I ask.

'What?'

I don't help her out, just keep looking at her. She knows what I mean.

She returns my gaze, face serious.

'From that first day,' she replies. 'When I asked to use your phone.'

The whole week. When she was flirting. Giving me her number. Asking me to come and work with her.

'So what,' I say, trying to keep my voice steady. 'You like criminals?'

She glances down at the pavement, and we keep walking. Then, after a moment, she says,

'Well, not *all* criminals.'

Her voice is different to how it usually is. She sounds coy. And she looks it, too, as she glances over at me. Now there appears to be two separate Stephs: the sweet one I spent the week chatting to on the hill and this one. She keeps on giving me that gaze from under her brows, the one which transfixed me at first but now seems manipulative.

'What,' I say again. 'You saw my phone, you knew I was inside, and you thought it was hot?'

I know I'm repeating my question, but I want to be sure, to double check that the Stephanie I thought I knew has gone.

And sure enough, she gives this silly giggle, and sweeps her hair away from her neck.

'Look, we all have our tastes, don't we?' she says. 'I bet you do. Tall. Blonde. Asian. Whatever. It's no different.'

We're passing Londis now. I come to a halt, so abruptly that she continues for a few paces before stopping, too.

'All right then,' I say.

She looks back at me, frowning, confused.

'Come on then.' I gesture to behind the Londis. 'Car park over there.' I look at my bare arm as if checking a watch. 'I've got a couple of minutes.'

My voice is loud – a couple of passers-by turn to look. I start towards the shop, boiling with rage and now something else, too: a feeling that's been buried for seven years. Lust. I start towards the car park, fuelled by the thought of pressing Steph up against the back wall of the supermarket, my hands squeezing her bare arse, my heavy breath in her ear, hearing her pant. The image is so fucking powerful, for that moment I would risk my release for it. Go back to prison for another seven years.

As I reach the side of the shop, I turn back. Of course

she hasn't followed me. She's just standing on the pavement, arms hanging limp, staring at me. I stop and look at her for a moment, for what must surely be the final time. Then I turn and start running up the hill, as fast as I can go. In four minutes flat, I'm at the gate.

7

Steph

On Saturday morning I have a long-standing date with Roxie. We're going to a sauna as a belated birthday present – her treat. She's even persuaded my mum to look after Liam for a couple of hours. I'd forgotten about this and only remembered on Friday evening, on the tube, coming back from the hill. It was rush hour and I was squashed immobile against a woman, and in my eye line was a newspaper. I stared ahead, trapped, as the woman flicked through the paper and paused on an article about Roxie. 'Roxie Miller: Me and my Vits' – an interview about her supplement intake.

I don't feel in the mood to meet her, with everything that's just happened with Rob, and I'm ready to make up an excuse and cancel. But then something happens to change my mind. After I've collected Liam from after-school club and we get back to the flat, I can immediately tell that Tony's been in. The air feels different, as if it's been stirred. As I move inside, I spot tiny signs of his presence: cupboards and drawers not fully closed; the pile of post in a different order to how it was. Beside the bed, one of my slippers is at an angle, as if it's been kicked. My laptop is still on the bed where I left it but now it's just slightly ajar. He wants me to know he's looked at it. I'm used to this, and I don't think he'll have found anything – I'm careful, and delete continuously, and my secret phone is in the locker downstairs. Nonetheless, today it upsets me so much I need to turn my back so Liam doesn't see my face.

I suppose it's no mystery why I'm so affected by it. After my disaster with Rob yesterday, I feel like I've kicked my escape hatch closed. This is going to remain my life and it'll only get worse. I think of Tony in the restaurant: *Do I need to pay you more attention?* I must get out of the flat, if only for a morning.

Also, it occurs to me that Roxie might be able to help.

So, on Saturday morning, I drop Liam off at my mum's, as arranged by Roxie. Mum greets Liam awkwardly, patting him on the shoulder, and he steps away from her, backing into me. They barely know each other. She was all over Liam when he was a baby, but then her interest and affection started to drain away and now, for the past couple of years, she hasn't wanted to take him at all. She claims she doesn't know how to handle him, although he is the most placid boy on the planet. That she agreed to babysit today is evidence of how much she adores Roxie.

But Mum's favour doesn't appear to extend to wanting to get to know her only grandson; she walks Liam straight into the lounge and hands him the TV remote. I kiss him and explain I'll be back after eight episodes of *Octonauts* before hurrying away, trying to shake off the guilt at leaving him with someone who once suggested I should sue the IVF clinic for the result I got.

The sauna is a Russian place in an unlikely spot in the basement of an office building in the City. Roxie was introduced to it by one of the oligarch girlfriends she hangs out with these days. I've been here before with her; it's where she kicked off her hen night, the limos waiting outside to take us on to cocktails in Soho and dinner in Mayfair, for an evening that cost so much that Tony still brings it up two years later.

The sauna itself is hardly luxurious. You're made to wear an unwashed felt hat and the famous treatment involves being beaten with a bunch of leaves wielded by a silent old man in a white vest, before a bucket of freezing water is tipped over your head. In the café, laminated menus offer boiled potatoes and pork fat by the hundred grams to a soundtrack of dated, mournful music. One of Roxie's friends explained to me that the lack of glamour is the point: it reminds them of their humble roots, their life back home before they ascended to the world of open Amex cards and £40 fillets of miso cod. Also, the place offers them the chance to have a few hours off from their role, as they wander around topless, scrolling through their phones and being rude to the staff.

I'm not late, but the receptionist tells me Roxie is already here and waiting for me in the café. Walking in, I immediately spot her. It's impossible not to immediately spot Roxie. She's at a table, sitting very upright, her hair wrapped in a towel, hand on her phone. No doubt she's already updated her Instagram with one of those make-up free selfies, gazing up at the camera with a vulnerable expression, as if she's being brave for revealing her bare, gorgeous face.

'Doll!' she shouts when she sees me, rising from her seat. As we hug, I feel the contrast between the delicacy of her frame and the full, hard breasts squashed under the towel. Over her shoulder, I notice the two women at the next table have stopped talking and are looking over at us – or, rather, at Roxie. Maybe they recognise her, but I guess, from their expressions, they're just responding to her looks. They're ordinary middle-aged women out on a treat, and they might have been feeling OK about themselves until now.

'So clever of you to suggest this,' I say, as we untangle ourselves and sit down. 'I've forgotten how crazy this place is.'

'Honestly, I think I'd be dead without it,' she says, pouring me a cup of murky herbal tea. 'I'm here once a week. You should come too. Roxie orders.'

I smile weakly. Even if I wanted to come here every week, it's impossible. The place is more expensive than it looks, but even if it was a tenner I still couldn't do it. Roxie knows all this. She changes the subject.

'Oh my god, I've got to show you this,' she says, picking up her phone and scrolling through to a video. I dutifully watch a clip of her baby niece licking a slice of lemon before grimacing and saying, 'Ugh, sour, lemon.'

'Isn't she the cutest?' says Roxie. 'Almost makes me want one of my own. It's just amazing. At first I was like, shuddup, she's not even one – no way can she be talking already. But she is! Amazing. Maybe girls are more advanced than boys, but . . .' She looks at me and trails off.

'Oh god, hun, I'm so sorry,' she says, hand flying to her mouth. 'I am such a dick.'

She looks genuinely contrite, her eyes huge, and I feel tears threaten to well up too, as much due to everything that has happened recently as from her going on about her extraordinary niece.

'It must be so hard for you, hearing about other people's kids,' she continues earnestly. Roxie has never known quite when to stop.

'It's OK, really,' I say, forcing a smile and standing up. 'Shall we go in and sweat?' She nods and follows me next door, where we put on the ugly felt hats before going into the sauna and reclining back on the wooden benches. For now it's just us in here so there's space to stretch out. I take the higher level.

'Oh god, I must tell you who I bumped into the other day,' she says, eyes closed and one thin leg cocked. 'Gloria!'

Gloria is an old colleague of ours from the beauty counter; a tiny, fierce Brazilian. She was open about the fact she was working in retail purely to meet someone to take her away from it, and efficiently achieved her ambition when she assisted a man who was buying some last-minute Christmas presents for his wife. By the New Year, she was holed up with him in Milan.

Roxie tells me that Gloria's now left that guy and married someone even richer and is now living on Lake Geneva and breeding huskies. Relieved to have moved onto safer ground, we start to swap stories of the old days at the department store, and finally I start to relax. Roxie has a good memory and is funny about some of the old regular customers, like the one who would buy £140 creams and return them the next day, the pot scooped out and refilled with Ponds. As she talks I look down at her; in the dim light, her sculpted face in profile, skin glistening, she looks fit for a men's magazine, even in that stupid hat. A tiny diamond stud in her nose, a present from Luke, glints in the gloom. Since the TV show it's like she's joined a different species, and it's hard to remember that once we looked quite similar. She was always being mistaken for my little sister.

We met eight years ago when we worked together on a beauty counter at Fenwick. I was the counter manager and she was one of the new hires, still just a teenager. It was the second job I'd had and I took it very seriously. I liked learning the business of retail, sales techniques, relishing the buzz words – *purchasing decision, basket spend, till codes*. I felt like I was getting tooled up for the future, getting the qualifications I didn't achieve at school. At home, I studied diagrams of the five stages of the point-of-sale journey, hiding the books behind magazines in case Tony got suspicious. At the counter, I practised giving the customer the space to make a hassle-free decision; noted the exact timings of the Power Hour, when the lunchtime crowds upped sales. The products we sold promised to transform the customers, and I'd decided that this job was going to transform me. It was my domain. I was good at it, and I was happy, for the first time in a long time. Then Tony got wind of my enthusiasm, my ambitions, and announced that the time was right to have a baby. And then it turned out we needed IVF, and it was decided that I should stop work to concentrate on it all.

Roxie was a great saleswoman; better than me. She'd started off promoting teeth-whitening kits at trade shows before joining the company and within a month of working for me she broke the counter record, when a customer dropped over a grand on a single sale. She'd flatter and seduce the customers, asking questions and appearing to listen to the answers, as if she truly cared about their moisturising routine and water consumption. Her beauty could have counted against her in that job, intimidating the customers, but she got round it by being really warm and animated.

These days she's not nearly so expressive – another of the changes in her, along with her lips and breasts getting fatter and the rest of her skinnier. Maybe it's down to the Botox but I think it's also that she feels she has to treat her face with more care these days, now she knows how much it's worth.

'I owe you so much, Stephie,' she says, now, lifting her head to look at me. 'Not just for introducing me to Luke. You hiring me. I honestly think the acting I learned there, laughing at their stupid jokes, helped me get on the show.'

She smiles to herself and I guess she's remembering our earlier, simpler lives. But her mentioning Luke makes me think about him, and the situation he's led me into, and which I've now fucked up, and any warm, fuzzy feelings I might have had are snuffed out.

I sit up.

'Rox,' I say. 'I need to borrow some money.'

I don't say any more. I'm feeling trenchant, but I must be careful. I know she knows something of what I'm up to, but I'm not sure exactly what. I suppose I'm testing her – a test of whether I mean more to her than Luke does.

She doesn't speak but her eyes are now open, looking at the ceiling.

'Five grand,' I continue. 'And I'll pay you back as soon as I can. With interest. You know I wouldn't ask if it wasn't important.'

She turns her head to me and reaches up with her arm to touch mine.

'Darling,' she says, her voice thick with regret. 'I'm sorry. I just can't.' Then she adds, 'You know why.'

I look away, back towards the wooden slats on the ceiling. I'm not surprised by her response but I'm upset that I ever asked. We're both silent. I become aware of how much I'm sweating; my entire body, even my kneecaps, are slick with moisture. And along with the sweat it feels like other things are welling to the surface – like how I feel about what happened with Rob on the hill yesterday. The full realisation of how I've fucked everything up, and what that means for me and Liam.

The sauna door opens and we both look up. A female staff member enters, holding a bunch of leaves, and nods at us, unsmiling.

'You first,' says Roxie quickly. She still sounds upset.

I forgot that Roxie has arranged for us to get the branch treatment. There's a stone table in the sauna, like one in a mortuary, and the woman places the leaves at one end and indicates for me to lie down, with my face pressed into them. The leaves are wet and cold against my cheek. I close my eyes, trying to relax, relieved that it's a woman doing the treatment. But then I hear the sound of the door again and open my eyes to see that the woman has been replaced by a thickset middle-aged man, now standing over me, a bunch of leaves in each hand. Without a word he starts sweeping them over my bare back, almost sensuously. I feel as if I'm being felt up by a tree. My eyes are squeezed shut and my whole body is clenched tight too, contracted as far as I can, as if I've been chained down for this. The man picks up pace, the leaves slapping harder and harder against my skin, and now I find I'm fully reliving what happened yesterday on the hill – the moment of Rob marching over to that shop, that look in his eye, what I knew he wanted to do to me in that moment – and Tony is there too – and the next moment I find myself rearing off the table and pushing the man away with all my strength and stumbling out of the sauna, hearing Roxie call after me.

8

Rob

Weekends weren't so bad when Deller was here. On Friday our canteen would be delivered, and we'd each have ordered specific ingredients to make a recipe that we'd then cook together in our cell on Saturday evening. In the days we'd read and go for a run in the yard, if they let us out. And because he was so popular he was often with the other lads, playing poker or whatever, and I got the place to myself.

But now Deller's gone, and Marko's here. Even if I did have any desire to cook with Marko, his diet consists almost solely of Pot Noodles. And, devastatingly, he appears to have no interest in leaving the cell. His one job of the week is delivering the canteen, which involves wheeling a trolley around the other wings, but he declares this task so exhausting that he has to spend Saturday recovering, laid out shirtless, pale and slug-like on his bed. Having Marko four feet away from me would be trying enough in normal circumstances, and after all that happened last week, things don't feel too normal. On Saturday morning, after Carol informs us it's going to be another beautiful day for those who aren't entombed as we are, and Marko observes how she looks the sort who'd like it up the arse, I take *A Suitable Boy* and head out onto the wing.

All three landings are teeming, shouts of 'Ai!', 'Fam!', 'Bruv!' and 'Blood!' filling the air like bird calls, supplemented by the click-clack of pool balls from the tables on the ground floor. At 9 a.m. the wing is already stuffy. The screws have their office door open, and I glimpse their 1990s model table fans on full. No such fancy ventilation for us; we get the stagnant, degraded air. I wander around trying to find somewhere quiet and private, as if such a space might have miraculously sprung up in the past week. The poker guys are set up in their usual corner; it's the first time I've seen them since Deller left. One of them waves me over.

'Heard from him?'

I shake my head. I'm pleased they haven't either; it would have stung if he'd written to them and not me.

'Tech?' says one of them – meaning, Deller got busted because of a phone?

I shake my head. 'He wasn't supposed to be here in the first place, so they sent him back to closed.'

They shrug and turn back to their cards. The positive effect Deller had on my popularity seems to have disappeared along with him.

There will always be guys who want to chat, though: random knuckleheads who think that I'm only reading because I've got nothing better to do. They prowl around the wing like toddlers on steroids, seeking stimulation, and every time I perch somewhere and open my book, one starts talking at me. I could be a chair or a dishwasher for all the back-and-forth he requires as he tells me how many upper tricep curls he's done that morning and how that ranks with his personal best, the progress of his appeal, his grievance with the guy in the cell next but one, his hopes that the cheeseburger will be on for lunch.

And sex, of course. I never welcome the subject in here, and especially not now.

'So I was rumping her, yeah,' says the guy now leaning on the wall beside me, 'and she was all right and everything but her friend was proper dench, yeah, you get me, and so I started rumping her too, the friend, and then the first girl she found out yeah and she went fucking ape, and then there was a . . .'

I pat him on the shoulder and move away to the other side of the landing. The guy immediately turns to the nearest person on his other side and seamlessly continues his monologue.

When I first arrived here, the atmosphere in the wing reminded me of being on a cross-Channel ferry crossing. The confinement makes you restless and unsettled as well as sort of sapped and depleted. These weekends are worse when you've been working out during the week and had a taste of the real world. In closed conditions, every day is pretty much the same as any other day, and once you've accepted that your sentence is the same shit twenty-four hours, stretched over years, you shut down the part of you that seeks change. Your horizons contract to fit the space you've got, and you accept that time is something that's being done to you, instead of something you do things with.

Of course, some people don't accept this and try and control time, either with spice or intensive exercise. In closed prisons, where hopelessness runs high, it's usually drugs. In open conditions, when the end is in sight, it's weights. *You go gym?* is our wing's standard greeting; I must hear it a hundred times a day. There's a clear division in personality types between those who are into weights and those into running. Basically, runners are more thoughtful; or so I like to think. I go for as long-distance as possible, so you can reach that lovely state when your limbs settle into a rhythm and your brain gets rinsed. But when I ask a screw if there's going to be any yard time today, he just shakes his head, with no explanation.

There's no one I want to visit, nowhere to escape to. Moments from the hill keep coming back to me, as fierce and unwelcome as a sudden blast of music from a cell. What Steph said and my reaction to it; that burst of anger; the march towards Londis, fuelled by boiling lust. Pacing the landing, I feel similar to how I did when jammed in the window of the shop with Sami: hemmed in, unable to consider and digest. I don't have space to think about it properly, and I don't have the chance to escape it and get out of my head.

I wish I could chat to Deller. I don't think I'd tell him about what happened with Steph. He might not understand, and say I was an idiot for not seizing my chance. But he'd take my mind off it, and make me laugh.

After another half hour pacing around, I admit defeat and head back to the cell. At the door, I stop. Marko has someone in. I don't recognise the guy; he must be another new arrival on the wing. He's youngish, wearing a vest, his kids' birthdays tattooed on his neck. He's drinking out of my cup. Leaning against my bunk. The TV is on but they're talking – their conversation appears to consist of this new guy itemising the cost of the contents of his house, like a bailiff.

'Stereo, two hundred. Blu-ray, a hundred. Fridge freezer, five hundred.'

Marko is nodding along to all this, as if it matches his own mental inventory.

'One of those instant hot water taps, you know? Three hundred and fifty quid they cost. You got one, bruv?'

Marko shakes his head.

When they notice me standing in the door, the new guy says to Marko,

'The fairy?'

'What was that?' I say, stepping over the threshold.

'Relax, mate,' says Marko, sniggering. 'Was just telling Carter here that you're squeaky clean. Like Fairy liquid.'

I want to turn around and leave, but I must stand my ground. So, ignoring them, I climb up onto my bunk, and find an envelope addressed to me lying on the covers. I recognise Deller's writing, and my mood lifts. Picking it up, I see that the top of the envelope has been sliced open, showing it's been read. The chances are it was the prison rather than Marko – opening a cellmate's post is pretty extreme behaviour – but I look over at them, just to be sure. No, it wasn't him: he's not checking my reaction. Instead he and his new mate have lapsed into silence, staring open-mouthed at *Saturday Kitchen*.

I turn my back to them and open the envelope. Inside is a single sheet of paper. Deller has an education of sorts – well, he did his GCSEs – but always writes in block capitals, and with little truck for punctuation.

Robbo Robbo Robbo,

Greetings from B Wing. Well that was unexpected and unwelcome! Back to closed for me. Though guess I've been on borrowed time for three months. We thought they'd forgotten about me, eh. Anyway, at the risk of sounding soft, I miss

you. It's shit here, a completely different vibe. A lower class,
know what I mean. There's this one guy who licks anyone
who comes in his way, on the cheek, just to fuck with them
I suppose. And a posh twat down the hall who run over a
little kid and says it doesn't matter because the kid 'was just
a chav.' Honestly, they make the goons on your wing look
like fucking statesmen. Eric the Moose is Barack Obama in
comparison.

Hope your alright, mate. Home soon for you! Write to
me please.

Your Deller.

P.S – if you get the chance could you throw those birthday
cards in an envelope and post to me?

Cheered, I get my paper from my shelf and start to write in reply. Someone once told me that a turning point in prison, when you know you've been in a long time, is when you correspond with more people inside the system than outside. I'm well past that point, but while I've written to friends inside before, never within the same actual building. Deller's wing is only a few walls away, but it might as well be on the other side of the country.

I keep my letter light, complaining about Marko mostly. There's a certain satisfaction in writing about what a twat he is when he's four feet away. I don't mention Steph.

On the way down to lunch I post the letter, and it's only then that I remember about the birthday cards, which are still stacked in a pile on the cell windowsill. But I couldn't have posted them to him now anyway: I don't have an envelope big enough, nor enough stamps. I'll have to order them on my next canteen.

Cheeseburgers are on today, to the approval of the general population, but the queue's long and by the time I get to the counter, they've run out. Instead, I get handed a dry bun and, randomly, a dollop of curry sauce. The server tells me the kitchen miscalculated the amount of food needed for the weekend – they've used the same numbers as for weekdays, somehow forgetting that the men who work out during the week also need to be fed. He says it with a shrug and no apology.

The guy behind me isn't having it

'I want a cheeseburger, bruv.' He jabs a finger at the server. 'Are you listenin'? Are you listenin'?'

In all the prisons I've been in, the worst aggro has been at mealtimes. Something primal gets unleashed when a group of captive grown men are denied proper food. The escalating tension is made worse by the terrible acoustics in here; the raised voices are bouncing off the walls.

'That's all we have, innit,' the server keeps repeating.

Normally I would stay well out of this sort of scene, but today, because I'm already upset and unsettled, I feel myself heat up.

'What are you going to do about it?' I say loudly. 'Tell me. What are you going to do?'

The server is trying to look nonchalant, but I can see a shift in his stance; from enjoying the power of telling grown men they're getting a dollop of sauce for their lunch, to realising he's close to trouble.

'Not my fault, bruv,' he protests. 'Not my fault.'

I look at him for another long moment and then glance away, and notice a screw watching the scene from across the room, hands at his hips. He catches my eye and the thought occurs to me that perhaps this is a test: a set-up to see how we react. How *I'll* react. They'll be marking me down in the office later, adding it to my probation sheet, citing my quick temper as a reason why I'm not fit for release. So I mumble an apology to the server, take my tray and head over to an empty seat, next to a bin brimming with discarded food, sauce oozing down the sides. As I chew my dry bun, I do my exercises and count to ten.

Back in the cell, it turns out Marko's new friendship was short-lived. Apparently the other guy started talking about his double garage and how everyone needed one and Marko said he was bored now, and the guy stormed off.

'I wanna go back to the other wing, man,' Marko grumbles. 'Everyone's so fucking petty here.'

I know I'm included in this 'everyone'. Marko is so starved of friends that he's complaining about me, to me. If I liked him more, I'd tell him I know what he means. Everyone is made small-minded by being inside, but that mentality gets much worse in open conditions. When you first go inside, into a B Cat, nothing is expected of you. Everyone's lumped together, from lifers to millionaire white-collar guys to Lithuanian dealers, and you're all in it together, scrabbling to survive in chaos. It's an Us and Them thing. But when you're here, in the final straight of your sentence, there are far fewer dramas to distract you, and you're being observed much more. The stakes are much higher; a wrong move can scupper your parole, so you have to stay on your best behaviour. But aggression and one-upmanship still have to come out somewhere, and so pettiness thrives: blind rage over using the wrong coffee cups or not wiping down the equipment in the gym.

After his grumble, Marko turns back to the TV. I lie on my bunk, but my thoughts are drowned by his running commentary on the value of the houses in *Location, Location, Location*. At 7 p.m., a young female officer bangs us up. She's one of the nicer ones; she even calls me by my first name sometimes.

'Has she smashed anyone yet?' Marko says, as the door shuts. 'I'd have a go.'

On Sunday morning, I go to church. The building is an old Gothic-looking number, built with the original prison. Back then, everyone had the same God, but now the room is on a time share with Islam: there's a stained carpet to kneel on, Arabic symbols painted on the walls, and screens to clumsily conceal the altar.

The chapel is the one place where you can mix with the other wings, and I was hoping Deller might be here. But no, it's just the normal shower. A handful of white-collar guys, labouring under the illusion that attendance will give them a tick on their record. A bunch of junkies, because it's a good place to do deals, with a singalong thrown in. And some genuinely committed Christians, who've found God inside; invariably nutters who are as aggressive about their new faith as they were about protecting their patch before.

The chapel has its own cool microclimate; the chaplain is wearing a fleece over his dog collar. The sermon is about self-forgiveness, as usual. I close my eyes and inhale the stale, chilled air and try to empty my mind; clearing the way for the chaplain's words to have an impact. As if they were a sort of chemotherapy, attacking the hard mass in my stomach. That moment when I marched towards the back of Londis; what I was willing to do to Steph in those few furious seconds.

At the end, I slip away quickly to get into the queue for the phone – there's one in the corridor outside the chapel that isn't usually as busy as the others. Me and some other guy join the queue at the same time.

'Oh please, you go first,' he says, in a posh accent, stepping back and ushering me forward.

'Thanks mate, but you're all right,' I say.

'No, I insist,' he says. 'Really.'

'I think you were first.'

We carry on like this for a few moments, as if we're in a Waitrose checkout or something, until he concedes. I haven't seen the guy before, but he's clearly white collar and obviously new: in his early fifties, maybe, still with a bit of colour to his cheeks and shaggy hair, as if he'd rather look like that kid from *Scooby Doo* than have the kind of haircut on offer in here.

'Why's he doing that?' he says to me, gesturing to the young black kid on the phone in front of us. The kid has put a sock over the receiver so there's a protective layer of wool between him and the mouthpiece. I shrug and smile. The white guy must be new if he's never seen this before; it's fairly common. Someone probably once thought doing it might protect them from AIDS or some nonsense like that, and then it caught on. It doesn't take much for a habit to spread in here. Obviously it's completely unnecessary and doesn't stand up to scrutiny, but that applies to most things in here. Guys still wear their boxers in the shower, even when it's a private cubicle, or walk around the wing swaddled in a thick coat as a shield from stab wounds, as if this was a Mexican hellhole.

The kid finishes up and pulls off his sock before handing the receiver to the white-collar guy, who carefully inputs his

PIN before dialling. When the recipient picks up, he launches straight in, his tone far brisker than when he was talking to me.

'Yes, the boiler is still under warranty,' he says. 'The bottom drawer of the kitchen unit. No, the far right. Yes. *Yes*. How are the little ones? No, not yet. You've spoken to Simon? Tell him I'll call him. What? No, legal visits are different, they don't come off the quota. What? No, it has to be serviced at a dedicated BMW garage . . . What I really miss are those interdental brushes, you can get floss here but it's not the same . . . Yeah you could try, but I doubt they'd get through . . .'

He carries on for a few more minutes before checking his watch and hanging up with an 'OK, 'bye Lambchop.' He hands me the receiver with a brief smile before hurrying off out the door to B Wing.

When I dial the phone rings, and I allow myself to feel expectant, just for ten seconds, before it goes through to the familiar answerphone message, the one I've been hearing for years. It's the default recording from the phone company, with no name; I don't even know if this is her number any more. I should have given up on these calls ages ago, but it's a weekly habit I can't seem to shake.

'Hey, it's me,' I say after the beep, keeping my voice low. 'Don't know if you got my last message, but, er, my release is looking like the fourteenth of July. I'll need to go before the parole board one last time first but can't see any reason why they would put it back. Unless I fuck up, of course.' I force out a laugh. 'Anyway. The job's going well. Deller's gone, and my new cellmate's a dick. But never mind. Out of here soon enough. Um, I hope you're well. It'd be nice to see you . . .'

'Aiiiiiiiiii!'

There's a screech in my ear; I turn to see Tubey has joined the queue behind me. He grins at me, swaying like a cobra.

I hang up. I'd run out of steam, anyway.

'Missus good?' he says to me, as he takes the receiver.

'Good, man.'

'Don't worry bruv, I ain't telling her nothing,' he says, and then laughs hysterically and thumps me hard on the shoulder. I stare at him, confused, before I realise what he's on about. He saw me with Steph on the street last week.

I feel the urge to explain, which is stupid because the existence of a partner has hardly stopped anyone else here trying to fuck about.

'Tania's moved up north,' I say, not meeting his eye. 'Makes it difficult to visit. But I'll go up there, move in with her, when I'm out.'

Tubey nods vigorously.

'Important to have love, man,' he says earnestly. Then he slaps me on the shoulder again before turning to punch in his PIN.

'Aiiiii, bitch!' I hear him shriek, as I walk away.

That afternoon, it's visiting time. Outside in the corridor, I watch the guys gather ready, wearing clean jeans and their tightest T-shirts to show off their freshly inflated arms. An officer hauls a laundry bag of bibs along the corridor, as weighty as a corpse.

To my surprise, Marko joins the throng, looking particularly shrivelled next to these meatheads. Unlike them, he hasn't dressed for the occasion, but at least he's put on a top. When he spots me, he sidles over. I suppose I'm the closest thing he has to a mate.

'Got my missus and kids coming,' he says. 'Blessings of my life.'

Right, I think: a family he loves so much, he hasn't seen fit to mention them at all since I've known him, let alone put up any photos. I know he's trying to rile me, and for a moment, it works. But my indignation that Marko has people who bother to visit him is quickly subsumed by joy. If he's on a visit, I have two hours alone in the cell. I hot-foot it back and lie on my bunk, alone at last, tuning out the noise from the landing as best I can. I fix my gaze on a spot on the ceiling. Deller used to say that even the Taj Mahal hasn't been gazed at as much as the peeling ceilings in this place.

Finally, I'm alone and with space to think. I focus on all the good moments of last week. That soft little hand in mine, signalling the start of it all. That *Middlemarch* quote. KFC. Those eyes. Me telling her about my walk down the Thames path. Those easy silences. How, just by showing interest and listening, she made me feel that things might be OK. As my release approaches there are times when the real world seems visible but unreachable, as if I'm looking at it across a chasm. But I felt that if someone like her was interested in me, then I might be all right.

But she knew. I thought she liked me for who I was, and all along she knew.

Music starts up in the cell next door; a burst of drill, full volume. After a few seconds it stops just as abruptly, and there's a hyena laugh from somewhere, before it starts up again.

But maybe, I think, this *is* who I am. Perhaps prison isn't something I can escape from, and I was kidding myself to think otherwise. I wanted Steph to like me for myself; well, now 'myself' is someone who's spent seven years inside. And rather than being upset, I should feel grateful that she doesn't mind – indeed, that she thinks it's hot. Deller would say so. He'd have no truck with my negativity at all.

She's out there now, somewhere, enjoying Carol's fine weather. I never got round to asking about her idea of a good weekend. Maybe she's at a barbecue with her son, gently rubbing suncream on his face, telling him to lay off the ketchup as he goes in for his second burger. Or sunbathing in a park, her skirt hitched up, reading a long novel. Or lying next to a friend, faces offered to the sun and chatting in low, giggly voices. Maybe she's telling the friend all about me, what a scumbag I am.

Too soon, the door slams open. Marko is back from his visit, face twisted with anger.

'So I ask her to bring something in next time, nothing really, just a few little things, and she says no.' He picks up the kettle and slams it back down on the table. 'Says she can't risk it. Loving the fucking power, she was, I could tell.'

From my bunk I watch his face and remember, again, my own moment of fury on the hill. Did I look like Marko does now, puce and ugly and raging?

'She looked fucking hot, too, sitting there all prim,' he says.

He struggles out of his T-shirt and flings it in a corner before turning on the TV. Later that evening, when the lights are out, I hear him wank furiously, cursing his hot, selfish missus as he does. When he's finally still and quiet, my thoughts return to Steph.

9

Rob

On Monday, on the way to work, I search for her. I go right up to the window of the café and scan the customers, getting odd looks, until I'm certain she's not amongst them. Then, as I continue walking down the hill, I find myself twisting around every few seconds to search the crowds. I'm so desperate to spot her, I glimpse her everywhere – now all the women on the hill are her height, have her hair, are dressed like estate agents. But none of them are her. Of course not. Why would she be here, after what I did?

By the time I reach the furniture place, I'm breathing hard with desperation. In her absence, I want to shout my apology to everyone I pass, as if these strangers on the hill were witnesses to my malfunction. Maybe some of them were.

It's overcast today, the brightness of the weekend snuffed out. The crowds moving down the hill seem heavy-footed, reluctant to go to work after their weekend on heaths and in pub gardens. I wince as I pass Londis, the scene of the crime. Then the Job Centre, and soon I'm at the KFC, the end of the road.

Carl's back from Aylesbury today. As I approach the shop I see him peering in the window, frowning at the new display, and I realise I'm actually grateful for his return. Unlike with Sami, I know where I stand with him, and his low opinion of me chimes with my current self-loathing.

'How was the course?' I ask.

Carl nods, noncommittal. I notice he's trimmed his beard and is clutching a St John's Ambulance first aid certificate, already laminated for display.

'I've got one of those,' I say, gesturing towards the certificate. It's true, I did a course at my last prison. I'm trying to be friendly, but from the look he gives me it was the wrong thing to say. Within a minute, I've pissed the guy off again.

Our journey across the shop floor is slower than usual, as Carl notes the changes wrought by Sami in her morning of madness. He makes odd noises as he spots the differences; little huffs and exhalations.

'No raincoats in May,' he says sharply, more to himself than me, and he starts to dismantle one of Sami's mannequin outfits. I wonder what he'll say about Sami accepting those bags of old books, sitting out the back. I stand there, staring ahead at the boxes of games packed haphazardly on the shelves behind the mannequin, and remember counting those jigsaw pieces, the feel of that damp cardboard in my fingers; the impossibility that even a thousand of those little brown scraps could ever add up to a beautiful picture.

Then I remember. Before I deleted Steph's number from my phone, I wrote it down on the inside of a jigsaw box.

Carl is continuing to grapple with the display; the raincoat belt has got tangled in the wire mannequin. I take a step closer to the boxes. I can't remember which one it was. I think it had a picture of a haystack on – or was it a horse and cart?

'Mate?' I say.

Carl glances over.

'Those jigsaws I counted last week. There's a couple I need to double check.' I smile humbly, like the illiterate he thinks I am.

'I've been worrying about it all weekend,' I add, stepping towards the shelf. 'I'll give them the once-over now.'

I might have overplayed my hand. Carl has now left the raincoat and is focused on me, head tilted. I remember what Sami told me, about how the previous lag used the shop as a drop-off point.

'Of course, you'll want to check the boxes first,' I say.

I suspect this only serves to intensify his suspicion, but really, what can he say? I select an armful of boxes, all the predominantly brown ones I can see, bring them over to him and awkwardly prise off the lids, one by one, so he can check for illicit contents. I can see I've wrong-footed him by showing I know he doesn't trust me, and being cheery about it too. As I open each, I scan inside the lids. In the third box I open, there it is. A scrawl of blue biro.

My work is done, but of course I have to go through the rigmarole with the other boxes before I can take the whole armful into the back, to my nest of bin bags. Within five seconds of being alone back there, I've ripped off the precious piece of cardboard and put it in my pocket.

So I've got a way to contact her. Now, how to do it? I don't have any credit on my phone, otherwise I'd take the risk and use that. Officially, the prison-issue mobiles are just for keeping in touch with the prison and your workplace, in case you're held up. Although there's nothing actually stopping you using it for other calls, it's not a clever idea. Once your number's out there, there's always the chance that someone will call or text in the evening, when you've handed the phone back into reception. I've heard of several guys caught out like that. Once your number's out there, you can't really relax again.

Of course, most of the other lads working out wouldn't have this problem. They have tech secreted in safety deposit boxes at a shop on the high street, which they collect as soon as they're released for the day and then spend all day on fake social media accounts. It occurs to me I could find one of them at lunchtime and ask to use his phone – but no, that won't work. To my knowledge, no one else stays in this area; they're scattered around London, mostly on building sites. I could use a payphone instead, at lunchtime – except that I don't have any money.

Wait. That pound coin I found in a pair of trousers last week and hid underneath a pile of *Auto Traders*.

I dig my hand under the stack of magazines and – yes – touch the nub of metal. Triumphantly I unearth it and stick it in my pocket, beside the stiff strip of cardboard. As I pointlessly re-count the jigsaw pieces, I can feel the coin and the cardboard strip through the fabric of my trousers. Together, the keys to Stephanie.

After the jigsaws, I'm put to work cleaning baby stuff. As I rub the plastic with disinfectant, I urge the morning to pass. I even break one of my own rules and keep an eye on the clock. Finally, it's 1 p.m. and Carl comes to the door with my sandwich.

'I think I'll take it outside,' I say, getting up and moving towards the door. 'Have a walk. It's such a nice day.'

Carl looks at me askance, but again, what can he say?

The high street is as swarming as ever. Music booms from stalls in the market. Motorbikes tear up the road, fumes visible in their wake. A street preacher bellows outside the tube. As I pass by a barber shop, I hear a terrible shriek and glance inside to see a young boy having his hair shaved, in tears, his mum holding him down. But the disorder doesn't affect me today. I'm on a mission.

I wolf down the sandwich while walking briskly to the end of the high street and then back again. Near the tube I spot a phone box, but when I reach it I find the box is just a shell. I keep on searching, walking faster, frustration mounting as I weave through the crowds. Across the road, outside the cinema, I spy what looks to be an old-fashioned red box, and in my excitement I run across the road without looking, narrowly missing a van. When I near the box, I see a woman standing beside it and a man half inside, fiddling with something, and a warm smell hits me. Despite these clues, it takes me a long moment to realise that instead of a phone, there's a coffee machine. A tiny fucking café inside the phone box. I watch the man carefully drawing a heart in the coffee foam for the customer, and wonder whether I'm in an alternate universe.

I check my watch: 1.12 p.m. A few feet away, at the bus stop, is a small queue.

'Where do I have to go to find a working pay phone?' I say loudly, in their direction. Of the half dozen people in the queue, half are glued to their mobiles and ignore me, and the others look at me as if I'm insane. Then one of those on their phone finishes her call and looks over to me.

'Who uses pay phones?' she says.

Her tone isn't unkind. I step towards her.

'Please, I need a favour,' I say. 'I desperately need to make a call. One quick call. To my girlfriend. My phone has run out of battery. Can I use yours? I'll pay you.'

I hold up the pound coin and smile at the woman, trying to channel Deller's charm. The woman is black, middle-aged and striking, with high cheekbones and long dreadlocks mottled with grey. As I speak, she looks at me steadily, her expression that of someone who's heard some shit in their time.

'I'll be so grateful,' I say, and I could not be more sincere.

She glances up at the electronic bus arrival display.

'OK. You've got two minutes.'

I gibber my thanks and offer her the coin, but she waves it away. After passing over the phone, she surprises me by taking hold of my T-shirt in her fist. She doesn't say anything, but it's clear she's going to keep hold of me for the duration. And who wouldn't? So, with this woman clutching onto my top with her strong grip and the others in the bus queue staring at me, I take out that little strip of cardboard and dial.

10

Steph

The air conditioning is broken, again. I phone down to the concierge, but no one picks up. Three Eastern Europeans are supposed to man the front desk on rotation, 24/7, but like so many things in this building – in life – the reality isn't quite what was advertised.

I stay on the line, listening to the phone ring on that unattended desk all those floors down, long after it's clear I'm not going to get an answer. The air in the apartment feels as if it's setting around me, and without that low burr of the machinery, the place is even more hushed than usual. The lack of fresh air is a small disaster, because the windows here don't open. I've grown used to most other things in this place – the absence of character; the lack of storage; the impenetrable convection hob; having to wait five minutes for the lift – but the windows still bother me. I'm not even allowed my own air.

Tony bought the place off-plan, and I didn't know about the windows before we moved in. The developers boasted about a 'winter garden', so I assumed there'd be outside space, but this turned out to be a tiny, glassed-in balcony. Almost worse than nothing at all. When I protested about the lack of access to fresh air, Tony said that sealed windows are standard in luxury developments now. Besides, it was safer; we'd never have to worry about Liam falling out. I suspect he wouldn't be so bothered about that risk now.

I hang up and move over to the winter garden, pressing my forehead against the warm glass, inhaling the trace of the morning's Windowlene. No river outlook for me – the bulk of the view is taken up by the neighbouring apartment building in the development. All the other windows look unoccupied; no plants or signs of individual life. These are starter luxury apartments, kept empty by overseas investors or owned by young City boys who work eighteen hours a day. I occasionally glimpse the latter in the lift, sweaty, with holes for eyes and some poor mute woman in tow.

Above the building is a strip of palest blue sky, threaded with aircraft trails. The triple glazing ruthlessly insulates the flat from noise, even all the building work going on around here. If those two passing planes collided in mid-air, I'd barely hear a thing. From here, so removed, it feels impossible I was ever a passenger on one. And it has been a while. Back when I'd actually wanted to spend time with Tony, and him with me. Or, rather, with us – with me and Liam. That long ago.

It was a trip to Amsterdam, accompanying Tony on some work thing. Liam was a month away from turning two. We hadn't been abroad since he was born, because I'd been busy with him and Tony had been setting up his business, and so I suggested we came along, reminding Tony that soon we'd have to pay for Liam's plane seat. And Tony was keen. He really only ever saw Liam at weekends, for the odd hour or so, and he claimed to be excited to spend some proper time as a unit of three. I think he really was.

Not long into the flight, I looked out of the plane window and, through a gap in the clouds, saw a field of white crosses far below. I pointed them out to Tony and suggested they were war graves in France, and he replied that it'd be impossible to make out graves from this far up, and anyway, we'd barely left Britain; what I had seen was in fact a crowd of tidal turbines just off the Kent coast. I remember his tone as gentle and affectionate, or at least his version of that – he'd smiled and pressed my nose with his finger, in his way of saying 'you're so cute!' Also on the flight he commented proudly on how good Liam was being. Other kids were squealing and acting up, but our son was just sitting dead still on my lap, not squirming or making a sound. For that hour, at least, Tony appreciated his placidity.

One of the things I once liked about Tony was his focus. When he turns his attention to something, it's intense, to the exclusion of everything else. At the very beginning the subject was me; then, for the next decade, it was his business. And, that weekend in Amsterdam, it was Liam. He had read that by the age of two children should have a fifty-word vocabulary and the odd two-word sentence, and as we pushed our son around the streets, he tested Liam, pointing things out and asking what they were. First, he went through all the obvious things – *father, mother, dog, tree, bird, boat.* Then, when Liam didn't respond, Tony said that maybe he was skipping all the basic things and going straight on to the more advanced stuff. *Canal. Streetlamp. Lemon. Bicycle.* Of course, Liam wasn't. And it wasn't just the absence of speech, but of any engagement at all; he only responded to his name after several attempts and even when Tony got right down in his face, Liam preferred to fiddle with his coat button than look at him.

Tony grew more and more frustrated, bumping the pushchair ever more roughly over the cobbles as the weekend went on.

'It's like there's nothing in there at all,' he said, pointing at Liam's head. 'It's completely empty.'

Then he turned on me.

'You told me he'd said lots of stuff recently. *Juice, mummy, choo-choo.* Every day, when I came in, you said there'd been a new fucking word.' And it was true. I couldn't explain Liam's sudden silence, and I admit I felt annoyed and frustrated with him too. Why choose this weekend to clam up, when finally we were all together and he had his father's full attention?

Of course, now we know what was happening – a regression, common with autistic children, where they seem to lose their speech overnight. But that weekend, long before any diagnosis, was the turning point, when Tony's love for Liam started draining away – along with any affection he had for me, too. On the flight home, as we flew over the Channel, he pointed out the turbines.

'Look, there are your war graves,' he said with a short, cold laugh. 'Now we know where he gets his brains from.'

Today, as I stand in the winter garden, the sun is hitting the green reflective windows of the building opposite. All those units, just like this one; only happier places, surely. I can glimpse the tangle of cranes over the new development. Way down on the street below, miniature buses and specks of people go about their business. A spider's web clings to the outside window frame. It's been there for a while. A spider went to the effort of climbing sixteen floors, and for what?

There can't be any insects up this high. I wonder when she realised her mistake. Maybe insects make bad decisions, too. Or maybe some are born different, just like humans.

I move back inside and put in another call to the concierge. This time Abdul answers, and says he'll log a complaint with the management company. His sluggish manner annoys me – he actually sounds stoned – and my tone sharpens. Abdul has always riled me, and recently I've started to suspect that he's in Tony's pocket. I can well imagine him agreeing to report on my movements for a tenner a week.

'You're the only one who's complained,' says Abdul, when I've finished.

'That's probably because I'm the only one here,' I reply. 'Sort it out. Please.'

As I hang up, it crosses my mind that perhaps it's not the building's fault. Maybe Tony has the air conditioning controls linked up to his phone, too, as well as the heating and lights, and he's turned it off for some reason.

It hits me heavily, once again, that I'm not getting out of this place anytime soon. I managed not to dwell on it too much this weekend, instead devoting myself to Liam, but now I'm alone I can't stop turning over what happened on the hill. How I misjudged Rob. Or rather, how I thought that at heart he was an ordinary bloke who would be thrilled to have it handed to him. I've failed at a lot of things, and I freely admit I'm ignorant, but the one thing I've always managed, that I thought I was good at, was men. That moment when he marched off towards that shop – maybe that had something to do with lust, but mostly I saw fury, and humiliation.

This wallowing isn't my style. I mustn't let myself succumb to these thoughts. I move to the sofa and pick up my laptop to try and distract myself. Usually, that means lurking on online forums, anonymously venting my hurt and hatred of Tony and worries about Liam, but today I don't have the strength, and I choose instead to scroll through flats on Rightmove. Normally I find it easy – soothing – to put myself in those empty spaces and bring them to life, but not today. The flats all look like dumps, with mean windows and cheap floors and '90s kitchens, their white goods rudely jutting out from under the worktops. And what's the point in looking now, anyway? I'm going nowhere.

So I give up and turn to my other task for today: photographing Liam's old clothes to sell on eBay. Strictly cash on collection. I've already retrieved the bag from my locker in the building's basement gym. My one secret place. I don't think Tony knows there are lockers down there – even when he lived here he never used the gym, claiming the machines were shit. The locker acts as my secret bank account, too, although there's barely anything there, due to topping up my Oyster card to get to the hill, and coffees in the café.

I tip the bag onto the floor. These are Liam's baby clothes: expensive, designer ones. Back then, when Tony saw Liam as his heir, he spent loads of money on him. I'm going to sell them as complete outfits; I reckon they'll fetch more that way. I smooth out each item on the floor and then put them together, styling them as if I'm dressing a two-dimensional infant: stretching out the little arms of the tops, folding over the sleeves, tucking a blue shirt inside a green cashmere jumper, collar neatly out, pairing it with some Armani jeans. As I work my memory leapfrogs over everything that's happened in the years since, back to that sweet, innocent, self-absorbed period of late pregnancy, when I was preparing for my life to change for ever. And then on to when Liam was a newborn, and the fierceness of my love for the tiny human I'd created felt like it would protect me from anything. Before I discovered that things could still go wrong.

As I'm angling my phone to take a picture, it starts to ring, making me jump. The display shows a mobile number, but one I don't recognise. Not Luke's. But wait – he could easily be using someone else's phone, or changed his SIM. I don't want to risk it. I know I'll have to deal with him soon, but I'm not ready yet. So I mute the phone and place it on the sofa, watching the screen until the call rings out and goes to voicemail, then turn back to the clothes. But I can't concentrate. My mental energy is being sucked into that slim silver box. I can sense Luke's voicemail squatting inside, impatient. My brother really doesn't like being ignored, much as he doesn't like his schemes failing.

I hold out for another few minutes before leaning over to pick up the phone. Best to get it over with. Walking over to the winter garden, I dial voicemail and then put the phone on speaker and hold it at arm's length, to lessen the impact of his anger.

The recording starts, and it's a male voice, but not the one I was expecting. And he doesn't sound angry.

'Hello. Yeah, it's Rob. From the hill? I just wanted to say I'm sorry about before. What happened. What I said. I shouldn't have done that.'

There's a pause, and traffic noise fills the call. The sigh of a bus door opening. Then I hear just the briefest snatch of a woman's voice before the call cuts off.

I stare blankly out of the window, looking at the trace of my reflection in the glass, as I digest this turn of events. This

123

reprieve. Then, I look back at my phone. 2.10 p.m. Plenty of time. Of course, I'm not dressed up in my normal smart Rob outfits – just in jeans and a vest – but I decide not to change. There's no need for all of that pretence now. I stuff Liam's clothes back in the bag and head out, waiting impatiently for the lift to take me down to the gym, where I hide the bag in my locker and head back upstairs.

Abdul is slumped at his desk, watching some video on his phone. The air conditioning seems to be working just fine down here. I head through the revolving doors, and emerge from the cool, stultified lobby into a blast of traffic noise and gritty air.

11

Rob

I'm out the back, under-occupied, twisting the top of a bin bag then releasing it to twirl, when I hear the bell over the door ring, signalling a customer. Then voices. I don't bother to listen – it's a strain to hear what's being said above Magic FM. Carl never used to play music in the shop, but he's had the radio on every day since returning from his management course. Perhaps he learned that sentimental music increases sales. Maybe he's secretly in love.

'Your Song' fades away, and in the relative quiet, before the DJ starts speaking, I hear a woman's voice say,

'. . . *really* long books?'

It's only three words but her voice is strong and clear, as if she's projecting on stage.

It's her.

I can't hear Carl's reply, but I guess he points to the books section.

'Oh yeah, I see it,' she says. 'Thanks.'

Her.

I lay down the bin bag carefully, as if it were full of glass rather than rags, and creep to the door. My first glimpse of the woman gives me doubt. She's standing with her back to me and although she's blonde and the right size, she's dressed very differently to how I know Steph, in tight, pale jeans and a white vest. Her hair is roughly bundled up on the crown of her head, like she hasn't given it any thought.

But then, the woman turns profile on and I can see that it's definitely her. I pull back into the gloom of the back room, heart clobbering my rib cage. I made that phone call and, somehow, I summoned her.

On the radio, the adverts finish and another song begins: 'Against All Odds' by Phil Collins. I creep back to the door and stick my head out a little further than before, so I'm visible, willing Steph to turn and see me. And then she does. It's just a glance over her shoulder, the briefest of eye contact; but it's clear to me that she knew I was there all along.

Carl turns in my direction; I duck back inside and stand to the side of the doorway. I realise I'm holding my breath. Then I hear her voice again.

'OK to try this on?'

I can't hear Carl's reply, but imagine him shrugging his assent.

A moment later, I see a flash of white vest as Steph comes to the door of the stock room and ducks into the changing room. The curtain goes right down to the floor; once she's inside, there's no sign of her. She is standing dead still in there, and I'm frozen too, three feet away, as if we're playing musical statues.

Then, finally, she speaks, as softly as a person can without actually whispering.

'Rob.'

I close my eyes to relish the sweet word. My worries about being discovered dissolve away.

'Rob,' she says again.

'Yes.'

Silence from her. And then I notice the slightest shift of movement in the curtain, at shoulder height. As if she's brushing it with a finger. I stare at the fabric, unsure how to respond – or whether I'm meant to at all.

Then the blue material moves again, but more decisively, as if she's pressing her hand against it. Now there's no mistaking that she wants a response. I step to within touching distance of the curtain and raise my hand. I'm hyper alert, conscious that the radio means I can't hear what's happening out there, whether Carl is about to catch us. My nerves are singing.

My fingers touch first the curtain, then her hand behind it, until we're pressing our palms together. The curtain is thin enough to feel the contours of hers, the soft mounds under her thumb and fingers. Neither of us speak. Then she presses the tips of her fingers in between mine, as if to interlace them, but the material prevents it, so instead she takes two of my fingers and squeezes them in hers, bunching up the rough fabric around them. I close my eyes so I focus on just the pressure of her hand. I can also smell her – her perfume, the smell of spicy roses, overpowers the mustiness of the curtain. I'm acutely aware that her hand leads to her arm, and her arm is attached to her body: that the whole of her is there, just a foot away, separated only by a thin piece of fabric, and that she might be expecting me to wrench back the curtain and grab her. But the gap between knowing this and taking action feels impassable – the curtain might as well be a steel door. I am just going to remain here like this, plugged into her socket.

Then she loosens her grasp on my fingers and drops my hand, and for a moment I think she's going to pull back the curtain herself. But instead, the material shifts again and now a far larger shape presses against it. I take a step back and see the outline of shoulder blades through the fabric, and I realise, with a surprising sense of relief, that she's offering me her back rather than her front. Her head is bent forward, revealing the line of her neck. I reach out my hand and again make contact, first touching her nape and then running my fingers down and across her left shoulder and down her left side, across at the waist, feeling the ridge and rivets of her jeans, and then up the right, tracing the outline of her with the lightest of touches, as if she'll disappear under pressure. Now I can hear the sound of her breathing, and I'm breathing hard, too. I'm pretty certain that I'm in the midst of the best moment of my life.

Then there's a sound from outside. Carl. Suddenly the radio loud again, as if it's been turned right up. We both freeze, my hand on Steph's elbow.

'OK in there?'

'Yeah, fine,' Steph calls out.

Her voice is perfectly calm and composed – I'm not sure mine would be. Then, as Carl moves away, back into the shop, she says, one last time,

'Rob.'

Promise, acceptance, recognition: it seems impossible that one syllable can convey so much meaning, but that *Rob* does. Then she moves away, leaving the curtain hanging lifeless, and she's gone, emerged back onto the shop floor. I remain stuck to the spot.

'Too big, I'm afraid,' I hear her say to Carl. A moment later the door bell tinkles as she leaves the shop.

The next morning, as I step out onto the hill, I know she'll be waiting. And there she is – standing just down from the café, holding a coffee cup, her gaze turned in my direction. As I walk towards her she watches me, smiling, showing those neat, luminous teeth. Her hair is pulled up on top of her head, with two long strands at the front. No sunglasses. After yesterday's casual outfit she's back to the smart dress and the invisible tights.

I reach her and, seamlessly, we start walking together. There's a few feet of pavement between us, so an observer might not necessarily think we were together, but it's as if that gap is electrified. It's the perfect distance for holding hands; if we both reached out, we'd touch. I feel like she's also aware of this, and, like me, thinking about our palms pressing together in the shop, sandwiching that rough blue curtain. Our strides are perfectly matched. We don't speak, but I realise I'm smiling to myself – on the verge of laughing, really. When I glance over at her, she's doing exactly the same.

I've only experienced this mutual heightened state once before, at the beginning of my relationship with Tania. It was after we first spent the night together and, walking to a café on Upper Street for breakfast, we both knew that we were at the start of something life-changing and were trying to digest this momentous new realisation; feeling simultaneously en-twined and separate; at peace and over-excited. It was one of the few times Tania was lost for words.

Today, too, I feel that Steph and I could happily do this whole walk down the hill in silence. But then again, our time together is so precious, I feel I should say something. As we're passing the furniture place, I start to speak, and, at the same time, so does Steph. We laugh.

'You first,' she says. 'I insist.'

What I really want to say is *will you be mine for ever?* But instead, I ask the question that crossed my mind last night, as I lay in my bunk reliving the day, as Marko shouted abuse at *Big Brother*.

'How did you know where I worked?'

She looks at me, bemused, and gives me a nudge with her elbow, breaching the magic space between us. 'I worked it out. It wasn't hard.'

'But I just said I worked in a shop.'

'Yes, well . . . prisoners often work in charity shops, don't they? So I just poked my head in all of them. Then I saw your manager and remembered you talking about a fat bloke in a maroon jumper, so I guessed it was that one.'

The fact that prisoners work in charity shops is common knowledge? I'd assumed it was kept within the system. I wonder what else the general public knows about us. This is the kind of train of thought – a reminder of the indistinct barrier between the inside and outside worlds – that on other days would leave me feeling insecure and anxious. But not today. I can't imagine what could unsettle me today. We continue to walk. The pavement is scattered with the spiky balls fallen from plane trees, which we crunch underfoot. The blackbirds are out.

'Your turn,' I say.

She looks at me thoughtfully.

'No, actually, I think I'll wait. Another time.'

I don't press it, in case it's something that could puncture this moment.

Her heels are higher than the ones she wore yesterday; when I look over at her, our eyes are almost level. She yawns, delicately, holding her fingers across her mouth.

'God, sorry,' she says. 'I didn't get much sleep.'

'Me neither.'

It's true. I twisted about in bed, semi-aware, until the cell started to lighten. Of course, I've had many sleepless nights before, thanks to prison ambient noise and the habits of pad-mates, as well as visits from memories and, of course, my conscience. But not like this. She has disrupted me, changed my chemical balance.

I don't want to tell Steph I dreamed about her. What goes on in my head at night will be the last thing I tell anyone. So instead I say, by way of explanation,

'I share a room with a snorer.'

It's not true. Marko does lots of maddening things, but that's not one of them.

'God, that's not what you want in a padmate,' she says.

It's funny hearing that phrase coming from her: I'd have thought she'd only know 'cellmate'. Another example of surprising common knowledge.

'How do you deal with being cooped up with a stranger like that?' she continues.

'Um, well, you set out ground rules from the start,' I say. 'Like, having respect for the other person's stuff . . .'

'Mentally, I mean,' she says.

'You don't,' I reply, after a pause. 'You never master it. Or at least, I haven't. You just get used to it. You just sort of contract into yourself, so there's a space between you and where you are. Like a moat or something. And then you live inside yourself.'

131

'I can imagine,' she replies. 'Or rather, I can't. I'm really impressed you're still sane.'

We're passing the Londis now. I glance at her face to see whether the spot still has any resonance for her, but she doesn't react at all.

'What do you notice when you're out here?' she continues. 'How has the world changed?'

'Vaping,' I reply, immediately. 'And everyone is obsessed with coffee. And with their phones. Although we can hardly talk – prisoners, I mean. iPhones are probably the number three topic of conversation, after women and the gym. Oh, and food. So number four, then.'

Steph smiles and nods, encouraging me to continue.

'Actually, the thing that's really different out here is time,' I go on. 'It's hard to explain, but inside, time is sort of – useless. Dead. There's such a surplus of it. But then it can also do odd things – like, an hour takes for ever, but a year can go by in a flash. Out here, there just isn't enough of it.'

Steph is having this effect on me. I didn't realise how much I have to say. I'd forgotten what it's like to talk to someone genuinely interested. Even back when I had visitors, none of them would ask me proper questions. My mother said she found it too upsetting to talk about my situation, and so during her visits she'd tell me about herself and what she'd been doing and her latest row with her sisters or how the sculpture classes were going, and the bloke she'd met who wanted to start a B&B in Croatia. Occasionally a friend would ask questions, but they'd either be something big and vague like 'how are you?', to which the only answer was 'OK', or they would want to know what it's like taking a shit with someone else in the room. Or they'd want to hear tales of shankings or whatever, things they've seen on telly, and I'd have to tell them there wasn't really much of that. That life inside is mostly pretty dull. No one wanted to know – and, to be fair, I didn't know how to properly explain – that time is the threat inside, the thing you battle, rather than predatory psychopaths in the showers. The knowledge that the best years of your life are being taken from you, and your identity eroded, and you only have yourself to blame.

There is the occasional man inside who's thoughtful enough to talk to about this stuff, but why would we discuss it? It'd be like being stuck out in the middle of the ocean with someone, both treading water, no help in sight, and them asking you what it feels like to be on the verge of drowning. Also, you have to be careful about what you say, and not reveal vulnerabilities, because they can be used against you. Even with people like Deller, it's best to be cautious.

Now, though, I can't stop talking, and answering questions Steph hasn't even asked yet.

'It's amazing what you don't miss,' I say. 'All the little luxuries, like nice food and coffee and a good mattress and a bath and that sort of thing. You adapt really quickly to all that. And the big stuff – well, you sort of shut those impulses down. Well, I do. You have to. You can't let yourself start fixating on what you haven't got, otherwise you'd go mad. Your horizons adjust to the space you've got, you know? Some guys are always going on about sex or an ice-cold beer or whatever. But I never did that. That's the path to madness. My old padmate Deller, the one before Marko – he did that, before I asked him to stop.'

At that, I notice that Steph has turned away, and I fall silent. Maybe I'm boring her with this rabbiting on, finding my voice after years of monosyllables. I stare at her little ears, noticing how neatly her hair is tucked behind them. We're still keeping the two-foot distance between us. I wonder when we'll touch again. There seems to me to be a mutual, unspoken understanding that when we do, it won't be some rushed, secretive thing like before, in the stock room – magical though that was. How it can happen, and when and where, I don't know.

Or maybe it won't happen. She's still not looking at me. I really hope I haven't somehow blown it. Maybe she's wondering about my crime. It's all very well me talking about life inside – but what did I do to deserve it? Perhaps she's annoyed I haven't volunteered the information. Perhaps that's my duty.

We've reached the lights now. We cross the road and come to a stop on the pavement, outside the KFC – our parting place. Neither of us move. She's looking at me again now, and smiling, but I'm still worried about her earlier silence. I want to part on a bright note, to recapture our earlier spirit.

'Actually,' I say, 'I tell a lie. There *is* something that I miss.' I pause, for effect. 'I'd kill for a KFC.'

I gesture over to the restaurant behind us.

She laughs, gratifyingly.

'If only all dreams could be so easily fulfilled.'

I explain about how some people get lunch money but I don't. Part of the deal with the charity shop is that they provide lunch for me.

'So you haven't had one since you've been out?'

As I shake my head, I notice a small change in her expression, the flicker that comes with a good thought. But then, all she says is,

'You should lower your expectations.'

We say goodbye and she briefly touches my arm before turning away. I watch until she is claimed by the tube.

At work, the day proceeds like any other, except that I no longer feel I'm alone back there in the stock room. The sounds from the shop floor are muted as I sit, my hands in bin bags, looking at that blue nylon curtain a few metres away, and relive the events of yesterday – the feel of Steph's body parts as she presented them to me, in turn, pressed against the cloth. Then, as the day ticks on, I start to elaborate, imagining what could have happened if I had pulled open the curtain; if she had pulled open the curtain; if Carl and Sam had left the shop for some reason; even if they hadn't. At one point in the morning, when I'm deep into this fantasy, a woman slips into the changing room. I only catch a glimpse of light hair and for a moment, I'm fully convinced that it's Steph. That again, I've somehow conjured her into being. I find myself rising to my feet, but then freeze as the woman coughs, and even from just that sound, I know it's not her. I sit down again, feeling a surprising sense of relief. As Steph almost said earlier, dreams shouldn't be so easily realised.

The next morning, she's waiting there again, in the same spot. Even though I'm expecting her, the sight of her floods me with a sweet, warm feeling – the fastest-acting drug ever invented. Her hair is different again today – dead straight and ironed, flat as a veil down her back. As I approach, I wonder what governs her hairstyles; whether she decides each morning according to mood, or whether the styles are on rotation, like the dinner menus inside.

'Where do you live, by the way?' I say, as we start off down the hill.

'You won't have heard of it.'

'Try me.'

'It didn't exist when you went inside,' she says. 'It's this new development Nine Elms. On the river, near . . .'

'. . . Battersea Power Station.'

She glances at me and smiles.

'How do you know it?'

'I read the papers.'

She nods.

'I thought nobody actually lived there,' I continue. 'That it's just for foreign investors.'

'Well, yeah, you're mostly right,' she says. 'But there are a few of us actual people.'

'The reason I know about it is –' I pause. 'Well, I'm not really interested in property and stuff. But there's a new tube stop, isn't there?'

'There will be. In a couple of years.'

'I like the tube,' I say.

I'm conscious that this is in theory a moronic thing to say, but somehow, with Steph, now nothing I say seems stupid. I feel she'll understand exactly what I mean by that statement – that I love the design of the map, how it simplifies a huge, messy city, and the fact that you can get inside a bullet deep below the pavement and cross London in twenty minutes. And I also know that while we may be talking about the tube, or whatever, both of us are really just thrilled at being close to each other, and anticipating the next time we'll get our hands on each other.

'It's going to be on the Northern Line,' she says. 'Which is a shame. Why not the Victoria?'

'Everyone loves the Victoria,' I say.

We walk in happy, buzzy silence for a moment.

'Our building is called Driftwood House,' she says. 'Ridiculous name, right? They have these big lumps of wood randomly dumped around the lobby.'

I note the 'our'. I hope she just means her and her son, but I don't want to ask right now.

'And these stupid sealed balconies,' she continues.

'Well,' I say, 'when I'm doing my walk to Hampton Court I'll wave at you.'

'No good,' she says. 'No river view, you see. But if you're in a plane over London, then give me a wave.'

'Well, I won't be doing that,' I say. 'Not for a while, at least.'

'You don't like to travel?'

'No,' I say. 'It's not that.'

I feel myself deflating, punctured by reality. When I get out, on the fourteenth of July, I'm not going anywhere for a long time. Maybe ever. You can't travel abroad when you're on licence. And as an indeterminate sentence prisoner, I might be on licence for ever. Then there's the small matter of having enough money to buy a plane ticket . . . It's a moment of unwelcome clarity about the future, and now I'm aware again of all the other people on the hill; of the traffic noise, the fumes. We walk in silence for the last bit, down to the Job Centre, and wait at the lights in silence. I feel desolate and folded in on myself; I can't look at her. I wonder if she can sense my change in mood.

We cross the road and stop outside the KFC.

'Listen –' she says, and I know from her look she's not thinking about my inability to travel – 'I need to apologise. For what I said last week, about liking prisoners.' She says the word without embarrassment, not lowering her voice. 'I was just nervous and being an idiot. Talking shit. For what it's worth, I don't like *prisoners*. It's only you.'

And with that she smiles and turns off towards the tube. I watch her until she disappears, and then turn and start for the shop, my buoyancy restored. I didn't ask whether I'll see her again, but I don't need to. She'll be there on the hill tomorrow, I know.

The rest of the day, I am extremely patient with Carl, and at peace with the rest of humanity – even when I find a stash of dirty nappies at the bottom of a bin bag. My sense of invincibility persists when I get back to the cell that evening. Although Marko tries his very best, there's nothing he can say or do to wind me up. In my bunk, turned to the wall, I replay the morning's encounter moment by moment, examining each detail I've learned about her before committing them to my memory. I imagine her in her Nine Elms flat, in Driftwood House.

Then, something snags my memory. She said that the development hadn't begun when I went inside. How did she know that?

The next morning, Thursday, she's there, in the red dress, her hair back to careful waves around her shoulders. I fall into line beside her and she gives me her coffee cup. Our morning routine.

'So, I need to ask you a question,' she says, as I take a sip.

I hand her back the cup, and look at her as we walk. From her serious tone, I know exactly what that question is. The moment had to come. I've steeled myself.

'Manslaughter,' I reply, my voice steady. 'A one-punch thing. Outside a club.'

I look across at her. This is the first time I've told anyone on the outside what put me inside. And this is not just anyone.

She nods, thoughtfully. No hint of shock or revulsion.

'Anyway!' I say, as if that's the end of that. 'So, what's in store for you today? More flats without bookcases?'

'Manslaughter,' she says. 'That's a long sentence, right?'

'Yeah. I'll have been inside for seven years.' It's a slightly evasive answer, but I want to avoid revealing I got an IPP sentence, where there's no fixed term and you have to convince the parole board you're fit for release. It doesn't sound good.

'And you're nearly out?'

'Yep. Fourteenth of July.'

She nods. This is the moment to ask about her comment yesterday, about how she seemed to know I'd been in for a long time when we spoke about Nine Elms. But I'm not sure how to put it, and anyway, do I really want to know how she could tell? That I give off the scent of a lifer?

'Have there been any good things about it?' she says.

'About what?'

'Being inside.'

I must look surprised, because she adds, 'I'm hoping that isn't the most stupid question of all time.'

'It's not a stupid question,' I say. 'It's an interesting one. I've just never been asked it before.' I consider for a moment. 'It's safe. I know that sounds weird, and prisons are meant to be hellholes where you're constantly on guard, but if you stay away from drugs and debt and are sensible, then you can stay out of trouble. Especially in open conditions, because the mad people don't usually get that far. There's a sort of structure to it and once you get your head around how it works, it's OK. I've made friends. Well, one friend. No one's judging you inside, no one really cares what you've done, it's just how you behave inside. Erm. And all your needs are catered for, I suppose . . .'

'Except sex,' she says.

I glance over at her, but her expression is thoughtful, not suggestive.

'Yeah,' I say.

We continue to walk in silence for a bit. I wait for more questions about my crime, but none come. She appears to be unperturbed by it, or at least incurious about its details. I feel both grateful and surprised.

'Are you ever going to tell me anything about you?' I say.

'Ask me anything,' she says. 'I'm an open book. I always feel I should be more mysterious, actually.'

'I think you're very mysterious,' I say.

Now I've brought up the subject, though, I realise I don't actually want to interrogate her. In theory, yes, I want to know everything about her, and there are doubtless some complicating factors – that child she mentioned, for a start, and probably a man on the scene. After all, women like her are rarely on their own. Right now, though, all that feels important is that I'm attracted to her, and she to me. I'm relishing this limbo – the sense that here, on the hill, it's just the two of us in the moment.

So, instead of talking, I do something I've wanted to do for a long time – I reach over, take her hand and hold it tight, for the first time since the first day we met and I helped her off the pavement. We continue walking, holding hands, for the final stretch of the hill, and the fear of being spotted by someone shrivels to nothing in the face of the pure joy I feel.

Before I know it, we're outside the KFC. Time has moved so fast today. I give her fingers a final squeeze and smile goodbye, knowing I'll see her again tomorrow. But instead of heading off towards the tube, as usual, she puts her hand on my arm.

'Not so fast,' she says.

She smiles at me, and then tugs at my sleeve, moving towards the door of the KFC.

'Come on!' she says, holding open the door for me. 'I want to make your wildest dreams come true.'

Before I know it we're inside, and Steph has joined the queue. I pause, digesting this unexpected development. Time is a concern; I only have a few minutes. But the queue isn't long. If we're served quickly, and I run, I might still make it for 9 a.m.

I make my decision, and join her in the queue.

The chain has had a makeover at some point in the past seven years. There are large touch-screens planted around the restaurant floor, and people appear to be ordering on them. But other elements of it are familiar: the smell of oil and salt, the torn salt sachets littering the floor, the depressed-looking servers and customers. It occurs to me that I've never been in one of these places during the day; it was always a late-night thing, after a night of drinking. Now, in daylight, it's certainly no place for someone like Steph. Queuing up she looks hilariously out of place, like a celebrity on a photo opportunity. But she doesn't seem to mind; in fact, she's grinning at me, eyes gleaming, as if hanging out in a KFC at 8.55 a.m. is the best fun she's had in ages.

God, I think, awestruck. I wish I could buy you breakfast, rather than the other way round. I wish I could buy you dinner at the Ritz.

141

I move closer to her until we're just touching. The powerful smell from the kitchen competes with the delicate fragrance that laces her hair, right under my nose.

'I'm glad I lowered my expectations,' I say.

Her smile tells me she remembers the reference, and gets the joke. Standing close, our bodies just grazing, we smile at each other, completely surrendered to the moment – or, at least I am. We only break off when we reach the counter and the server asks us for our order.

It turns out all they're serving is the breakfast menu, so Steph orders me a chicken burger before going for her wallet, putting the bag on the counter to rifle through, disgorging its contents as she goes. The server is waiting with a glazed expression and Steph is getting sweetly flustered as she scrabbles through her belongings. Watching her, I'm taken back to that first moment on the hill; how I first saw her, kneeling on the pavement, belongings strewn all around. Was it really only last week?

As she rummages, items are thrown up from the depths of the bag, things that I recognise from that first meeting. Her keys, her lipstick, her sunglasses. And then, something unfamiliar. A letter. It's half open, and the words at the top of the paper are visible for just a few seconds before it disappears back into the bag. But a few seconds is all I need. That crown logo and those words, in that font, are as familiar to me as my own name. I'd recognise them from twenty feet away.

HM Prison and Probation Service.

A moment later, Steph pulls out her orange wallet.

'So sorry,' she says, handing a ten-pound note to the server. She's not looking at me, and her hair has fallen in front of her face. I have a matter of seconds to decide on my next move.

The server turns away to fetch our order from the kitchen, and Steph glances up at me. I watch her smile falter as she registers my expression. Her mouth falls open in confusion, but as I keep staring at her, something registers, and she glances down at her bag before looking back at me.

'Oh, wait,' she says weakly. And I do find myself waiting, because despite my stone-cold demeanour I am desperate for her to somehow explain away what I just saw. But instead of speaking, she does something else, as unexpected and violent as a punch. In one rapid, seamless movement, she presses herself up against me, standing on tiptoes so that our cheeks are touching, and raises her left arm. Too late, I see that she's got her phone in her hand and is taking a photo of us. I blink, and then lurch away from her and towards the exit. As I turn and shoulder open the door, I hear her call my name, but I don't look back.

12

Steph

My first thought is to wait for him at the café, but on the tube over, I change my mind. If I meet him up there, right by the prison, I'll only have a few minutes, and with the gates just there, it'll be easy for him to shake me off and duck inside. Whereas, if I catch him here at the bottom of the hill, we've got the whole fifteen-minute walk to talk. If he agrees to speak to me, that is.

So, here I am, back in the KFC, the scene of this morning's bomb. I take a seat at the window, where I have a clear view of the pavement. I'm premature; it's not even four thirty, and Rob doesn't finish at the shop until five. I could tell myself that I'm here now because he might leave work early, after his shock this morning, but I know that's unlikely. I suspect the prison wouldn't be that understanding about a prisoner leaving early for some unspecified emotional reason. It's hard enough to get compassionate leave for your mother's funeral. Besides, from what I know of Rob, he'd prefer to be feeling that his world had ended when alone in that dim stock room, rather than cooped up with his awful padmate.

The real reason I'm here early is because I'm popping with anticipation. I've been pacing the flat all day, unable to keep still, knees jiggling even when I sat on the loo. I haven't felt so hyped since the morning of my wedding, when I was almost rebounding off the walls of our suite at the Marriott, soundtracked by the nylon swish of that ridiculous dress.

I should have listened to my nerves then. I hope that's not the case now.

This morning was a success. Everything went as planned. I played my part well, and Rob reacted as predicted. But, amidst all the adrenalin, I don't feel any real sense of triumph. Maybe that's because triumph is usually associated with finishing something, and this isn't nearly over. But also, I keep thinking of Rob's reaction. I didn't account for feeling so bad about him. Maybe this is how a hunter feels when they make their first kill; pleased they can feed their family for the evening, but with a new weight in their chest.

From where I'm sitting now I have a clear view of the crossing, and the spot where we say our goodbyes each morning. Or rather, said. As long as I keep looking, I shouldn't miss him. I pull the HMP letter out from my bag, sweeping away some scattered salt from the counter before laying it down and putting my hand over it. Not that anyone should want to steal it, but then you never know, around here. My phone is staying firmly at the bottom of my bag. My brother has already called twice this morning, but I can't speak to him; not yet.

I gaze out, examining the passers-by as if the glass is a one-way mirror. It's a quite different scene down here, on the high street, to the one on the hill in the morning, with all those freshly laundered professionals. Down here, every second young man looks like a jailbird – grey tracksuit, hunched shoulders, either scurrying along oblivious to the world or hyper-vigilant. I keep doing double-takes, thinking I spot Rob. One guy, from behind, looks identical – tall and narrow with sloping shoulders, head down, hair in a neat fade, hands stuffed in his pockets – and I've slid off my stool and am heading for the door when I realise it's not him. His top has a hood. Prisoners aren't allowed to wear them; it's one of the prison's strictest rules, and one that no one bothers to try and bend. Status symbols, like shoes and watches, cons will do anything to get them in, but who cares that much about a hood?

I twist back and forth on my stool and rub my fingers over the grainy counter, continuing to monitor the street. When one of these men does turn out to be Rob, and I rush out to him, what then? I recall that moment of pure rage on the hill, when he marched over to the Londis. Now, he'll have spent hours stewing in that stock room, convinced I'm a honey trap sent to test him, to scupper his release. I bet he'll have spent all day going through different scenarios; replaying each of our walks down the hill; imagining the CCTV footage of us together being presented in court. I bet he's wondering whether I was filming him from behind the curtain of the dressing room. Every time the phone rings in the shop, or the door opens, his throat will constrict. Cons have persecution complexes at the best of times, and often with good reason. Like now.

And if Rob had even the slightest doubt of my ill intentions then, of course, there's the photo. I glance over my shoulder to the spot where it all happened this morning, now occupied by some giggling teenagers who should be at school. I couldn't bring myself to look at the picture earlier but now I decide I should, to take responsibility for this thing I'm doing. I take out my phone and, ignoring the missed calls from Luke, open up my photos. There we are – cheeks squashed together, me with a terrible rictus smile, him with an expression I've never seen on him before – on anyone. The one I've been remembering all day. Wide-eyed, mouth ajar; an unguarded moment of fear, before his face turned to stone.

Looking at the photo isn't helping. I put the phone away and instead mentally rehearse my story. Or rather, Luke's story. It seems madly, needlessly complicated to me, but Luke says that's why it'll work, and on that, at least, I must trust him.

Some kid is playing aggressive music on their phone. The grease in the air turns my stomach. I lied to Rob, of course, when I said I loved KFC. I never eat junk food. Even when I was a young teenager, and our headquarters was the Colchester McDonald's, I sat nursing a Diet Pepsi as my friends tucked in. Mum had drilled into me that my body was my main asset – my only asset, really – and had to be looked after. And look, didn't all that self-denial pay off, when I pulled Tony?

A trampy-looking man sits on the stool beside me, banging his tray down on the counter. He starts muttering and I look over, thinking he's addressing me, but see he's actually leaning into his tray, whispering to the lumps of chicken as if he's telling them his secrets.

It's just gone five. I stare at the crossing, barely daring to blink in case I miss him. The tramp picks this moment to really start talking to me. I can't understand what he's saying, and I'm short with him before turning back to the window just in time to see Rob passing by. He's walking fast, head down, hands stuffed into his pockets.

147

In a second I've slid off my seat and I'm out the door, the letter in my hand. By the time I've hit the pavement he's already crossed over at the lights and started up the hill. I follow and, when I'm a few feet behind him, call out his name.

He glances over his shoulder, not reacting when he sees me. I've never seen such a blank expression. He turns back and continues walking.

'Rob, will you just look at this?' I call. 'Please.'

I wave the letter uselessly at his back.

'Look at what it says. The date. I haven't joined up yet. Haven't even had the assessment day. I've just done the online test.'

He still doesn't turn around, but I notice his pace slows down a touch, so I draw up beside him and thrust the letter into his eyeline, holding it steady so he can read it while moving. I watch his eyes scan the text for a few seconds before looking away, and hope he's at least caught the first lines.

Dear Miss Winder,

Thank you for your interest in joining HM Prison and Probation Service. We invite you to come for a Recruitment Assessment Day . . .

'There's nothing funny going on,' I continue. 'I just didn't mention it because I thought you'd be freaked out.'

Still looking ahead, Rob snorts with derision. He weaves around someone and I keep pace with him, holding out the letter, like a reporter trying to confront a politician. Except, of course, here I'm the wrongdoer.

I persevere, matching his stride, and it pays off: after a minute, he plucks the letter from my hand and, still moving, scans it. We're already passing the Londis; I don't have much time and must choose my words carefully. This is my tiny window.

He hands me back the letter.

'If you're not here to fuck me over, then why did you take that photo?' It's barely a question; his voice is dull and drained.

I pause before speaking.

'Insurance.'

He shakes his head sadly.

'There's something I need to tell you,' I continue, my voice steady and loud. 'About why I'm doing this.'

We're at the furniture place now. Only another few minutes before the café, and then the prison gate. My timing is a disaster; I hadn't accounted for these long silences. It's vital to be clever about what I tell him now and how much I leave for another day. The last thing I want is for him to disappear inside, unreachable, and to fester away in his cell; letting his paranoia loose, chewing over sparse facts, coming to unhelpful conclusions. I've got to release just the correct amount of information, to make him want to meet me tomorrow.

I launch straight in.

'Do you know someone called Elliot Sturridge?'

He frowns, still not looking at me.

'He's in there. With you.' I gesture up the hill, towards the prison.

Rob shakes his head. We're at the café now. He comes to a halt, and so do I.

'Your boyfriend?' he says.

Finally, Rob's voice has some flavour to it: a trace of hurt. When I don't immediately reply, he pulls out his phone from his pocket and checks the display.

'I've got to go in,' he says, starting off towards the gate.

'No, he's not my boyfriend!' I call after him. I watch his long back, those sloping shoulders, and see him slow down. And then I say, loudly and clearly,

'He killed my son.'

At that, he stops and turns to look at me – but now it's my turn to run off, back down the hill.

The next morning, I wait for him right up by the junction with the prison side road. I don't think too much about it; just that I want to have as much time as possible to talk on the way down. But when, at nine, he emerges from the gate and clocks me, I see him react, even from a distance, and realise that I'm too close for comfort. He's in a small cluster of men and as they pass they all eye me up – all except for Rob. Making it pretty obvious, I think. If he really doesn't want our connection to be noticed, he should look too.

The men are bantering together as they walk down the side road from the prison, but as soon as they emerge onto the hill they separate. One gets straight on his phone and starts barking orders at someone, another sprints for the 93 bus. Rob and another start down the hill, at different paces, blending into the crowd.

I trail Rob until he's past the café and then speed up until I draw level with him. I've decided not to apologise for waiting too close to the prison. It's vital to set the right tone, make it clear that what I've got to tell him is important, So, instead, I just say:

'Elliot Sturridge.'

He looks at me, and I know that he's thinking I look a state: puffy eyes, hair flat, wearing the same clothes as yesterday. I haven't given any thought to my appearance: there are far weightier things on my mind.

'I don't know him,' Rob says. He's still holding back, but his tone is different from yesterday: a touch less hostile, a touch more curious. 'Which wing is he on?'

'Don't know. I think he came in a few weeks ago? Forty-seven. Shortish. Stocky. Curly, receding hair. Arrogant prick.'

No reaction from Rob.

'So, this guy. Sturridge,' I continue, keeping my voice low and steady, 'he was in his car, driving, on his phone, texting the woman he's having an affair with, the wife of his best friend, telling him what he was going to do to her that evening. *You're going to answer the door wearing just a towel, like I've surprised you in the bath . . .* And while he's concocting this fantasy, he's not paying attention and he knocks over a little boy on his scooter. Kills him.'

I pause for breath.

'*My* little boy.'

We walk in silence for a minute, me breathing heavily. I don't dare to look at Rob's face. Around us, the commuters are listening to their music, scrolling through their phones. I continue,

'So this guy, Sturridge, he kills my son. My little Mouse. And, essentially, he's killed me, too.' I give a dry laugh. 'So he's basically destroyed two lives. They charge him with death by dangerous driving, and the CPS tell me he's looking at a seven-year sentence. He pleads not guilty, hires some five-hundred-quid-an-hour barrister, this slick, Porsche-driving shit. We get all geared up for the trial. Then, a week before it's due to begin, we hear that his barrister has bargained the charge down to death by careless driving. A one-word difference. I don't want to accept it but the CPS tells me that because of some tiny, fucking little technicality, it could be argued his driving wasn't officially dangerous. And basically the CPS decides to accept the lesser plea. I had no say in it.'

I haven't been looking at Rob while I speak but now I do; his head is down and I can only assume he's listening. It occurs to me that he probably hears this sort of thing inside all the time. From the criminal's rather than the victim's point of view, but still. Maybe there's something about the ranting about the details of sentencing and injustice that makes him switch off. I cut to the chase.

'Long and short – he receives an eighteen-month sentence, but gets a third off for pleading guilty. So, a year. And of course he only serves half of that. So six months inside. Six fucking months. For killing my son. And essentially killing me.'

We're passing the furniture place now. The guy on the sofa is watching us – watching me – with interest. I lower my voice and continue.

'During mitigation Sturridge gave the judge this big sob story, in his best posh voice, saying how devastated he was but basically blaming my son for not looking where he was going. And me for not controlling him. No, not directly blaming me, because he knew the court wouldn't like that – but definitely suggesting I wasn't looking after him. *I assumed he was with his mother, but I didn't see her.* That sort of thing. He glanced in my direction once during this speech, he was obviously told to by his lawyer. But he didn't meet my eye. And when I saw him outside the courtroom afterwards, he blanked me.'

I pause to catch my breath. We're nearly at the Job Centre now.

'He'll be out in September. His wife has probably already

sent out the email for his welcome home party. Oh god, his fucking wife! She was so publicly loyal and forgiving about the whole thing – the accident, his affair. Sitting there in the court during sentencing, giving him this nauseating smile, doing this ridiculous wriggly finger gesture, obviously some secret code between them. And she didn't look at me once, either. He addressed her directly in court, apologising. Called her this stupid fucking pet name, Lambchop, pretending it just slipped out. *And to my precious Lambchop – oh I'm sorry, Julia – I can't apologise enough . . .'*

I'm getting overheated again. We're almost at the bottom of the hill now. Rob lifts his head and looks straight ahead, across towards the KFC.

'So you're going for a job in the prison service?' he says, frowning. And who could blame him for being confused? We've reached the crossing and wait for the lights in silence. Only a minute left now. I must choose my words carefully.

'You've got to go,' I say. 'Meet me here at five p.m. and I'll explain.'

He shrugs. I guess this has been the story of his life for the past seven years – being thwarted and frustrated, being made to wait. He nods goodbye and heads off towards the shop. I watch him get absorbed into the crowd, wondering how he'll digest this conversation during the day. My hope is he guesses what I'm going to tell him. He's got eight hours to work it out, sitting in that shitty stock room.

And he does. At 5.05 p.m., when we meet again outside the KFC, he says, with no preamble,

'So, what – you want to become a prison officer to take your revenge on us scumbags?'

153

I laugh.

'You say it as if it's common. Are there a lot of sadistic screws?'

The green man flashes and we cross the road.

'Word of warning,' Rob says. 'They don't like being called screws. Officers never call themselves that. It'd be like . . . I don't know, like you calling yourself a bitch, or something.'

'Ah, right,' I reply quickly. 'Anyway. I'm not a sadist. I only want revenge on him.'

'How?'

'Well, I think he should stay in there for ever. But that isn't going to happen. So I just want him in longer. Don't you think that the worst thing would be to know you're coming out, to see the light in the distance, to think your life is going to start again, and be counting down the days − and then to be told that's not going to happen? That you've got, say, another three years inside? That's torture, right?'

Rob gives a brief nod of agreement, and then keeps nodding, more slowly, as it dawns on him what I'm saying.

'You want to fit him up?'

Even though there's no one close by, his voice is low. I don't say anything, so he knows he's got it right.

'How?' he says.

'I'm going to plant something on him. Some drugs. Spice.'

He looks at me and then, when he sees that I'm serious, starts to laugh.

'Why?' I say, affronted. 'It wouldn't be hard, would it? It's always in the news, officers bringing stuff in.'

'Yes, you're right,' he says, and although he's shaking his head with incredulity, I can see he's making an effort to be kind. 'But let's say you did it. Did your training, started working on the landings, then got a load of spice in and somehow planted it on him. It's pretty likely you'll be caught. And you know what would happen then? You not only bringing stuff in, but fitting up a prisoner? Someone who you had past dealings with? You'd be fucking crucified. Not just a long sentence – they'd stick you in a protected unit. With a load of child killers and paedophiles. That woman who abused those kids in her nursery and sent the photos to her boyfriend – with people like her. For years.'

'I won't get caught,' I say quietly.

'You really might,' he says, lowering his voice so it's a copy of mine. Even amidst all of this, I register that move; there's something pleasingly intimate about it. 'They're really cracking down on bent officers,' he continues. 'Haven't you seen the news? Searches all the time. It's not like how it was. And – wait – for fuck's sake, this guy will recognise you! This is so ridiculous.'

'He won't,' I say. 'I told you, he barely glanced at me during the sentencing. And anyway, I didn't look like this then.' I pick up a piece of my hair. 'I wasn't blonde. And I was bigger, too.'

We walk in silence for a bit, and then Rob says,

'Was he your only child?'

I turn away from him, and don't reply.

As we pass the Londis, I gather myself and face him again. 'How long did you get?' I ask, clearly.

'What?'

'For the one-punch thing. How long is your sentence?'

When he doesn't answer immediately, it strikes me that this might be the first time he's had to talk about all of this outside the prison walls. Then, he says,

'I've been inside for seven years.'

'Right,' I say, briskly. 'So you've lost seven years of your life for defending yourself from some coked-up lunatic or whatever. And inside there' – I point up the hill – 'is a smirking posh twat who was texting his mistress as he was driving, and ran over my son. And he's going to be out in five months. Does that seem right to you?'

'Of course not,' he says. 'But fixating on sentencing disparities – it drives you mad, I see it inside the whole time. No, it's not fair, and it's not right. But that doesn't mean you should ruin your own life.'

'I won't,' I say. 'I mean, I might. But it's a risk I'm prepared to take.'

We're approaching the furniture place now. The sofa guy is stirring his tea with his finger and he sucks on it as he watches us pass.

'You think it's all right in there,' he says. 'Not so bad. You could cope. But you're wrong.'

'It's not that,' I say, hearing the desperation in my voice. 'Rob, the truth is, I don't have that much life to lose. I feel like I'm in prison already.' I notice him flinch at that, but I continue. 'A life sentence in solitary confinement. In one of those American super maxes, where the cells are underground concrete bunkers with no sound or light. I thought it would get better. I mean, it's been more than a year now. I knew there would always be pain, but I didn't realise it would get worse. The first year I was in shock, and now it's real and – I feel so hollowed out I'm barely alive. And the only bit of me that feels alive is the anger, not just towards him, but towards the system that allows him to have such a tiny sentence for taking away my son's life.'

I fall silent and walk on, not looking at him. After a moment, he says,

'What's your plan? Plant spice in his cell?'

I nod.

He does his incredulous head shake again.

'This is not a good plan.'

I sigh, exasperated. 'Well, I'm halfway there already.'

'What?'

'I've found someone to sell me the stuff. I met him in the market. I'm going to his flat tomorrow.'

'What? No,' he says, staring at me. 'No. You're not.'

'I am.'

'How much did you ask for?'

'Half a kilo.'

'Fuck. How much is that costing you?'

We come to a halt, a few metres from the prison turn-off.

'I sold my car,' I say.

'You're insane,' he says, and then, 'you're really determined to do this, aren't you?'

I nod firmly. Rob looks off to one side. A bus chunters by. He glances down at his watch and then over to me.

'The photo.'

'What?'

'The photo you took in the KFC.'

I flush and look away.

'Oh. Yes.'

'Why did you take it?'

'Because I knew I'd have to tell you this, and you could get me into trouble, so it was sort of insurance. Like, I've got something on you. I'll delete it, if you want.'

I take my phone from my bag and scroll through to the picture, before showing it to him and pressing *delete*.

He nods and starts off towards the gate. After a few paces,

just before he disappears around the corner, he turns around and walks back to me.

'Tell him to come to the hill,' he says. 'This guy. Tomorrow morning 8.45 a.m. Car park behind Londis. You meet me before with the cash.'

I stare at him, and say something stupid, out of all the things I could say to him.

'He might not come out that early.'

Rob laughs.

'For that much, he'll come whenever you want.'

He turns back towards the prison, and I watch him disappear down the side road. I notice the ex-con beggar stationed at the turning is watching me with interest, as if he knows exactly what's going on. I give him a hard stare back. Then, as I start down the hill again, I take out my phone to text Luke.

13

Rob

Steph wanted me to offer to meet this guy and do the deal for her – even if she didn't know it herself. Otherwise, why tell me about it? Unconsciously, at least, she wanted me to picture her picking through the market in her heels, a lost deer in a dangerous forest. Approaching a group of young men smoking weed, their waistbands under their arses. Asking them whether they can sort her out a load of spice. Them exchanging glances over her head, and silently agreeing for one of them to take charge. Telling her the price, that she should come to this flat tomorrow, bring the cash. Exchanging numbers. Then, as she walks off, watching her go and not even attempting to muffle their sniggers.

Steph thinks she's fearless but she's not. She's fuelled by rage and the desire for revenge, but it's not the same thing. And she's so consumed by it she's not thinking straight. I mean, putting the insanity of the plan itself aside, why buy the drugs now, before she's even had an interview for the prison service? But I suppose we don't act rationally when grief and injustice are concerned.

And, of course, that goes for love and lust too. Because why would she strike up a relationship with me, a prisoner, when she's about to become an officer? The only reasonable explanation – and certainly, the one I want to be true – is that she just couldn't help it. That once we started talking, and discovered this thing between us, putting a stop to it was beyond her control.

I suppose you could ask the same of me: why would I risk my release by doing this deal for her? But there's no way I could let her meet a random scumbag in his flat to be ripped off, or worse. To offer was a bit of chivalry as instinctive as holding open a door. Doing the actual deal itself holds no fear: I know what these people are like, and I know how to handle myself. The risk is significant, but I'll take it for her. Up until now, swapping my T-shirt last week was the dodgiest thing I've done in seven years. No phones. No drugs. No playing the system in even the smallest way, the way everyone else does: borrowing memory sticks of films and music, swiping food when working in the kitchens. It was one of the things that I clung to, to prove I was different to the rest and give me hope that being inside would be just a blip in my life rather than something that would define it. Marko's right: I'm Mr Squeaky Clean. Or I was.

When was the last time I did anything for the benefit of someone else, let alone risk my own neck? It would have been for Tania, of course. Dropping out of my course, coming to London, taking that estate agent job. Choosing her over my mother when their mutual loathing became too much. But of course, all that wasn't illegal. And because I ended up with Tania, it was for my benefit too – or so I thought.

But I suppose what I'm about to do for Steph is for me, too. Helping her will make me feel like a good person. And yes, it's a risk, but lots of the other guys do dodgy stuff when working out. Look at Wilko tootling off to his coke business every day. The smart ones get away with it – even Wilko gets away with it. I'm just temporarily joining their gang.

Contrary to the impression I gave Steph, her plan to stitch up this Sturridge guy isn't the maddest thing I've ever heard. Not even close. Inside you're bombarded with all sorts of crackpot schemes – most of them the product of mentally damaged, paranoid and amoral minds that never get beyond the bunk ranting stage. Some of them, though, almost come to fruition. Only last week, for instance, a woman visitor was discovered smuggling out a syringe of her boyfriend's semen that he somehow slipped over to her during a visit. A lad wanted to knock up his girlfriend and wasn't going to let the simple fact of not being able to touch her get in his way.

When the men in here tell me their plans, I don't interrupt or engage, because I couldn't care less about them. But it's different with her.

What Steph doesn't know is that I'm doing the deal to help her – but not in the way she thinks. As soon as I've got the stuff, it's going straight in the nearest bin. I can even picture the one; it's about ten feet down from the Londis. There was a tangle of black hair extensions poking out from it last week, like someone had been decapitated.

It's only that evening, as I lie in my bunk, facing the wall, trying to block out *EastEnders*, that I properly think about what she told me. About what happened to her child. My vision of her in the market, being eyed up by pound shop gangsters, is replaced by one of her on a road, hunched over the body of a little boy. Beside them his scooter, wheels still

161

spinning. A Range Rover stopped a few feet away, not a dent on it. A posh voice saying 'Oh fuck.'

The image is vivid and scalding. I've done the courses – so many courses – learning how to put myself in the victim's shoes, to fully empathise, to inhabit them, to understand that they are as real a person as I am. That phrase she used, about feeling she had a life sentence in solitary confinement – my victim's father said a similar thing to me in a letter.

So I feel her pain. But also his. The man, Sturridge. Because I've also experienced that moment when you realise you've done something unspeakable, the worst thing a man can do, but you haven't been struck down by a thunderbolt. You're still standing, still breathing. It's surprisingly easy to carry out the most heinous act in the world.

And his behaviour in the courtroom – his smirk. I have sympathy for that, too.

Marko has the TV on extra loud this evening. The characters are screeching at each other: *'What did you think would happen, eh? Numbskull!'* I hear a cough from the bunk below, then comes the rasp of a match and the smell of smoke. I shut my eyes and move closer to the wall, until my nose is pressed against the clammy brick. Memories of my trial float up, from where I thought they'd been securely buried. In here people moan about the injustice of their trials all the time, but none of them are interested in reliving the overall experience. They're especially not interested in talking to someone who believes their jury came to the right decision. Over the past seven years, a number of caring professionals have helped me comb through my background and my crime and its aftermath, but never the trial. No one is interested in hearing about that. The only thing that matters to others is the verdict.

The months of preparation by the QCs, sifting through the finest-grained detail of the event and your past, in order to present two versions of you – one too good and the other too bad. And the one that wins is definitive. If you're found guilty, all those mitigating factors melt away, and the 'too bad' you is what you are.

I've had no desire to revisit that time. But now, because of Steph's comments about Sturridge, I find myself back in the dock, in the middle of that row of bolted plastic chairs, with that smell of bleach and dust, separated from the courtroom by a scratched Perspex screen. The guard at the door, reading a weeks-old copy of *Metro*. The loneliest place in the world, where you're subject to both extreme, constant stress and an odd tedium, as the lawyers argue over arcane points of law, or drill down into the forensic detail of a situation you know all too well. To my horror, I found my eyes closing on several occasions. In the dock, every action is scrutinised as a sign of your character, yet the situation makes it impossible to behave anywhere normally, and you know that, despite all the solemn words from the judge, you won't be given the benefit of any doubt. If your eyes close, then you're on drugs, or bored, or contemptuous. I haven't read any news stories about my trial, and I never will, but I've no doubt they say that I didn't show any emotion when the verdict was announced. They always say that, don't they – and it makes the accused sound like a psychopath. But the truth is, when you hear a single word that will change your life for ever, it's like you've been zapped with a stun gun.

I admit, though, that my fist bump to the judge after he passed sentence – that was an act of insanity. Especially as, us being at opposite sides of the courtroom, it was a one-sided fist bump – and a one-sided fist bump is a pretty similar action to an attempted punch. I can still recall the collective intake of breath when I did that – not just from the public gallery to the side of me, but from the legal teams in front as well. All I can say is that it came from a place of profound, all-encompassing relief. Finally, it was over. The end of sitting there in that plastic box, of being watched, judged. Of combing over my terrible actions; of watching grainy CCTV footage; of hearing graphic medical reports of brain bleeding. Of hearing the victim's family describe their pain. Of hearing my own words twisted, my life distorted, and learning what people really thought about me. Of seeing my mother up there in the public gallery; of hearing the wooden bench creak as she left halfway through a day's proceedings. Then, towards the end, of not seeing her there.

For months it'd been like the world's strongest man was squeezing my head between his hands, and at that moment, when the judge sentenced me, I was released. Honestly, I have never known such relief. And my reaction was to smile and give the judge a fist bump in gratitude as I was led down to the cell.

So I have some sympathy for this man Sturridge, and his smirk. And I know that, however he appeared in court, he will be suffering. Because when you've killed someone, you've crossed a line and you are never the same again. You go to bed with the knowledge, and you get up with it. It'll be with him for the rest of his life, like a spirit attachment. Sometimes it'll screech, sometimes it'll keep quiet, but it'll always be there. Even when he's shagging his devoted wife, or cracking open the Moët at his welcome home party.

His wife. Steph said he called her Lambchop. The word nudges a memory. *Lambchop.* And I remember: the posh guy in the phone queue after chapel, who offered to let me go first, used that name on the phone.

So, that was Sturridge.

As a rule, I don't know or care what my fellow prisoners have done. I judge them on how they act inside. A true test of character is how you behave when cooped up in very limited circumstances with six hundred men. I hope it is, anyway. Psychopaths aside, we're all trying to live in the present rather than the past, and we all hope we're more than the sum of our crimes.

Once I shared a cell with this old bloke, Kavanagh. He was always extremely polite and considerate: made me the first cup of hot chocolate, respected my space, apologised for the tiniest invisible infraction, like for moving my shoes from one side of the cell to the other; gave away his canteen; helped youngsters with their appeals. He was genuinely one of the most pleasant people you could ever meet. It turned out he had stabbed his wife twenty-seven times. But to me, he's a nicer bloke than Marko could ever be.

On the TV, *EastEnders* is finishing and Marko starts singing along to the theme, aggressively loudly, but actually quite tunefully. When it's over, I hear a click and then silence. It's a surprise – maybe even the first time the TV has been off since he moved in – but I don't say anything, or stir.

'You awake?' he says.

When I don't reply, I hear him shift from his bed and move somewhere in the cell, and some indeterminate noises. Then he says,

'All right? Yeah, of course it's me.'

I had no idea he could speak so quietly, and it takes me a moment to realise that he's on a phone.

'Yeah. Yeah. Fucking no! What you . . .? Who? Thinking of you, baby. Yeah, course! Are you going to come visit me, then? Bring the gear? Yeah, I know. But I didn't mean it, like – I was going out of my head, you know . . .? Come on, mate . . .'

By rights I should be having a fit now. Marko having a phone could be a major problem for me. If the cell is spun and the phone is found, he has made it very clear that he won't admit it's his, in which case we'll both get done for it, and my release date will be pushed back. But as I lie there listening to his tone change from a cajoling whisper to a frustrated hiss, I find that I'm not annoyed as I should be. It's as if the knowledge of what I'm doing tomorrow, my secret, has anaesthetised me.

The next morning there she is, standing outside the café. She's in casual clothes today – those pale, ripped-knee jeans; a pink sweatshirt – and even from a distance I can see how tense she is. When I reach her she doesn't even smile, just starts off down the hill, me at her side. She's holding a cup of coffee and after a few steps hands it over. So far, so usual. But when I take it the cup feels wrong; there's something in there, but it's not liquid. I look over at her and clock her expression and the penny drops. The cup is full of money.

In bed last night, as I was falling asleep, I wondered about how she would deal with handing over the cash. I guessed she'd stuff the notes into my hand, too obviously, so I'm surprised by her nous. Impressed, too.

Her hair is in a tight, high ponytail. Her face is grave and drawn and, for once, she looks middle-aged.

'You told him it would be me, not you?' I say.

She looks up at me, stricken. 'Shit. No. Should I text him now?'

I shake my head.

'OK,' she nods. 'And where shall we meet afterwards? The café? No, that's going back on yourself . . . KFC?'

'No,' I say. 'I'll have to run straight to work. You go on and I'll meet you later.'

'I can't,' she says. 'Not this afternoon.'

'Well, tomorrow then,' I say.

'Will you text when it's done?'

I give a half nod, half shrug. Maybe I should – *Deal was fine, and now the stuff is in the bin! You'll thank me for this.*

Just before the Londis we come to a halt, and Steph gives my bicep the briefest of squeezes before walking on. I watch her go, her pink top marking her out as she merges with the commuter crowds, and feel her fingertips on my skin, like five tiny hotplates.

I check my phone. 8.13 a.m. There's a German shepherd tied up by the door. As I approach it starts to snarl, and then strains after me when I walk past and quickly slip behind the shop.

It's more of a goods yard than a car park, with a couple of loading trolleys chained to a railing and the ground strewn with torn cardboard packaging and wrapping plastic. There's a strong stench of urine. It seems unlikely that this is anyone's preferred spot for a quick fuck, even a lifer on his first release, but I spot a handful of empty condom wrappers amongst the rubbish. Looking around, I can see Deller was right – there doesn't appear to be any CCTV.

There is, however, a block of flats overlooking the yard – one of the looming Victorian mansion blocks, built around the time of the prison. Maybe even out of the same supply of yellow brick. I've seen studio flats there advertised in the window of the estate agent on the hill: £225 a week for a space not much bigger than a cell.

The way the light is falling means that the building's small windows are shrouded. It's impossible to see if anyone is there, idly looking out as they brush their teeth and think about their day ahead, about whatever job you have to do that allows you to pay £225 a week rent, on top of all the other costs of existence.

Judging from the state of this yard, I'm sure any onlookers would have seen a lot worse than me and a bloke doing a deal. Still, behind any of those blank windows could be the person who is going to point at me in a courtroom.

Nonetheless, as I wait for this dealer, clutching my coffee cup full of cash, I feel oddly calm. Not half as nervous as I did when I was just walking down the street alongside Steph, doing nothing wrong. It's as if I've been possessed by the person I was before prison, when I would have thought nothing of meeting a dealer behind a Londis. I've never done a deal like this – never bought anything more than a quarter of weed, or a few pills, for personal use only, when Tania and I were off to V Festival or something. But while I know this is a different ball game, with far higher stakes, it's as if that knowledge exists only in the abstract. I can't really feel it.

Maybe it's because I've mingled with many dozens of dealers over my years inside and know the type well – disorganised, greedy idiots who can't hold down a proper job. Or maybe it's because I'm doing this for noble reasons; I can justify it to myself, regardless of the consequences.

I'm alert as some guy comes into the yard; besuited, fiftyish and sweaty. Not the dealer, just some guy on his way to work, probably here to take a piss or have a toke. When he spots me, he backs out again.

8.47 a.m. He's late. I can give it until 8.50 and then I'll have to peg it.

Then another guy comes in, and I recognise him immediately. Not as an individual, but as a type. Twenty-something, well-built, black – every other man inside looks like him. The way they carry themselves is both slouchy-casual and surreptitious – simultaneously peacocking and paranoid. He's wearing a gilet, although it's not the weather for it. He clocks me, and I give him a nod. In one hand he's clutching a cup from KFC and in the other his phone. I see it's a burner, the same brand as the one in my hand. And the prison system wonders why it's hard for us to stay on the straight and narrow, when they send us out into the world with the same phones as drug dealers.

'Wha gaun?' he says.

'Lady can't make it,' I say. 'Sends her apologies.'

He squints at me.

'I don't talk to strangers.'

'Really.'

'Only the peng ones,' he says, unsmiling. 'Ain't dealing with no straight goer.'

Obviously he's pissed off he won't be able to rip off Steph, or try and sleep with her, or both.

'I've got the cash,' I say in a low voice, holding up the cup.

He shakes his head and turns to dial a number on his phone, still glancing around him as he does so, compulsively vigilant. I look at him side on, and there's something about his profile, the straightness of his nose and set of his mouth,

169

that I recognise. And I realise that I recognise him as a person, not just a type.

'Morris,' I say.

He glances up at me, eyes narrowed and wary.

'Wandsworth,' I say. 'G Wing. Twixes.'

The guy holds my gaze steady for a few moments, and then frowns as he starts to remember.

'*Stand By Me*,' I add.

'Fuck, man,' he says. 'That film. I cried like a baby.'

He smiles, his whole face changed, and lays his hand heavily on my shoulder. I last saw the guy six years ago, when I had just trained as a Listener. Morris was in for his first drugs offence, a two stretch, and came to see me almost every evening, confiding how he had fucked everything up, his sadness over his failed relationship and that he might never know his tiny daughter, his worries about the future: everything that came into his head. For hours, he talked and I listened. He'd always have a Twix and give me a quarter of it. One evening, he didn't want to speak, he just wanted company, and so we watched a film on TV, a coming of age story about a group of young boys, while he wept silently.

After a couple of weeks he stopped calling me out. He hooked up with a gang and I'd spot him on the wing, hand down his trousers, bellowing away, acting like he couldn't give a shit about being inside. Then, he was transferred and I didn't see him again. Until now.

Why he's now here in this car park carrying half a kilo of spice hardly needs explaining. As for me – I don't think Morris ever knew what I was in for, or how long I'd got. During our sessions he never asked about me, and I didn't expect him to: I was the Listener. The only personal thing he said to me was that I seemed too posh to be inside; but that was the end of his enquiry. He has no reason to question why I'm now out, buying wholesale quantities of drugs, just like him.

'How're things?' I say.

'Good good good. Empire building, you get me? Look, I even got business cards.'

He digs into his pocket and hands me a card – black, with just a phone number on it. I nod, and slip it in my pocket.

'And you, fam, where you living? Got a woman?' He cracks up. 'What the fuck. Of course you got a woman. A nice one, too.'

He means Steph. I feel myself colouring, just at the thought that someone might think we were a couple; that that possibility might exist in the universe. Then, a flurry of horns from the street snaps me out of the moment and I remember what I'm doing here, and how risky it is, and how I'm almost certainly late for work, and images of me and Steph together are replaced by one of Carl, standing outside the shop with his lunchbox.

'Yeah.' I awkwardly pat his back. 'All good, man. Sorry she couldn't come. Look, I've got the cash.'

I hold out my coffee cup, and in return Morris hands me his. It's one of the mega-sized ones, half a foot tall. It's heavy. I wonder how he and Steph both knew that this was how the deal was to be done, the goods and cash in cups. Had they discussed it? Is this just how things are done these days, another thing that everyone knows except me?

Morris prises off the lid of the coffee cup and peers inside. I follow suit and glance inside the KFC cup. From what I can see the spice has been pre-divided into a load of little bags, all stuffed inside one larger one. I note that Morris doesn't count the money – a mark of respect. We replace the lids. The deal is over in a matter of seconds. Even if that block of flats is watching, there isn't really anything to see.

'Man, good to see you. I have to get going,' I say. 'But listen, I got a favour to ask.'

'Anything, blood.'

'If that girl – my girl – comes asking for stuff again, don't sell to her. And ask your friends not to. She's in a – situation – and I'm trying to help her, you know?'

I'm counting on him not to ask why, and that he just assumes the most obvious explanation – that my girlfriend has a drugs problem and I'm trying to keep her away from the stuff. And why wouldn't he?

'Sure, big man. You were good to me, won't forget that.'

He gives me a fist bump, and I watch him slide away. I know there's little chance of him keeping his promise, however indebted he feels to me for those evenings. If dealers didn't sell to the vulnerable and fucked up, they'd be out of business in a day. I check my phone. 8.55 a.m. As soon as Morris is out of sight, I walk briskly back out onto the hill and then run, my hand pressed over the lid of the cup. It's only when I reach the lights that I remember I intended to throw the stuff away in the first bin I came to, that one by the bus stop just down from Londis. There's another bin between me and the shop, but I find myself passing it by, and I arrive at the shop still clutching the cup. Carl's waiting, and he immediately clocks it.

'No food or drink out back.'

'It's empty,' I reply. 'I'll throw it away,' and before he can reply I walk through to the back, as though he's just making

172

conversation rather than giving me an order. Sami is in today, already arrived, and to my annoyance she follows me into the back room. There's a waste bin just there, so I feel obliged to put the cup in there, ever so casually but carefully, so the weight of its contents isn't obvious, and listen impatiently while Sami tells me about how her daughter might be leaving her husband, and that the father of someone she knows is getting an OBE, and then, lowering her voice to a whisper that's more conspicuous than a normal pitch, sharing her thoughts about how Carl is stressed because the shop isn't meeting its targets.

Finally, she goes back to the shop floor and leaves me alone. I hear her talking with Carl, lavishly sympathising with him over his hay fever and bemoaning the particularly high pollen count. I figure I've got a few minutes alone at least. I take the cup from the bin and put it inside a bin bag of clothes to shield it. If Carl comes in then it'll look like I'm just rummaging through some rags. With my arms in the bag, I prise open the lid of the cup and inspect the stuff, as far as I can. I've never seen it in bulk before; only glimpsed it in the little Ziploc bags it's sold in inside. It looks just like the weed I smoked as a teenager but is actually completely unnatural; some anonymous herbs sprayed with a grim manufactured chemical that eats away at the brain.

From what you see on TV and in the papers, you'd think that all prisoners spend their days smacked out on the stuff, but it's not the case – for me at least. I found it easy to resist. Those who take it are the ones whose non-existent impulse control led them here in the first place, or who have totally lost hope. When I was a Listener, I'd get these calls from men in psychosis – I saw them pretending to be dogs, cackling like hyenas, beating each other up. It was like some medieval freak show. Anyone with a drop of self-respect or sense wouldn't go near the stuff – for me, it'd be like the equivalent of spending months constructing the Thames Barrier and then punching a huge hole in it. However, on the whole, self-respect is in extremely short supply inside.

I wonder about the prison value. A huge mark-up, that much I know. It's usually sold in tiny quantities, a fiver a bag, enough to blend your brain for a few hours. Half a kilo could be ten grand. Possibly twenty. Of course, I have absolutely no intention of taking it inside and selling it. It really is the last thing I'd do. But at the same time, my plan to throw it away now feels like I'd be chucking a rolled-up wad of notes in the bin. Twenty grand is two years of living in a studio flat.

It strikes me that my job is done. I did the deal to stop Steph doing it, to keep the drugs out of her hands and so prevent her going through with her suicidal plan to bring it into the prison. So whether the spice goes in the bin or is just squirrelled away somewhere, out of her reach, doesn't really matter.

My hands still inside the bin bag, I ease the spice out of the cup and look around for somewhere to hide it. On the shelf is an ancient combined TV and video player. I remember Carl reprimanding Sami for accepting it and then explaining to me, at some length, about the law concerning selling second-hand electronics. They have to be tested and no one here has the energy or money to sort that out. In short, that TV isn't going anywhere for a while. I go over and try to wedge the packet inside the VHS slot. It's too thick to go in, so I remove the little bags from the big one and manage to stuff them in, a handful at a time.

I drift through the rest of the day in a heightened state of tension, feeling both bad and saintly. I wonder how Steph will react when I tell her I'm not giving her the spice; I wonder what the hell I'm going to do with it. At lunchtime, I have a change of heart and decide to go out onto the street and throw the spice into a bin, but instead I find myself staying inside to eat my sandwich and leaving the stuff in its hiding place. I feel something I haven't felt for a very long time, and it takes me a while to realise what it is. Power. Not in the sense of having power over another person; more that I'm taking action, doing something bold, making something happen. Or not happen, in this case. I've done something that will have some effect, and will lead to some good.

Although, I will admit, a small part of me also enjoys the knowledge that others would kill for what I've got, for those packages stuffed in the mouth of the VHS.

Marko, for example. That evening, when I'm back in the cell, he badgers me as usual and I think: if only you knew.

I lie in my bunk and contemplate the fact that I've just done something that could ruin my life for the second time. That could send me back inside for another decade. And I realise that it's not just that I haven't had this power since coming inside – I've never had this power before, ever, even in my twenty years of free life. And the feeling is immense, a bigger kick than spice could ever provide.

14

Rob

My eyes flick open. Someone or something is too close. Since being inside I've developed an exclusion zone around me, a foot or so of fiercely guarded personal space, and even when unconscious I can tell if someone has strayed into it. Without moving my head from the pillow, my eyes swivel to the left. Marko is standing just there, beside the bunk, uncharacteristically still, looking at me with those mouse-dropping eyes. I return the look, not saying anything, trying to suss out what's going on before reacting. In my experience, this kind of motionless is usually the precursor to some act of gratuitous violence, like that moment just before a cat lashes out. But I didn't think Marko had it in him – he's too uncontained and impulsive.

I can't see my clock from here, but from the light behind the curtain and the noise on the landings, I guess it's around seven. Time for me to get up. Marko is usually asleep when I leave for work, one weedy white leg hanging off the bunk.

We continue looking at each other for a few seconds, and then I say, as casually and evenly as I can,

'All right?'

'I have to tell you something,' he says, gravely.

'Yeah?' I'm on full level alert now.

'You've got a probation meeting today,' he continues.

This isn't what I expected. I sit up and twist around to lean my back against the wall, further away from his face.

'You got a slip,' he says. 'When you were out yesterday. I hid it, innit.'

'Why?'

He shrugs. It's perfectly possible he doesn't know exactly why he did it. He was bored; it was something to do; he doesn't like me. I've known a lot of men like Marko over the years and they're missing some vital part of their brains – you can't judge them by the same standards as normal people. They'll do things just for the hell of it, because they can and because they don't care about the repercussions, or because they just crave some attention, whether good or bad, like a three year old.

'Wanted to get you into trouble, like,' he says. 'Would have been funny, no? Mr Squeaky Clean.'

'But you had a change of heart.'

Marko shrugs again, and it's possible he really doesn't know the answer to that, either. Maybe he's as surprised as I am by this unexpected flash of decency, or maybe he belatedly realised the consequences of my missing a meeting – which would have been serious, possibly delaying my release – and he just couldn't be arsed to deal with them. He raises his hand and drops a crumpled slip onto the bed, before ducking back down to his bunk.

'Where's my thank you then?' he says from below. 'Won't fucking bother next time.' He puts on the TV, loudly –

the Russia Today breakfast show, with its eerie automaton presenter. I haven't seen Carol for a long time now.

I look at the slip, with its scant information. The meeting is at 2 p.m. That means no work today. No leaving the prison. No Steph.

She'll be waiting for me, loitering beside the café as usual. She'll watch my fellow workers emerge and, soon enough, she'll realise that I'm not coming out. And then she'll wonder why; and what I've done with her money, and the drugs. Whether I've stitched her up. She'll feel something of how I did the other day, in KFC, after I'd glimpsed that letter. Punched. And then, when the shock has worn off, a surge of panic, and the rest of the day waiting for the knock on the door by the authorities.

And she really does have something to worry about. Before, she had the power; now, I feel we're equal. But my overwhelming urge is to comfort and reassure her. I can't bear the thought of her upset and thinking badly of me.

Lying back in my bunk, still clutching the slip, I think of her at this moment getting ready in that little flat of hers, in Driftwood House in Nine Elms. Invisible tights drying on the radiator. Long novels piled beside the sofa. A breakfast DJ's cheery prattle on the radio. Hair styling tools lying on the carpet. Looking through her handbag and that leather folder to make sure she's got everything she needs for her day ahead, viewing houses and making deals. Thinking about meeting me.

No, wait. Of course, I'm wrong. That image is the old her; the person I thought she was, before that moment with the letter in KFC. I restart my fantasy, but this time the cosy flat is a silent, sad place; a two-bedroom apartment where only one is now needed. Upon waking, she has a brief, sweet moment of innocence, before she remembers, before bleak reality sets in. Her son, gone forever. Elliot Sturridge, out of prison in four months. Now, I see her pulling on her clothes listlessly, without checking in the mirror, distracted by the thought of getting the drugs off me, and the next stage of her plan. Going out to the kitchen, not looking as she passes the second bedroom door. The contents of the room left untouched; his name spelled out in wooden letters on the door.

What was his name? Did she call him Mouse, or am I imagining that? It must have been a nickname.

At least this probation meeting means I can postpone the task of telling her that the plan isn't happening – that I've hidden the drugs to stop her going through with it. I think of the package stuffed in the mouth of the VHS player. My day off work, a day when I'm not in the stock room, means a whole eight hours for Carl to go back there and fuss around with his stuff, like Tutankhamun arranging his tomb, and decide that today's the day to finally deal with that defunct TV . . .

The prospect of the stuff being discovered should terrify me. But all I can focus on is Steph believing I've fucked her over, or gone off her.

I sit there thinking for a moment, and then slide down from the bunk, being ostentatiously careful not to brush against Marko's mattress. He's staring at the TV – *Escape to the Country* now – and filing his nails with a pan scourer.

'Mate?' My voice is low and quiet.

He glances up, blank.

'Can I use your phone?'

I watch my words register and his expression turn to glee.

'Ha ha ha ha. I knew it!'

He wants me to ask, 'Knew what?' so he can then tell me how he saw through my holier-than-thou shit from the beginning, that he knew I was corruptible.

'I just need to send one text,' I say instead. 'How much?'

He looks away, towards the wall, and I can see that he's calculating how desperate I must be to ask him.

'Forty,' he says, finally. 'For the iPhone. Thirty for Beat the Boss.'

'Not cash,' I reply. 'I don't have anyone on the outside. I mean something on canteen. Tuna. Pop. Burn. Whatever.'

He slowly shakes his head in cartoonish astonishment at my cheek, and I realise that he's intending to barter like he's on Petticoat Lane or something. I watch him as he looks around the room, thinking, and see his gaze land on my shelf.

'Four mackerels,' he says. 'Three Cokes, a Bounty, half pack of burn.' He's itemising all the items on my shelf. Then he frowns, trying to remember. 'And garlic. And that thing beginning with T. Orange powder.'

'Turmeric,' I say, coldly. The herbs and spices – they're the ones that Deller left me – are kept in my cupboard, and by including them in his demand, Marko is letting me know that he's looked in there, and wants me to worry that he might have gone through the other stuff in there, more precious than turmeric.

'And that's for the Boss. Not the iPhone.'

'OK,' I shrug, and watch a look of disappointment pass over his face, because I've given in so easily. He's as transparent as a toddler. Arms folded, I watch him as he goes to my shelf and gathers everything up, and then into my cupboard for the garlic and turmeric and transfers them to his shelf. Then he rifles in his cupboard before coming back over to me, arm outstretched. His fist is seemingly empty, but then he opens it to reveal in his palm a two-inch-long, half-inch-wide black oblong. Beat the Boss: an all-plastic phone expressly designed to cheat the BOSS body scanner chairs when you smuggle it in. I look down at it, thinking about how it was transported here, and how it came out, before reluctantly picking it up.

The strip of cardboard with Steph's number on it is under my pillow. I surreptitiously retrieve it and turn my back on Marko as I start to text. It's the first time I've handled one of these. The phone's keypad is so minuscule, barely half an inch across, that it's almost impossible to hit only a single button. The whole exercise is so laborious that my eventual message is as short as it can be.

Rob. Not 2day. CU Mon.

I hope she doesn't think I'm a moron who can't spell. After a moment, I add

All ok.

She'll know what I'm talking about.

I send the message, although the phone is so basic there's no sign that it's successfully gone, and go back to delete it. Next, I try and delete the number itself, and I'm fumbling to find the call log when Marko plucks the phone from my hands, delicately, between two fingers.

'I want to delete the number.'

'Don't worry mate,' he says. 'I don't need to text your gash. Got enough of my own.'

He puts the phone back into his cupboard and grabs the remote before flopping back onto his bunk. I climb back onto mine. After a minute, I call down to him again. No answer, but he must have heard me, so I go on.

'Mate,' I say, to the man who is very much not my mate, 'you know when you're doing canteen . . .'

He grunts.

'When you're on B Wing, have you clocked a posh bloke? Sturridge, he's called.'

'What, posher than you?'

I give up, and pick up *The Museum of Innocence*, but only manage a few pages. The descriptions of romantic longing feel too close to the bone. Some aggressive rap starts up next door; on Marko's TV, a presenter bellows 'Now what do you think of this lounge diner?'

Our cell door is open. People pass by along the landing, a steady stream of grey tracksuits, punctuated by the occasional black and white uniform of an officer. One guy stops at the door, and I look up. I recognise him – he used to come round scratching for Deller. He's looking dejected, and his face falls even further when he sees Marko lolling on Deller's bunk.

'Oh yeah, he's gone,' he says, flatly. He turns to leave.

'All right, mate?' I call after him. He stops and half turns back.

'My appeal result, innit,' he says. 'Fucking joke.'

Amongst men who've been in here for a while, troubles are usually one of three things: their baby mama is refusing to let them see their children, their Proceeds of Crime bill has come through, or their appeal has failed.

'That's rough,' I say. I learned from my time as a Listener to say as little as possible when people are upset. People just need to vent.

'Knew it was a fucking bad idea. In the court, staring down at a year-old stain on my trouser leg, like a total mug.' I know the stain he's talking about: I have a similar one on my court clothes, and I'd guess most of the others here do too. When remand prisoners go to trial, we're held in a tiny windowless room below the court, on a too narrow bench, with not enough room to manoevure your arms. During the interminable wait, they give you your lunch – something microwaved in a plastic container – and the combination of the cramped conditions and your shaking hands means it inevitably spills on your clothes.

'I'm sorry.'

'You appeal?' he says, to me.

I shake my head.

'Wise man.'

He's right: not appealing my sentence was the best decision I've made in here. Even though I got given an IPP, and even back then there were rumblings about them being unjust. I felt I deserved my verdict, and I deserved the sentence. So it never occurred to me to do it, even though my lawyer assumed I would. And that was before I saw what it does to people, holding onto false hope, the months of waiting, the stress of being in court again, being judged, having the biggest mistake of your life rehashed – and then the devastation if the sentence is upheld. Most don't succeed. In fact, I know several men who have had their sentence increased when the judge has taken a second look.

As the guy continues to tell me about his failed appeal, I notice the TV volume increasing; Marko is pissed off we're disturbing his programme. Finally, he gets up off his bunk.

'You two can sit around talking shit,' he says, 'but I've got work to do.'

The other guy has run out of steam anyway, despondency getting the better of him. He slopes off, and I turn to Marko,

'Can I come with you? To do canteen?'

He stares at me.

'Why?'

'To get out. See some mates on B Wing.'

He smiles.

'Ah right. You want to see your posh mate.'

'No, no,' I say, lamely. 'I just . . . Just want to get out. You know.'

He squints at me, and heads for the door.

'Anyway, you can't leave the wing,' he says. 'You're not a Red Band.'

'I'll just grab a clipboard and say I'm helping you out,' I reply, following him. 'Say you're too much of a useless cunt to do it by yourself.'

It's a gamble, this sort of aggressive banter, but it seems to work. Marko shrugs and doesn't protest as we head down the landing. Maybe he secretly wants the company.

We pass along the landing and through the centre of the prison, Marko opening the door that leads onto the closed wings. While our open wing is a relatively new addition to the building, constructed in the '60s, the closed wings are part of the original Victorian structure. As we make our way into the wing, I'm taken back to the places I started out in – Wandsworth, the Scrubs. Proper dank old pits, atmospheric, but not in a good way. Within these old brick walls the air feels more condensed, you're aware of a higher density of grubby men expelling CO_2. The acoustics are also much worse, and the volume of clacking pool balls and screeching inmates hurts my ears. It seems unbearable to me now, as we pass through, but I know from experience that if I had to I'd get used to it soon enough.

It's more international here, too: as we pass down the landing, I hear Polish, Russian, and some other languages I can't identify. Most of them will be deported before they make it to open conditions.

When we arrive at B Wing, the other canteen workers are getting the boxes in from the yard under the supervision of an officer. Every Friday morning the whole prison goes into lockdown while a few trusted inmates deliver the canteen. A few trusted inmates – and Marko. He's somehow managed to become a Canteen Red Band, supposedly in charge of the whole process on this wing, so he doesn't even have to do any of the grunt work. We stand and watch as the black DHL boxes are dragged onto the ground floor of the wing and then carried up to the right landing. There's a bit of banter but because of the officers present, the men are relatively well behaved as they break open the packing boxes and unload the bags. The canteen arrives pre-sorted and in sealed bags, clear plastic sacks too big for the job in hand, the size of a spoilt kid's Christmas stocking. The delivery guys pull the bags from the boxes, squinting at the labels to ascertain which cell they are destined for, and then carry the sacks down the landings to dump the bags outside the cell doors.

All these products with their bright packets, expensively designed to entice people to choose them over dozens of competitors on the supermarket shelves, and then finishing up here, in the cells of non-consumers with no choice and twelve quid a week disposable income.

Back at Wandsworth, tins of mackerel were the main currency. In this place, it's Coke. One bag I see now contains just eighteen cans. Other orders are clearly for personal use, rather than debt repayment. Garlic and ginger and Tunnocks tea cakes. Pork scratchings. Wordsearch books. *Top Gear* Top Trumps games. Birthday cards for their mothers and children. Rosaries. Flip-flops. One sack I spot contains just a single, pathetic Snickers bar. Others are stuffed full: men who have been getting paid for work and saved up their money.

My own order is in one of those boxes, back on the open wing. It's mainly toiletries, ordered a week ago, in a more innocent time when I was beside myself about Steph and wanted to look my best. Dax Short and Neat hair cream. Dove deodorant. Even some St Ives face scrub.

When the bags have been carried to the correct cell door, it's Marko's job to deliver them to the cells. It's not hard to understand why he went for this position. Although an officer goes round unlocking the doors for the deliveries, doing the canteen is still a good gig for a thief. Marko wouldn't blatantly nick the goods before they get to their recipient – the bags are sealed and labelled, and not even a moron would just tear into them. Still, there are opportunities for sleight of hand, such as when a recipient has moved cell in between order and delivery, and so isn't there to immediately claim their stuff, which can then disappear into the ether. Not today, I hope. I don't want to get involved with any of that. Marko's going to be handing over the bags, presumably so he can get a good look at what's in them, and I'm carrying the clipboard with the prisoner lists on it, in case someone queries my presence. But the officer doesn't seem remotely bothered about me being there. Most of the screws just count the minutes until their shifts end, like a micro version of a prison sentence.

All the cell doors are locked; nobody is allowed out while canteen is being delivered. As we move down the landings, the men are lounging on their bunks, TVs blaring, or doing press-ups. They're waiting for us, and they spring to their feet as the officer unlocks the door. Marko just chucks in the canteen bag, like a jaded zoo keeper feeding his animals, and then the door is slammed shut. As he does so, he keeps up a running commentary of whingy nonsense. His latest complaint is his hay fever; his eyes are red and streaming.

'How do you get hay fever if you never go outside?' I say, which is a mistake, as he then launches into a theory about how the authorities deliberately infect the building with pollen to weaken and demoralise.

I tune him out and, as we walk, I scan the list for the information I'm after. And there it is: *Elliot Sturridge, B4-33.* He's ordered some salt and dried basil. Some Pringles decanted into a small plastic bag, rather than in their original tube, because the tube was once fashioned into an offensive weapon and so is now forbidden inside prisons. PG Tips. Pitted prunes. Rennies. Dental floss, which sparks a memory of him on the phone, telling his wife – his Lambchop – that he misses interdental brushes.

As we approach his cell, I realise I'm stiffened and tense. We stop outside. The officer opens the door and, as Marko rummages through the bags, I peer inside to see an old guy sitting on the floor, pinching the loose skin on his forearms and examining the flesh as if he's never seen it before. He glances up at me. His greasy dark hair is plastered to his forehead and his mouth opens to reveal a toothless cavern. This isn't Sturridge – or, at least, it's not the guy from the phone queue.

'Sturridge around?' I say.

He looks at me and smiles, too broadly.

'I'm alone,' he says, starting to giggle. 'But not alone. Never alone!'

I give up and instead glean what I can about Sturridge from a quick scan of the cell. Not much – even if I assume that all the stuff belongs to him rather than his mentally ill padmate. On the wall are a few photos of a dark woman and two little children, wearing woolly hats and standing on a fallen tree trunk. On the shelf some books, intellectual by the standards in here – Robert Harris, Malcolm Gladwell. Several boxes of herbal tea bags. He's neat – the J cloths are folded carefully over the sink and the duvet on his bunk is straight.

'Come on,' says the officer to me, as he and Marko move down the landing.

I follow, disappointed. I don't know exactly what I expected from coming to Sturridge's cell, but I suppose it was to get some idea of him – to make a connection, however faint, between the monster who killed Steph's son and the guy who let me go first in the phone queue.

We stop outside another cell, a few doors up. The officer opens the door; no one's in.

'Aw, your boyfriend isn't home,' says Marko, as he dumps a bag inside.

I'm confused, my mind still on Sturridge, until I glance around the cell and see familiar pictures on the wall – including a newspaper photo of Roxanna Miller walking carefully down the prison steps in high heels. Deller's cell.

We walk on, me feeling both deflated about Sturridge and mildly disturbed at forgetting Deller. Only a few days ago I was so keen to see him. He was the centre of my world.

But now my head is filled with new people – with Sturridge, and with Steph.

When we get back to the cell, I ask Marko to check his phone to see whether Steph has replied. He insists I turn my back while he rummages for it in the cupboard, as if I don't know where he hides it.

'Woooaahhh,' he cries. 'Wooaaaah!'

I look round to see him peering at the screen, giggling, eyes watery.

'So she has replied, then.'

'Fucking hell, mate,' he says. 'I'm not sure you're ready for this. It'll blow your brain. Dirty little bitch.'

The cell door is still open, and an officer passes by, glancing in as he does.

'Keep your voice down,' I hiss. 'So, can I see it?'

Marko raises his hands in a fake gesture of regret.

'Price was just for sending, not receiving.'

I stare at him, and he grins at my annoyance.

'I've got nothing left to give you,' I say, evenly. 'You've taken it all.'

'Bring me in some Piriteze when you're next on the out,' he replies. 'Hay fever's doing my nut.'

To my surprise, I find myself nodding. From the expression on Marko's face, he's pretty astonished too. I don't know – maybe I feel emboldened, knowing what's now wedged in that VHS slot at the charity shop. Compared to that, a strip of pills down my pants is nothing.

'But,' I add, reaching for the phone, 'I want to read the text now. Not wait until Monday.'

Marko gathers himself enough to insist on shaking my

hand to seal the deal before handing it over. The plastic feels moist from his palm. I squint at the message on the tiny screen.

OK.

Marko starts cackling at the prank. I'm careful to keep a neutral expression and not feed his glee.

For most men in here, probation meetings last a few minutes and happen on the hoof – on the landings, on the stairs, wherever one can find a quietish spot. The officer won't go into the man's cell, in case they're kidnapped, but anywhere else in the building is fair game. But I get a proper meeting room: a privilege of the IPP prisoner. I'm familiar with this place now. Two chairs, one stained with something that I can only hope is coffee; a chipped table, a pair of posters on the walls, one giving information on benefits and the other advertising a suicide prevention hotline. That sense of low-quality, degraded air that infects the whole place seems especially acute here. Funny that this is, in theory anyway, the most hopeful room in the place, the antechamber to freedom. You'd think that at least they'd have put up some sort of inspirational poster, like the ones you get in Chinese takeaways, with sunsets and sprinklers and kittens. Maybe the ambience is intentional, trying to prepare us for the fact that actually, things are going to be pretty bleak on the outside, too.

I haven't seen Bill, my probation officer, for several months now and when he looks up from the desk, I'm taken aback. He's lost a load of weight – his face has a yellow tinge and a caved-in look, and a hundred more wrinkles. I hope he isn't dying. He's one of the good ones.

The smell of warm, greasy pastry drifts up from a sausage roll on the desk, sitting on top of its Greggs bag.

'Rob,' he says, as if he's pleased to see me. The screws use our surnames but probation officers are civilian workers and they generally use first names. With Bill, his pallyness seems vaguely sincere. 'How's the twitching?'

The last time I saw him, we spent much of the time talking about birds. I was massively into them then – not actually watching them, of course, but reading about them – and when I mentioned it Bill revealed that he escaped with his binoculars onto Wanstead Flats whenever his work shifts allowed. That's as much personal information as you'll ever get out of a probation officer. They're trained to be opaque, in case we get our associates to threaten them on the outside.

I smile noncommittally. It's nice he remembered, and I don't want to tell him my interest has waned. He leafs through some papers on his desk. My record. On the top is my escape file: the one they turn to if I abscond, with my known addresses.

A commercial radio station is on, turned low, but I'm still distracted by the chatter of the DJ. No one seems to want quiet in this place, except for me.

'So, your end is in sight,' he says, looking at the sheet in front of him. 'Fourteenth of July. Very fitting. *Liberté, égalité, fraternité!*'

I look at him blankly.

'July the fourteenth. French Independence Day,' he explains, jovially. 'Come on, you're one of the bright ones.'

'Oh yeah. Of course.' He's right, I should have known that. Seven years in here has rinsed away my expensive education.

'Look at all these courses,' he says, leafing through my

paperwork. He gives a guttural cough, and holds up a wodge of certificates a centimetre thick. I've got copies in my cell: my prison life measured out in offender management programmes. I am accredited in controlling my anger, taking responsibility, expressing remorse, increasing my empathy, being aware of my victims. I suppose they are an achievement. The courses themselves aren't difficult to complete, but getting on to them involves waiting lists and moving from prison to prison, because not all places host them. Over the years I've felt like Pac-Man trundling around a grid, gobbling them up.

And then, late last year, when I had consumed enough, I stood in front of the three women and two men at the Parole Board and told them I was ready to be released. It's not easy convincing people that you're rehabilitated and pose no risk to society, when you're still inside. How can you prove it? You can't. So you collect these courses – CALM, ETS, ARV. Most of them are as meaningless as their acronyms, but they're necessary for getting you to release. And that's if you're lucky. Some people can't work the system to get on the courses, usually because they're mentally ill or illiterate, and they're stuck in here forever. I'm one of the rare fortunate ones.

'Right. Employment,' Bill says now, looking up from the papers. 'You already know this, I believe, but the charity shop say they don't have a position for you when you come out.'

'Oh yeah,' I reply, smoothly. But I didn't know. Maybe I should have realised the shop wouldn't have me – it was so obvious it didn't need to be stated. In any case, the news shouldn't come as a blow. It's hardly my dream job. Still, I feel surprisingly gutted. I tried really fucking hard with Carl: swallowing my irritation and boredom; counting his jigsaw pieces without complaint; absorbing his suspicion and hostility and judgement; eating those old sandwiches. I did everything except bow to him every morning.

And then I think of the spice stuffed in the VHS, and I'm seized by the notion that Carl has discovered it and that's why he doesn't want me; that the next thing Bill is going to say, in that genial voice, is 'And who can blame them? What were you thinking, you plonker?' As if that's the way a crime like that would go down – just a gentle reprimand. It's completely absurd, and the idea quickly dies away, but left behind is the hard, cold fact of those bags. This illegal act of mine that could keep me inside for many years. Could stop me from moving on from this antechamber into the light. I realise I'm sitting taller in my chair, stiff and formal, hands squeezing my kneecaps.

'So, other options,' says Bill, apparently oblivious to my new tension. 'Timpsons? You're bright, you'd have a chance there. Some opportunities at Pret, too.'

His voice betrays the fact that he knows that the chance of getting a placement at one of these well-intentioned companies is small.

'And there's always good old biohazards,' he goes on. 'You've done that here, haven't you?'

He's right, I have. Inside here, mopping up shit, blood and puke is actually considered quite a good job, and one of the higher paid ones. Outside, though, I suspect it doesn't have the same cachet.

'Or building sites,' he continues. 'You know, Brexit is going to be useful for you lot. All those Poles going home.'

When I don't respond, he continues,

'Personal training?'

This is the post-prison occupation of choice amongst my contemporaries. It's the thing they're most qualified for, after all, and it means they can work for themselves, advertising on Instagram and in newsagents' windows. No CRB checks or HR departments. And, of course, the chance to manhandle girls in their Lycra.

'Not really my bag,' I say.

'Yeah, I can see that,' he says cheerily, eyeing my thin bare arms.

I smile along, as it strikes me, not for the first time, that even those in here who care, like Bill, can only care up to a point. However much he likes me and thinks I'm different to the others, he can't have the headspace to really be concerned with what happens to me after I leave this place.

Of course, there's always the option of applying for a proper job, to aim for the same sort of life as those men trotting down the hill in the morning. Nothing to stop me doing that – except the certainty that it'd be a dead loss. Why would anyone ever hire me? I wouldn't. I'll have to declare my conviction for every job I apply for; every loan, mortgage, house rental. Even if I could afford to buy a car, I probably wouldn't get insurance. Officially I've served my time and earned my release, but my sentence will continue when I leave prison, and for the rest of my life. Because of the length of my sentence, my conviction will never be spent.

I've known all this for a long time, of course: since those weeks leading up to the trial, when I spent fourteen hours a day at my computer, researching my immediate and long-term future. But inside, in our warped, airlocked world, surrounded by people in the same boat, it's quite easy for the true picture to be obscured. When you're surrounded by chancers and blaggers and villains, you can find yourself believing that you'll be the exception to the rule, that you can buck the odds. The outside world seems so remote, it's impossible to translate your experience in here onto it. But then occasionally you get a little flash of insight into how things will really be when you're out.

'You could look into volunteering as a peer advisor,' Bill says. I look at his caved-in face as he studies my notes. 'You might be good at that. Helping others who've been inside. Advice, support, that sort of thing.'

'Look, fair play to them,' I say, 'but I want to get away from all this. Do something new. And earn.'

He nods, understanding, and then runs through a list of set questions about finances, and how I'm going to support myself when I'm out. They always go through the three risk factors for ex-offenders: employment, accommodation, and family ties. I'm not sure of the point of asking all this when they can't do anything to help. As you walk out the door they give you your £47.50 and that's that. Bill tells me about signing on and benefits, which I knew about already, and which can be summed up as: good luck. It takes six weeks to start receiving housing benefit, and you have to pay rent at the probation hostel. If you don't have family to help you out, what do you do? Sleep rough? From what I hear, that might be preferable. The hostels are notoriously grim, worse than prison by most accounts.

Bill pauses for a coughing fit.

'It says here you haven't been taking any RORs,' he says, when he's recovered. 'Why's that?'

By this stage, I'm supposed to be going out on regular overnight visits to family as part of my resettlement programme. Re-establishing family ties, impregnating my girlfriend, getting pissed on the sly. I turned it down, ostensibly because my mum lives too far away for an overnight trip and I don't have anyone nearer by to stay with. I told Bill this during our last meeting, but now I explain it again.

'What about accommodation on release?' he says. 'After the hostel.'

I look at him. This is the one place where I don't have to pretend I'm going to be reunited with Tania and live love's young dream.

'Then I'll go to my mum's,' I say. 'Persephone Prideaux.'

He raises his eyebrows. 'You'd better spell that for me.'

As I do so, I realise that I've never actually said her name out loud in here. It does sound ridiculous, like it's made up. As indeed it is – she changed her name by deed poll when she was in her twenties. I give him her address and watch him carefully write it down.

'Remind me about your mum,' he says, although the subject has never come up before. 'She employed? Live alone?'

I hesitate.

'She's not employed. I mean, she's an artist. Or she was, anyway.' I feel my cheeks getting hot. 'I think she lives alone.'

It's unclear whether this is just chit-chat or not, but always best to be careful not to give too much away, even with a relatively chilled probation officer like Bill. I feel my right leg start to jiggle under the table, and, with only that tiny warning, I start to cry.

Bill glances up and holds my gaze for a long moment, before looking back down at the table. I close my eyes and breathe, and count to ten, and try to calm down.

I've never cried in here. Not even in my darkest early weeks at Wandsworth. Not on anniversaries or at Christmas.

What was the source of this ambush? Maybe it's not just about Mum. Maybe it's about Tania. Or Steph. Or all of them. I don't know, the emotion is too dense to unpick. I know it's not just to do with my crime. I've lived with that, I know what that feeling is, how killing someone poisons your soul and turns food to shit in your mouth. This feels more abstract: just a sense of horror at the waste of it all. How quickly and easily lives can be taken or ruined, and how those who survive are like the walking dead. The victim. Tania. Mum. Steph. Regret and hopelessness are the two enemies in here – I feel like I've spent my time inside with my arms permanently outstretched in front of me, holding those feelings at bay. But now they've got to me.

Bill's kindness has its limits. He lets me heave for a couple of minutes and then gently boots me out. I walk slowly back to my landing and by the time I reach the cell, my face is dry.

Marko has clearly been awaiting my return and he springs up, sniggering, when I come in. Even the TV is off.

'There's been another one,' he says.

He holds out his Beat the Boss. Steph has texted again? I take the phone, suspicious as to why he's allowing me to read this text for free. Most likely, it's a wind-up. I cautiously scroll down, my finger vast on the tiny buttons.

He's not winding me up. There's another text from her number, sent an hour after the first one – just after I went out to the probation meeting.

One can begin so many things with a new person!

'Whooooah,' crows Marko, snatching the phone back. 'She's fucking someone else. Bad luck, mate.'

Ignoring him, I stare into the middle distance. *One can begin so many things with a new person!* It must be a quote – Steph wouldn't use 'one' in a text. No one would. And the line is ringing a bell. The words aren't so memorable in themselves, but that exclamation mark is. My guess is it's another quote from *Middlemarch*. I take the book up to my bunk and, as Marko watches *Location, Location, Location*, I skim through, eventually locating the line in the middle of part two. It's Lydgate, thinking about the possibilities of forming new relationships, of reinventing oneself. And it turns out there's more to the quote; it continues, *even begin to be a better man*. I lay the book on my chest and smile up at the ceiling, feeling swung to the top of the seesaw again.

Now I'm facing the prospect of a weekend stuck in here before I can see Steph again. There is a small release, though: on Saturday morning, just as Marko's settling down for *Saturday Kitchen*, comes the faint bellow of 'Exercise!' Marko stays put, of course, but I'm straight off my bunk and down the landing. I greet the yard as if it's glorious countryside. The rolls of barbed wire on top of every fence, wall and railing are hedgerows; the shouts and cackles of my fellow lags birdsong. Immediately I begin running, looping around the yard, past the guys doing chin-ups on the rusty outdoor gym equipment, the ones huddled in groups, doing deals and talking boastful bollocks. The air out here is warm and gritty, not fresh by any standards, but I draw it down deeply into my lungs.

In the closed prisons I've been in there were a number of fellow runners, but it's not the same here. Everyone chooses the gym, except Deller and me. And now it's just me. In all the yards I've known, the unofficial track moves clockwise around the yard, whereas I run in the other direction. I always have done, from my first weeks inside. It makes me feel that I'm on my own.

I keep going, increasing my pace, sticking close to the perimeter fence. I run the whole time we're allowed out, non-stop, like a slow whirling dervish, past the same faces, increasing my speed so those faces come round quicker. Someone in here told me that running can add years to your lifespan and it occurred to me then that my circuits of the exercise yard might eventually compensate for the seven years I've spent in here. But I don't run like this to live longer. It's my escape. For me, running feels something like freedom. I do it to rinse my mind; to blur out the past and the future, and see the present more clearly. Also, I admit, to punish myself. I'm not satisfied unless I feel the bones in my feet crunch, my hamstrings twinge.

After fifteen minutes or so, when my breathing and limbs have settled into a rhythm, I can view the Steph situation with some clarity. The path forward is obvious. On Monday, when I'm back at the shop, I'm going to retrieve the spice from the VHS, call Morris and get Steph's money back.

What was I thinking of, keeping it? I'm so close to the end. I acknowledge the possibility that a small part of me wants to get caught, because I'm scared of that end, of what will happen when I'm pushed out into the world. Sometimes in my bunk, when I'm thinking about leaving, I imagine that on the fourteenth of July they'll open the gate onto a sheer drop; like those doors you see in warehouses down by the docks in London. Or maybe it'll be like the balcony that Steph described in her flat in Driftwood House – you

199

step out onto it, expecting fresh air, but actually it's still boxed in.

I keep going, examining my thoughts, picking up speed until the faces I pass blur into one. Then I clock that someone has joined me. The only other person running anti-clockwise round the yard, and at the same pace.

Deller.

My surprise slows me right down but he keeps on running, glancing back over his shoulder and beckoning me on.

'Come on!'

I increase my speed to catch up and, when we're running in sync, we smile at each other. This is like old times. He's looking a bit fuller in the face than I remember. Or, more likely, he hasn't changed, but I've just grown accustomed to the shrivelled Marko.

'I hear you were on my wing this morning,' he says. 'Gutted I wasn't in.'

Of course, he thinks I went over there to see him. I feel a pang of guilt, as if I've been caught out cheating on him with Elliot Sturridge.

'How did you get here?' I say, meaning, out in the D Cat exercise session.

'My new friend Elsa,' he replies. 'I told her what happened, me getting moved and not saying goodbye, and then you coming over to see me but me not being in. I asked if she could get me out here.'

As we circle the yard, he tells me more about this Elsa, a new officer on his wing, fresh from training and only twenty-two years old. She's already innocently let slip that she's single, he reports, and some of the other lads are circling her. He's had to warn them off. And, of course, this makes me think of Steph's plan to come in here, and the kind of things that would be said about her when she first walked the landings.

'How's the new me?' he says.

I tell him a few stories about Marko's horrible habits, and he responds and laughs, but I realise that while it's good to talk to Deller, and he hasn't changed, being with him doesn't feel the same as it did. More distant, and less easy. Maybe it's inevitable, due to him moving on. Or maybe it's a residual effect of the probation meeting, that reminder that soon I'll be out of here while he'll remain. Before, our lives were exactly the same – running in the wrong direction together, keeping the same pace – but now there's a crack between us that is widening by the day, and soon enough we'll be in different lands, as we were before we both did what we did to get in here.

Or perhaps, I think, it's because this huge thing has happened. That's really my only news, the only thing in my head. For a moment I consider confiding in Deller about Steph – but no. The story is too involved and complicated for what remains of our exercise time and besides, even with Deller, telling is too risky. So we continue to gossip about cellmates.

'I'll have Marko,' he says. 'Jesus, the fuckers on my floor.' He tells me about a guy who licks people's faces. I smile and don't let on that he's already told me this before, in his letter. I'm panting slightly by now, but Deller isn't; somehow in the last fortnight he's become fitter than me. Then he says, 'There's this guy, posh bloke – nothing against posh blokes, you know that – but this one is a right arsehole. Got a nothing sentence for knocking over and killing a kid, and he's still bitching about it. Like he's the victim. Got a driving ban and he's whining that it doesn't start till his sentence ends.'

I realise I've slowed right down. This is the second time Deller has mentioned Sturridge; he wrote about him in his letter. I want to ask him more about the guy, but don't know how to without showing unnatural interest. And maybe there's nothing more to know. Deller appears not to notice my reaction and has happily moved onto the next subject, telling me about how he's finally managed to finish reading *Shantaram*, on my recommendation, and how he's managed to get hold of a memory stick containing the new season of *Billions*.

A whistle blows from across the yard, signalling the end of the exercise. We slow to a walk and join the pool of men heading inside. At the door, as we part ways to our respective wings, Deller slings his arm around my shoulder.

'Rob, if you've got a moment, could you send me those birthday cards? I know I'm pathetic.'

'Oh shit, sorry mate,' I reply. 'I don't have enough canteen for stamps this week. Next week. I promise.'

'Oh no,' he says. 'Forgot about the stamps. You shouldn't fork out for them. Don't worry, I'll think of something.'

Then there's a shout of 'Luke Deller, as I live and breathe!' and one of the poker lads pushes through the crowd to sling his arm over Deller's shoulder. I turn away, ready to join the trail back to the open wing, but instead I stop still for a few minutes, my head churning, processing this new information I've received. It's only when I'm the last one left outside and an officer chivvies me along that I start moving. As we head inside, I turn to him.

'How long does it take to become an officer?' I ask. 'I mean, how long's the training period, before you get to work on the landings?'

He squints at me.

'What, thinking of applying?' he says. 'They won't have you, you know.'

15

Steph

On Sunday morning I receive a brief text from Luke, telling me to expect a call later. At least I assume it's from Luke. I don't recognise the number, but that's not unusual: he has a deck of SIM cards and is always swapping them. The text puts me on edge, which is usual when Luke's involved, but especially so today because of what I have to tell him.

Liam is busy in his bedroom playing games on his tablet, sucked into another world. I try and channel my nerves into keeping busy – doing my nails; filling out another of the endless forms for another educational psychologist about Liam, which make me feel like a terrible mother for not remembering exactly when and how he started pointing as a baby; preparing for the accounts session with Tony tonight – but I'm aware of Luke's constant mental presence. Tony and Rob are there, too, in the background. Three men, circling me.

I've done my meal plan for the week. I could go to Aldi, but I don't want to risk being out when Luke calls. He doesn't like it when there's background noise or a chance of being overheard. I even consider reading. There's a copy of *Middlemarch* on the coffee table, which I haven't touched since I bought it for 99p on eBay – much easier to just look up quotes online. *One can begin so many things with a new person! Even begin to be a better man.* I wonder whether Rob's worked out where the quote comes from. I bet he has. I wonder what he thinks about it – what he's thinking about right now.

I end up cleaning the windows. The outside world looks particularly unreal today, the sky a uniform eggshell blue with no planes in sight. I feel like I'm polishing the glass of a framed photo. I go over what I'm going to say to Luke. Basically, that I'm getting the money from elsewhere, a friend's lent it to me, so we don't need to go through with the scheme. What a stroke of luck! I'm going to present this lie as positive news, maintain the façade that this whole scheme was hatched for my benefit.

He's going to be fucking furious.

Perhaps I should be telling him in person. If I'd booked ahead I could be there now, this afternoon: Sunday visiting hours are between 3 p.m. and 6 p.m. It might be safer, even easier, with other people around.

But. I think back to my last visit, the one a few months ago that started this whole thing off. For once I was alone. I usually went with Liam, but this time I begged Mum to look after him for a couple of hours, making up some excuse about Luke needing my advice on something, some problems with Roxie, and because it was her precious boy she agreed. But really, it was me who needed to talk to him.

I was early for the visit, and so I loitered in the posh café beforehand. I was saving my allowance from Tony for the visit hall, so I didn't have enough for a lattè; instead I gulped down glass after glass of that free, mint-infused water before joining the trail of relatives to the visitor centre. It was February, but the Christmas decorations in the waiting room were still up; the wonky white tinsel tree, its arms bald from many years of being tugged at by small children; a few of those springy gold decorations Sellotaped to the ceiling, giving off that distinct filmy smell and, above the desk, some Christmas cards addressed to the staff. How sad and lonely must someone be, I thought, to send a card to the staff here. The people who take your name without a hello, or even eye contact; who refuse to give you change for the locker, or make any allowances or exceptions, or show even a drop of kindness or understanding for the situation visitors are in, as if it's somehow of our own making.

Or maybe, I considered, as I sat down to wait, the senders are actually charitable and imaginative. The staff here are so obviously miserable, a product of low-level abuse and bad pay and a depressing environment, like bus drivers, that they need some cheering up. If they feel valued and appreciated, they might pass on good vibes to the visitors. If that was the case, though, it didn't appear to have worked.

Amongst the usual shower of us – quiet, sad parents, the loud wives and girlfriends and their kids – there were a couple of people who stuck out. One was a young male lawyer, pink-cheeked, clearly newly qualified and here to visit a client for the first time. He didn't know about the system, that legal visitors have to use the same lockers as the rest of us, and he hadn't got a pound coin on him. He asked the desk for change but of course they wouldn't give him any, it's against their policy, and he was getting in a real fluster, clearly thinking he was going to miss his meeting. This woman standing nearby offered him a pound coin. She was one of the posh ones. There are more and more of them around as the SFO come down heavily on boiler-room schemes. They're different, these middle-class wives. They don't dress nicely or show off their bodies; almost as if they go out of their way to look unattractive. This one was wearing a big bright jumper like a kids' TV presenter and hadn't even brushed her hair. Anyway, she offered the guy this pound coin for the locker, and he said, 'But how will I pay you back?' and she said, 'Don't worry, it's only a pound.' And at that it was like the music stopped. Her phrase reverberated around the room and everyone stared at her. Only a pound! *Only a pound!* No one else there could afford to just give away a pound like that and make such a big deal out of how it was nothing to them. She was either being insensitive, or stupid.

In the visiting hall, I sat down at the allocated table and waited for Luke to emerge from the little door that leads onto the wing, my position allowing me a restricted view of the men struggling into their baggy blue netball bibs before entering the hall. My throat tightened when I glimpsed him. Even from this distance, I could see him making a joke with the unseen officer. After we'd hugged and he sat down, I told him the story of what happened with the lawyer in the visitor centre, as a sort of ice breaker, and he threw back his head with laughter. 'Only a pound!' he repeated. I remember thinking it was a far stronger reaction than the story deserved, but at the same time I was pleased to have amused him.

'You always made me laugh, Stephie,' he said. 'You know, you're the only woman who does. Don't tell Roxie that.'

I felt myself blushing, and so suddenly nervous that I then jumped up and said I'd go and get him a cup of tea and some chocolate, even though the kiosk queue was about twenty people long, and we both knew from experience that waiting would eat up at least a third of the visit.

'Nah, nah,' he said, rising from his seat to reach my arm and pull me back down into my seat. 'I want you more than I want a Bounty.' I was conscious of his phrasing and the men at the surrounding tables glancing over at us, and I guessed what they were thinking; that maybe it was over with him and that gorgeous telly babe, and he'd already found a replacement.

But, I thought, this is just how he is with women, whether he's related to them or not. It just comes completely naturally to him. And I hadn't really appreciated it before because my previous visits had been with Liam, which was always distracting, or with Mum, who dominated things. Now, without them, I felt exposed and shy, aware that having his full attention for an hour, was a privilege but not one I really wanted, although I had purposefully come alone to ask him a favour. Even when we were kids, he was always surrounded by people: mates and, from about eleven, girlfriends. The smart ones were surface nice to me, but they all wanted the same thing – to have him to themselves.

It was a big gamble telling Luke what was happening with Tony. After all, they were best mates, as close as anything – or so I believed. I kept on putting it off and making chit-chat, but then Luke has always been perceptive, almost uncannily so, and after telling me some funny tales about life on the landings, he directly asked me how things were going at home. No one ever asked me that. I think people don't, generally, once you get married. It's like once you're locked in, it seems like a bad idea to stir things up. Also, even if people did ask, I wouldn't tell them the truth.

But now my half-brother asked me the question, and it was my cue to tell him, and then ask him the favour I'd come here for.

I started speaking, watching Luke's expression grow more thunderous as I went on. He said he felt terrible that he'd introduced us. Tony had been all right once, he said – cocky but OK. But in recent years his ego had swollen, and he'd become hard to be around.

'It's like, how he feels about something is the only thing that matters,' Luke said. 'And if he feels bad then the world should drop everything to make him feel better. He can fake that he cares about other people's feelings if it makes him look good, but he doesn't really mean it.'

This description of Tony wasn't exactly news to me, but it felt amazing to have my own feelings confirmed like that, for the first time, by someone who really knew him. Luke nodded as I told him how Tony looked different from every angle; one minute sweet and supportive, often when I least expected it, like when I was ill; then switching with no warning to contemptuous and the next moment passionate and then icy or aggressive. It was as if his behaviour was deliberately confusing and all my energy went into trying to unpick it. It's like I couldn't step back far enough to see him clearly, to get a full-length view of him.

But Luke got it – 'it's like he ties knots in your brain, isn't it?' – and I found myself telling him more and more. How Tony had basically moved out, into another flat he owned, because he couldn't stand being around Liam, but still wanted to control every aspect of my life, even down to the lighting in the flat, which he changed with his phone. How my weekly allowance had been gradually whittled down and was now just £50. All on his card; no cash allowed. How he kept a strict eye on my weight, at first noting down his too and presenting it as a joint health thing, but then gradually it just became me. How important it was to him that everyone thought he was this exciting, dynamic man and that when I tried to tell Mum the truth she wouldn't hear it, and basically told me that all relationships had their problems and that I was lucky to have him.

Luke asked whether Tony had ever hit me. I shook my head, but added that I feared it was coming. Recently, he'd started deliberately bumping into me. And then, finally, just as the hour was coming to an end, I told Luke the worst things. About how Tony treats Liam. How he calls him The Thing while Liam mutely gazes at him. How he refuses to pay for any extra help for him, because there's no point, because he's just a retard, isn't he? As I spoke, I watched Luke's face. He kept on looking off to the side, over to the next table where a family of five kids were fighting for their father's lap. His teeth were clamped over his top lip. Luke had always been very protective of Liam, even more so when he got his diagnosis.

An officer bellowed that time was up, and the visitors started getting to their feet.

'Sis, you've got to get out of there,' he said into my ear as we hugged goodbye. 'Get Liam away from him.'

It's what I wanted him to say, but I needed something else from him, too. Still pressed against his shoulder, I whispered,

'Luke, I need money. For a flat. Will you lend me some?'

At that, he'd pulled away from the hug and held me at arm's length, appraising me for a long moment, his expression unreadable, before turning and heading back to the wing.

That night he'd called me from his secret phone and without even saying hello told me straight off he wasn't going to lend me any money. Before I could react, he continued – he wasn't going to give it to me, but I could earn it by doing a little job for him. It wouldn't involve any real risk on my part, as long as I kept up the act. I had to pick up some lag working out on a day licence and convince him to bring some gear inside. Luke would then sell it and split the proceeds with me. It wouldn't be hard, he said, because he knew the target well: he could tell me exactly which buttons to press with him. What he liked in women, which books he read, how to connect with him; which sob story would most likely get an effect.

Since then, I've thought about that day. That period of time between the end of the visit and him making the call to me. When he'd sat in his cell and thought about everything I, his flesh and blood, had told him. When he knew he had enough money in his bank account, that between his ill-gotten gains and Roxie's earnings he could easily afford to lend me what I needed. But instead, he came up with this scheme. And I'm sure he doesn't see anything wrong in it – it comes so naturally to him, to turn situations to his advantage.

Yet still, despite all this, despite knowing he thinks nothing of using my desperation for his benefit, I still feel guilty about what I'm about to tell him.

Luke calls just after 2 p.m., when I'm cleaning the kitchen. He's on one of his old numbers.

'You're a goddess,' he says, straight off. 'He's completely fucking besotted with you, you know that? And who can blame him?'

'Did he talk about me?' I say, surprised.

'No, no. But I can just tell, from the way he acted. Sort of distracted and dreamy.'

I don't reply, but I cross the living room over to the winter garden, and gaze out over the cranes doing their dull, slow dance. Luke goes on,

'And I spoke to Morris. He said Rob did the deal.'

'Yeah.'

'Whatever you're doing, however you're doing it, you're killing it,' he says. 'Proud of you, darling.'

I don't speak, just press my cheek against the warm glass of the window and shut my eyes. Luke is usually good at picking up on mood, even from down a phone line, but not today.

'I got him fired up about Sturridge, too,' he continues. 'Told him he'd been boasting about killing some chav kid. He looked like he was going to throw up. Thought he was going to storm up to the landing and put Sturridge in a headlock.'

'Really,' I reply weakly. I wish he wasn't so cheerful.

'So what's happening, then? Is he going to offer to carry it in, or are you asking him?'

This is the moment. Clearly, this is the moment.

'I'm not sure yet,' I say. I look across at the building opposite, where, in the window of a flat on a similar floor to mine, I spot a tiny, indistinct figure crossing the room. The sight strengthens me, for some reason: the knowledge that I'm not the only one around. I speak again, my voice stronger.

'Look, I must tell you – this crazy thing has happened. You know my friend, Susie, up in Liverpool? You definitely met her. Petite, dark hair, dolphin tattoo on her shoulder . . . really cute.' This description is unscripted; I'm hoping that by conjuring a picture of the kind of woman he likes, I'll soften him up. 'Anyway, I was talking to her about everything with Tony, and she said that she'd had this inheritance come through, her grandad, and that she could lend me some of it. Ten grand. Enough to get me back on my feet.'

I'm hitting my stride. Luke's not the only actor in the family.

'So I don't need to get Rob to bring the stuff in!'

No reply. I can hear him breathing, and a faint background whine of drill music, I guess from a neighbouring cell. He's thinking about how to react, or using that interrogator tactic where they don't speak and wait for the other person to blab away out of nerves.

'I'll get you your money back for the gear,' I add. 'Of course.'

'Ah, OK,' he says, finally, in an even tone. 'Well, that's very nice of – what's her name again?'

'Susie,'

'What a good friend!'

'Yeah. She is.'

'Thing is, sis,' he goes on, 'people are expecting the stuff now. Not very nice people. But I can go and talk to them, explain that Susie came to the rescue and the deal's off. Hope they understand.'

He lets the silence sit for several seconds before speaking again.

'Does Tony know about all this, by the way?'

'What?' I can't hide my astonishment at the question. 'Of course not!'

'Ah, OK,' he says. 'Right. Just checking, so I know whether or not to mention it.'

'No, please don't,' I say stiffly, as if our conversation in the visit hall never happened; as if Luke didn't know about the situation at home, and that the whole point of this enterprise was for me and Liam to escape.

'No problem. Of course not. So, remind me, do you have a good lawyer? Sorry if you told me this already. This place turns your brain into dregs.'

Why is he asking me this?

'I don't think you'll qualify for legal aid, what with the properties and everything,' he continues. 'Because you're married I think his income and assets count, unfortunately – even if you can't access them yourself.'

What are you on about? I think, panic rising. But I stay quite, because, really, I know exactly what he's saying.

'If I know Tony, he'll get a good one. He's a tight fucker but when it comes to this . . . Might even go to the family division at Withers or Mishcon. Pitch for full custody. So you've got to match him. Heavyweight with heavyweight.'

'He won't go after custody of Liam,' I say, too forcefully. 'He can't stand being in the same room as him. He'll be delighted he's gone.'

'Well, maybe. You're probably right. You know him best. Thing is, he doesn't like being told what to do, does he? Likes to be the one making the decisions. Likes to win.'

That's certainly true. I keep my eyes fixed on the strip of sky. Finally, a plane has appeared, zipping across the view.

'Anyway, he wouldn't get custody,' I say, eyes on it. 'He hardly sees him. He barely knows how old he is. What time he goes to bed. What he likes for tea.'

'Yeah, true,' says my brother. 'You know what, you'll

214

probably be fine.' He pauses. 'How is Liam, by the way? You were trying to get him some speech therapy, weren't you?'

'Um, yeah. The school has stopped doing it,' I say on autopilot, feeling floaty and adrift.

'Oh, that's shit,' he says. 'Listen, I can hear a screw on the landing. Better go. I love you.'

He hangs up. I lift my hand from the window, leaving a sweaty handprint.

That evening, I'm watching Liam in the bath, still feeling jittery, when a text comes through from Luke. It's a different number; he must have swapped SIM cards. He changes them far more often than his socks.

It's a photo of the picture Liam drew for Luke for his birthday - one of his *Octonauts*-inspired underwater scenes. The photo shows it propped up on the windowsill of his cell, the inside message visible: *Lots of love from sis and Mouse.* It's accompanied by a heart emoji.

It repulses me, him using Liam to get me to do what he wants. I don't want to reply, but I find myself responding with a thumbs up and a heart emoji. Because you always reply to Luke.

16

Steph

On Monday morning, I'm standing outside the café in time to watch him emerge from the prison side road. He's with another bloke, the bulky, dead-eyed one who comes out at the same time as him. Although side by side, they're not talking. Rob is wearing a dark blue sweatshirt and jeans; I know his limited wardrobe well by now.

All morning I've been feeling solemn and nervy, full of the decision I made last night after Luke's call. As I went through my normal routine – getting Liam up, dressed, fed and off to school, acting just like normal, conscious, as always, that Tony could be watching – these resolutions ran over and over through my head, like one of those strips at the bottom of a TV news report. I am not going to rise to my brother's threats. I am not going to use his dirty money and be forever in his debt. I am going to put a stop to this mad scheme and return the gear, and give Luke back his money. I will deal with the consequences.

Of course, the consequences are major. I won't be able to escape with Liam and start a new life in some sweet little flat, far away from Nine Elms and Tony. At least, not yet. But I'll find a way. Something will happen. Maybe I'll be able to get into a hostel. It might not be too bad.

I tried my hardest to be cheerful for Liam, but I think he could tell something was up. As we walked to school along Vauxhall Bridge Road, he kept his eyes down and didn't once look up at the cranes.

So, waiting on the hill, I'm in a serious mood. But still I find myself smiling at the sight of Rob. As he approaches, I think of the last text I sent – that quote. What did he make of it?

He spots me, his expression as opaque as ever, and I watch him say a brief something to his mate before sloping off towards me. Only as he nears me, when he's close enough so I'm the only one who'd notice, is there the flicker of a smile. Half of his mouth upturned; which in his language, I've learned, is the equivalent of a bear hug. We gaze at each other for what feels like a long while, but in our timeframe, on the hill, is just a few seconds. Then we walk, starting off in silence as we usually do. I'm not carrying a coffee today; I can't afford one.

I haven't usually paid much attention to my surroundings on the hill, as I've been too focused on Rob and my mission. Today, though, I clock the hairdresser opening its shutters with a jarring clang; a man careering through the pedestrians on his bike; a pregnant woman leaning against a tree and dramatically holding her mouth as if about to be sick.

'So you got my text,' I say eventually. He nods.

'I should warn you, that's not my phone,' he adds. 'It belongs to my idiot padmate. So everything gets read by him.'

'Oh!'

217

'But funnily enough, he didn't get the *Middlemarch* reference.'

'So what,' I say, teasing, 'you're the only one in there without his own tech?'

He glances over and raises an eyebrow.

'Didn't know that term was used outside the system.'

'Oh really?' I say, feigning surprise. 'I must have heard it somewhere.'

He nods, and gives me that half smile again. I think I've got away with it. He seems in no hurry to discuss the drugs, and neither am I, actually – I think both of us are just enjoying being near each other, occasionally brushing arms or hips, exchanging glances – but I'm also excited about what I've got to say. Although he doesn't know it, and maybe never will, I'm saving him.

We're passing the furniture shop now. That weird old guy isn't there, for once; he's been replaced by a white cat curled up on a cracked plastic chair, eyes squeezed tight against the morning sun. Without thinking I stop and crouch down to stroke it. I don't look round, but I know that Rob has stopped too, waiting for me. At my touch the cat twists onto its stomach, arms and legs outstretched. I move to rub its forehead with my index finger.

'So, thanks for meeting that guy,' I say, not looking round. 'That went OK?'

'Fine,' he replies. 'He wasn't bad, as dealers go.'

'How shall I get the stuff from you? Shall I come to the shop? Try and outwit purple jumper man again? Or meet here this afternoon?'

I pause before moving on to the important part: that I'm going to return the stuff to the dealer and not go through with this stupid plan. But, before I can continue, Rob says, 'Neither.'

I twist around to look at him. He's standing close, hands in his pockets, looming very tall as he gazes down at me.

'What?'

'I mean, I'm not going to give it to you.'

With that he turns and continues walking on, leaving me frozen, my hand heavy and still on the cat's head, until the cat gets annoyed and gives me a nip. I straighten up and stare at Rob's back, those sloping shoulders, before starting after him, running until we're level again.

'What do you mean?'

He doesn't reply, just looks ahead and keeps walking.

Fuck, I think. *Fuck*. I've read him wrong all this time. Now he's got his hands on the gear, he's keeping it – like the lowlife I was sure he wasn't.

'No!' I shout. We're passing the Job Centre now, and a man waiting outside glances our way. I catch up with Rob and thump him on the shoulder, overcome with rage at the betrayal, and at my own foolishness.

Now, finally, Rob stops, turns and addresses me.

'Stop shouting,' he says, evenly, 'and listen, right? I'm not going to give you the stuff, because I don't want you to take it in.'

I stare at him.

'I won't,' I say, firmly. 'I'm not going to. I was going to say – you're right, it's a stupid idea. I'm going to give the stuff back. Forget the whole thing.'

He looks at me with a hard-to-read expression, somewhere between pity and affection.

'Look,' he says after a moment. 'I totally get it. You want revenge. Justice for little Mouse.'

I glance away. I'm ashamed that I used Liam's real nickname for this imaginary dead child. It was Luke's suggestion: he thought it would help me be emotional when talking about the crime.

'Of course you're going to try and take it in,' he continues. 'It seems worth the risk, right?'

Still looking down, I shake my head and start to protest, but he shushes me.

'So I was thinking – maybe I should take it in for you.'

Now I do stare up at him, genuinely lost for words. His face is grave and Rob-like, but then he smiles, a proper one this time. Just as the lights change, he darts across the road towards his shop.

On the tube home I stand with my face pressed into someone's corduroy jacket, eyes closed and head jammed with thoughts. Rob has offered to do what I wanted. This is what the whole plan has been leading up to. Now all that's left for me to do is find out when he's going to carry it, tell Luke, and then, assuming Rob gets it inside without being caught, the stuff will be taken off him and sold on. Then, at some point in the coming weeks, a large amount of cash will find its way to me – courtesy of one of Luke's associates on the outside, or even Roxie. And I'll be able to escape.

I should feel some sense of triumph, but I can't find it. This unexpected development has rattled my resolution to abort the plan, but not dislodged it. In fact, standing here inhaling the dusty scent of this stranger's jacket, I feel even more sure that I can't go through with it. When Luke suggested the idea, Rob was just a tool for the job; a faceless lag who'd once got in a drunken fight and ruined his life. Then I met him and he turned out to be a person; someone who had made a bad mistake, who had a temper, but who wasn't awful at all. And now he's someone who is willing to do me a favour, at huge risk to himself. No one has ever put themselves on the line for me before, or come close. Even in the early days of Tony, when he was on his best behaviour and trying to impress me, he'd book *his* favourite restaurant for my birthday. That all seems a lifetime ago now.

For Rob, of course, the plan is lose–lose. Either he gets caught at the gate and has years added onto his sentence, or he gets the stuff in, is ambushed by Luke and his cronies, and realises that the person he thought was his mate has stitched him up.

As have I.

The tube journey from Brixton only takes a few minutes, but by the time I emerge at Vauxhall I've resolved to meet Rob this afternoon and tell him everything. Who knows – he might even forgive me.

As the door to Driftwood House slides open, Abdul leaps up from his chair.

'Good morning, Mrs Winder,' he says formally. 'You have a visitor.'

I'm immediately on high alert. Abdul is never polite to me and I never get visitors, apart from Tony, who Abdul knows by name. Then Abdul gestures me over to the seating area, and I understand the reason for his odd mood. Curled up on one of those concrete-hard leather sofas, clutching her phone, is Roxie. She raises her head and gives one of her megawatt smiles.

'You!' she says.

I smile hello and watch as she uncurls and gets to her feet. She's wearing the briefest of denim shorts with unseasonal large furry boots, as if the top and bottom of her legs have read different weather reports. She's fully made up, her eyebrows thick and sharply defined, her hair as slick as oil in a high ponytail.

'I've just been doing this shoot at the power station,' she says, hugging me, 'and I was standing there sweating in this duffel coat, some guy chucking autumn leaves at me, pretending it was bloody September, I thought, aha, I know who lives near here . . .'

There's an artificial tone to her voice. She's never shown any inclination to visit me before. Besides, Roxie isn't the type to drop in on people; they come to her. Luke must have sent her.

I hear a noise, somewhere between a sigh and a groan, and realise that Abdul is still standing beside me. Abdul can't be more than twenty; the right age to be a fan of Roxie Miller, to wank over her Instagram feed in his bedroom at his parents' house.

'Let me show you up,' he says, sweeping his arm towards the lift.

'No,' I say to Roxie. 'Can we go out? For a walk? I've been cooped up all morning.'

Considering I've just walked in this is clearly untrue, but she just nods her agreement.

'Your doorman asked for a selfie,' she says, as we head out onto the street, 'and copped a feel. Hand jammed right down my arse crack, the cheeky prick.'

She doesn't sound upset; she's told me before that being manhandled in public comes with the job.

'Sorry about that,' I say. 'If it makes it better, he's never tried to feel me up.'

She smiles and cocks her head.

'Aww, darling, well you know *I* think you're gorgeous.'

Again, it's a false, awkward note. This attempt at a casual conversation isn't working. We both fall silent, and I consider where to take her – one of the chilly, soulless coffee places around here, or down to the river. The river. She obediently follows as we wind our way through the building sites, the men stopping work to stare at Roxie. A couple whip out their phones to take photos, but, surprisingly, there are no wolf whistles or comments. Builders clearly have stricter codes of conduct than doormen these days.

Our development has a small section of river frontage designated for residents only, heavily featured in the pro-motional material for the apartments but very little used. No fear of amateur paparazzi here. We sit on a bench, Battersea Power Station in the distance; the scene of Roxie's autumn shoot. The sun is high and the tide out; seagulls pick their way around the stony riverbed. There's a dank breeze. On the opposite bank, a couple with backpacks on are striding along the path, and I think of Rob and his mum, setting off on their Thames walk. Of course, they never got this far west. The drilling from the building sites competes with the roar of planes overhead as they disappear into the haze above the city. Roxie and I sit in silence for a moment, and then in a sudden, decisive movement she turns towards me and lays a hand on mine.

'Doll, I'm worried about you.'

'Luke asked you to come,' I reply.

She hesitates, then nods.

'He's worried about you, too. I hope you don't mind, but he told me what was happening. With you, and Tony, and that guy.'

'Come off it, Roxie,' I say. 'You've known for ages.'

'I haven't!' she protests, eyes wide. 'Your brother is very protective of you, you know. He loves you a lot. But he told me just now, because, well, he's worried. After your phone call. He thinks Tony has been intimidating you, or something.'

She's staring ahead now, frowning, as she continues her speech.

'I'm so proud of you, Stephie, for taking the decision to put you and Mouse first, for once. It must be so daunting, to start again. It takes real courage. But this is such an opportunity. Luke was saying, he really wants to help you out . . . You're a good person . . . you deserve happines . . . a fresh start . . .'

There's something theatrical and breathy in her voice; I feel like we're in a scene in her show, except the lines haven't been fed to her by a producer, but by Luke. I feel a surge of annoyance.

'What about you?' I interrupt.

'What?'

'You and Luke. Don't you deserve better?'

She stares at me, astonished.

'You're not serious.'

I nod. I want to derail the conversation from where I know it's headed, but I realise I'm also genuinely interested in her answer.

'He's going to spend the next decade inside,' I continue. 'You could be with anyone. Someone who'd take you out for dinner. Take out the bins. Have sex with you! You must have thought about leaving him. Having a life. You don't have children. You've got no ties.'

'Stephie,' she says gravely. 'I'm surprised you ask. It's *Luke*. Do you remember, you said that when you introduced us? "He's one in a billion."'

I wince. She's right, I did say that once – and meant it, too. It feels like hearing a voice from the grave.

'What about children? You might not want them now, but . . .'

'I'll only be thirty-three when he comes out,' she says. 'Plenty of time for all that.'

'So you've never considered ending it?'

'Never, Stephie!' Then, looking out to the water, she softens. 'Although at the beginning it was a bit of a shock, wasn't it? Do you remember visiting him at Wandsworth? That bitch squirting hairspray in my face?'

I do remember. The visitor centre always contained a gang of women getting made up before going inside. Once, one of them, clearly jealous of Roxie, turned her aerosol on her.

'And then,' she continues, 'it was so shit seeing him sitting there and not being able to have him. So yeah, I did once think about ending it. But only because it was too painful for us both. Not because I want to see other people. I honestly would rather not have sex ever again if I can't have him.'

As she speaks I look at her profile, the heavy make-up making her look like an avatar, and her words make some sort of sense: in her world, where everyone wants something from you, there must be an appeal to pledging yourself to a prisoner and taking yourself out of the game entirely.

'You deserve what I've got, Stephie,' she goes on, and her tone has changed again now, back to the script. 'Someone respectful. Who worships you. But Tony – I mean, the way he speaks to Liam! Luke told me. And the money thing.

And being so angry.' She glances around, as if to belatedly check he's not in earshot. 'I've never liked him, you know that.'

Despite the warmth of the day, I feel cold. Luke really has told her everything, despite his promises to keep it to himself.

Now she's gazing at me, head cocked, eyes huge.

'Oh darling,' she sighs. 'You so deserve a good man.'

'So Luke's a good man, is he?' I say, stiffly.

'Of course!' she replies, straightening up. 'He made some bad decisions, but that doesn't change who he is. You know that. Not like that guy, Robin,' she continues. 'Luke says he thinks you feel sorry for him, but really, Stephie – how can you?'

Robin? I'd assumed Rob's full name was Robert. It bothers me that Roxie knows something about him I don't. But I suppose there's a lot about Rob that I've just assumed, and not properly thought about.

'It was a terrible mistake, of course it was,' I say, feeling that we've now swapped roles. 'But it was self-defence. He didn't mean to kill him.'

'Him?' she says, and now she's looking at me intently, frowning as much as she's able. 'Stephie,' she says carefully, 'you know it was a woman, right? He killed his girlfriend, because she was with another bloke?'

As I gaze at her, absorbing the words, I feel my face set into a mask, like Rob's does. A plane roars overheard, horribly loud, as if about to crash.

'Yeah,' I say. 'Of course.'

I look down at my phone, as if checking the time.

'Listen, I've got to collect Liam.'

I lean over to kiss her powdered cheek and get to my feet.

226

'So, shall I tell Luke you're on, then?' she says, gazing up at me. 'With the plan, I mean?'

I return her look, giving nothing away, and then turn and walk briskly back to Driftwood House, breaking into a run when I'm out of sight. As soon as I'm inside the flat, I fetch my laptop and start to Google.

17

Rob

I've never taken anything inside before, but of course I know how it's done. We all do. There are two main options. The first is the simplest but the most risky. Wait until the right officer is on reception, stick the stuff in your pocket, cross your fingers and walk in. The right officer is one who'll barely look up from reading the sports section of his *Mirror* as he waves you through.

But even the laziest screws occasionally search – they have to do a minimum number each month. Safer, then, to time it right: to coincide with a football match, say. The world's prisons must have been flooded with contraband during the World Cup. Chelsea matches are the best. But they're rarely played at 5 p.m. on a weekday, which is when I need to get in.

A disturbance in another prison could also work. The service are so petrified of unruly behaviour spreading, and not having enough elite officers to deal with it, that a dozen screws would be diverted from our jail to keep things calm elsewhere. But again, a riot is hardly something you can count on.

And then I get my answer. On Tuesday morning, as we're passing through reception on the way out to work, we each get pulled in turn into the grotty little room beside the reception and told to urinate into a cup. A mandatory drugs test. As I give my sample, the officer's back discreetly turned, I smile to myself. It's as if fate has conspired to help me. The tests are administered at random, but the timing of the results is set in concrete: they always arrive back from the lab exactly a week later. They'll come in during the day, when we're out at work, so if someone has failed then the screws will be waiting for them on their return that evening and then will cart them off. All the officers on duty will be diverted to that task, so the chances are high that there'll be no searches that day.

And I know that Wilko, who I work out with each day, will get caught. He knows it too: he swore under his breath when the officer announced the MDT and, as he goes into the room, he's looking less cocky than I've ever seen him. He's got a week before his dealing business and Tinder dates come to an abrupt end and he's carted off back to closed conditions. His original conviction was for dealing, so they'll come down heavy on him. Being busted for the same thing as you were put inside for – they're not keen on that at all.

When he's finished we leave the reception and head out onto the street.

'Maybe nothing will come up,' I say to him, unconvincingly, as we move away from the prison gates.

'Ah, fuck it, man,' he says, as much to himself as to me. 'Better make the most of this week.' And with that, he claps me on the shoulder and sprints off around the corner. I walk on and think, well that's settled then. The spice is going in a week today.

I'm not expecting Steph. Or rather, for the first time in a fortnight, as I emerge from the side road and start down the hill, I'm not thinking about her. My mind is still on the drugs test and what it means for me. So, when I hear my name, I jump.

She's about ten feet away, standing just up from the café. Her usual spot. But even from here I can see there's something different about her. Her posture isn't as upright; her face is drawn. Even the way she said my name was different, more of a bark than a call. She's wearing an outfit I haven't seen before, a long skirt and a billowy white shirt. Her hair is loose and sunglasses are on, although it's overcast today. No coffee cup. As I walk towards her, I give her a half smile but she doesn't respond.

I reach her and we start walking. There's a fair amount of space between us today; in fact, we're as far apart as we've ever been. She seems in no hurry to speak. She looks unfamiliar, too, in that hippyish outfit, as if she's on her way to Ibiza. She seems to have given up dressing like Carol the weather woman. It crosses my mind that we've never really discussed that whole estate agent thing; if that was true or not. Those sorts of details just sort of fell away the moment I saw that letterhead in the KFC.

As we approach the furniture place, she says,

'I've been thinking about what you said. Your offer.'

Her voice is tight and formal.

'And I'd like to accept,' she continues.

I nod, as much to encourage her to keep talking as in agreement. But she lapses into silence. On we walk, her lips tight and her wolf eyes shielded from me. I start telling her about the MDT that morning and explaining why next Tuesday is a good time to bring the stuff in. I can't tell whether she's listening. For all her response, I could be talking to one of the plane trees lining the pavement. Then, as we pass the Londis, I fall silent, and she says,

'Well, whatever. Yeah, that sounds fine.'

Then, she says, just as a single word, very deliberately, 'Robin.'

I look at her. This isn't like it was before when she said my name, and a little nub of joy was detonated inside me.

'Robin Prideaux,' she continues. 'Funny that you're posh. You hide it quite well.'

I pause before replying, 'Maybe I was once. I don't know what I am any more.' I fall silent, knowing what's coming next.

'Yeah,' she adds. 'I googled you.'

We're at the lights now, and we come to a halt. Finally, she faces me. I'm pleased she has her glasses on, because I don't want to see the look in her eyes. I know my face looks immobile and stony; I hate how she must see me.

'Of course, I tried to Google you before, when I first met you,' she continues, in this new, odd, airy tone. 'But I didn't know your surname and, you know, there are a surprising number of people called Rob who punch people outside clubs. I couldn't immediately find you, so I gave up. And then, after we'd talked and I found out more about you, where you grew up, how old you are, things that I could have used maybe, I could have tried again. But I didn't. Because by then it didn't seem to matter, actually.'

I say nothing.

'But it seems you were quite selective with your story.'

I wanted you to like me, I think, but don't say. Instead, I just look at the pavement.

231

'You lied to me,' she says.

'No,' I say, finally. 'I didn't lie. But you're right. I didn't tell you the whole truth. Maybe that's the same thing.'

We stand in miserable silence for a few moments, before she spits.

'Jesus, do you really have nothing to say?'

I make myself look at her.

'All I can say is that it was a terrible, awful thing. The worst thing a person can do. Unforgivable. Like the judge said.'

She frowns, unsatisfied.

'There are things I could tell you. I could explain the circumstances, exactly what happened. Why I think it happened. But to say any of that risks sounding like I'm trying to justify what I did, or excuse it. And I don't want to do that.'

More silence from her. Her teeth are clamped over her lip – a habit that reminds me of Deller.

'I've got to go,' she says finally, her voice flat. 'And listen – I don't care when and how you get the stuff inside. As long as it gets in. Cheers.'

The lights change and she crosses the road and heads towards the tube, without glancing back.

At the shop, I say good morning, get handed another pile of jigsaws, and head to the back room. I feel nauseous and disconnected, my mind unable to settle on anything. I sit there for some time, on my nest of bin bags, staring at the blue curtain. Then, from nowhere, the memory comes to me of exchanging my T-shirt for the Stereophonics one, for Deller's birthday present – an act belonging to another, innocent age – and I'm struck with the urge to find my old top. Not just an urge – a need. I start rifling through the bags of rejected stuff, inspecting fistfuls of garments all of which seem to be the same dark blue as mine. Although it could have gone to the ragman by now, I have the strong feeling that it's still here and I can find it, by smell and touch alone. It has my scent, carries my skin cells; it's distinct from all the others. It feels of vital importance that I reclaim it, I want my smell, and with increasing urgency I find myself tearing open the bin bags, pulling out the innards and flinging them around. But because of the softness of the clothes and the plastic bin bags, my frenzy hardly makes a sound. Even though the radio is on low today, I doubt Carl can hear anything in the front.

Time is behaving oddly this morning, and by the time I find my T-shirt, at the bottom of the eighth bin bag, it feels like I've only been searching for it for a few minutes. I put on the T-shirt and somehow immediately feel able to think straight. I stand there amidst the sea of fabric and calmly look around at the objects around me. A broken cafetière. A tangle of dusty, balding feather boas. A framed poster from a Nine Inch Nails gig. A rectangular child's pencil case, the kind with lots of different compartments to open. A tower of CD cases. The VHS stuffed with spice. Then I see the plastic bag containing the volumes of *Les Misérables*, and pull one out.

I don't register the hours passing, but then the song on the radio – 'Born to Run' by Bruce Springsteen – fades away, and the lunchtime news comes on. 1 p.m. I can hear Carl out the front, on the phone, talking to head office about getting permission to purchase a table fan for the shop. I take the opportunity to head outside, hurrying past him so quickly he can barely react.

The high street doesn't seem as hectic as it once did. I'm still feeling untethered – there's a complete disconnect between what's going on in my head and the way I'm feeling physically. It's like I've put a layer of bubble wrap between myself and my shell. People pushing past don't impact me. I'm aware of the car horns, the religious nutter shouting, phones ringing, but I don't really hear them. Unreality is a sense I'm familiar with, of course, but I haven't felt it this strongly for a long time. Perhaps not even since my last few hours of freedom, when I walked around the building sites of King's Cross before handing myself in to the police.

I clocked the internet café on my first time out, in the way I clocked everything on the high street, but I never thought I'd be using it. It shares premises with a vape counter – they seem to spring up like dandelions wherever there's a spare space in a shop – and is next door to the trainer shop, so I get a waft of that horrible, new-plastic smell as I enter. There are no other customers; maybe I'm the only person in London now without a smartphone. The Somali guy in charge is watching some video and barely looks up as I hand him the pound coin and take a seat at the terminal furthest from the door. The room is stuffy and shabby, with ripped posters and the stuffing escaping from the seat pads. Prison décor.

My pound coin wasn't enough for a KFC, but it'll buy me half an hour in here. More than enough time to discover who I am out in the world; how Steph now sees me, and how everyone else will soon see me, too.

This is the first time I've been online for over seven years. I'm prepared for the search screen to look different, to fumble about clumsily, having missed many stages in the evolution of web design, but the Google home page feels immediately familiar. Maybe, I think, long-term prisoners are used by tech companies as guinea pigs to test the intuitiveness of their design. Except, of course, most of them have iPhones and are completely up to speed with the internet.

I carefully type in *Robin Prideaux*, and then, without thinking, follow it with my prison number. I don't think I've written my name without it for the past seven years. I delete the number and then press the search button. I know I appear totally calm and casual; anyone glancing in at me might think I'm looking up the TV listings.

But then I don't feel so collected any more, because the first thing I see, on the right of the screen, is a photo of Tania. I was prepared for terrible words, for bleak mugshots of me, but not this. I haven't seen the picture before but I know exactly when it was taken. I was there, watching, just out of shot. It was from when she was a bridesmaid at her mate Liza's wedding. She's standing between two others, all in shiny, thin-strapped blue dresses, smiling demurely. She was actually miserable that day. Liza had been a demanding bride and Tania hated having to wear that dress, saying it made her look huge. I suppose she was quite big compared to her friends, but mostly she never seemed to care about it: she'd wear tiny shorts and bikini tops in the summer and walk around the flat naked, completely unabashed. That was her thing, that absolute, take-me-or-leave-me confidence. But for some reason this dress really wound her up – probably because she hadn't chosen it herself and felt forced into it. I remember repeatedly telling her that day how beautiful she was, how she was the only woman on earth for me, that I'd never leave her, and when she was still upset, I remember feeling I would turn my insides out for her, if that would prove it. And I also remember thinking that perhaps it was times like this, when the usual everyday ways of expressing absolute devotion didn't seem to be hitting home, that led people to propose. And I thought, briefly, about when and how I should ask her to marry me.

I wonder when Liza gave that photo to the press. Maybe there's an interview with her somewhere, buried in Google, in which she tells how she always thought I was dodgy, how she'll never forgive me for taking away her best friend.

I turn to the next photo, a police mugshot of me, taken when I turned myself in. This I've seen before, on my files inside. I look far more than just surly; quite demonic, the lighting turning my skin yellow and with purple circles around my eyes. Or who knows, maybe I did really look like that.

Then there are other photos I haven't seen, taken outside the Old Bailey – the shots you always see in newspapers of the defendants' families walking into court, flanked by their lawyer and supportive family member. Except that it's me in the picture, wearing the suit that's now stuffed into a box in the bowels of the prison, with the curry stain on the right thigh. Mum is beside me, her arm linked with mine. My head is down; hers is raised and defiant.

The door of the shop opens and I glance up. A man sits at a nearby terminal and opens an Arabic web page. The serving guy is chatting to someone on his phone. I shut my eyes for a few seconds and then click on the first search result. A news story, published when the verdict came in, with the headline, 'One Punch Boyfriend Found Guilty'.

Consumed by jealousy and rage, he swung at the couple . . . In his summing up, the judge said, 'while the court accepts that you were provoked, and were aiming for the young man rather than Miss Schofield, it doesn't alter your intention to cause serious harm to another person, nor the devastating consequences of that punch.' Prideaux showed no emotion as the verdict was read out . . . Cheers and sobs from the public gallery . . . Sentencing next week . . .

I notice I'm dry-swallowing continuously as I read. When I finish, I go straight on to the next one, determined to read everything, until I realise that they're all essentially the same, using the same news source.

Then, further down the page, I glimpse a different headline. This one is from a broadsheet newspaper website, and is titled 'A letter to . . . my son in prison'.

I pause before clicking on it. At first I don't recognise the woman in the photo, pictured sitting in a garden, cradling a vase on her lap as if it was a newborn. Her hair is shorter than I've ever known it, and her expression is one I've never really seen before: suffering, stoical. Mum was many things, but she was never a martyr.

The article is dated four years ago. As I read, my insides retract.

My darling. Where to begin? Shall I tell you about when you were born and placed, a bloodied bundle, on my chest, and we looked deep into each other's eyes and I thought out loud: all I am, all I have, I give to you?

No. You know all about that. Let me tell you instead about another moment in our life together. A more recent one. Me, sitting alone at a numbered table in a shabby, high-ceilinged hall. I am clutching a ten pound note, growing damp in my fist. Around me are other mothers, fathers, siblings, lovers. All different creeds and colours, but united by sadness. Such noise: shouts, clattering, wails of children. Then, out of a doorway, a young man emerges, wearing a bright bib, as if he's about to join in a game of netball. More men follow. Sons. Fathers. Brothers. Friends. And then, finally, you. My son.

We hug, passionately. No words are needed, for now. You start sobbing, silently. For a moment, you weep into my neck, before the officer motions for us to separate. Me? I do not cry. My role is to comfort you. Be strong.

We talk. I make you laugh. I buy you some junk from the café and watch you, my son, who used to help me dig up Jerusalem artichokes on our vegetable patch, eating a processed chicken pie. You tell me about how the prison have offered you a place on a dry-lining course, and you seem happy about it. You, my son, who I ensured had the best education possible, even if it meant sacrificing my own dreams. I smile, not letting my true feelings be known.

Let me be clear: I don't want pity. And I don't need support. As you know, I've always been brave and lived life on my own terms – whether it was being a single mother by choice, or giving up a high-flying career to become a potter, or moving to a croft in Scotland, or, when other mothers were trying to establish Gina Ford sleep routines, taking you to festivals and dancing until sunrise with you on my back.

It is something I must come to terms with, the fact that I will miss most of your twenties because of something terrible you did. I need to give myself permission to accept that it was nothing to do with me. Not my fault. And while I do so, I will be there, for you to weep into my neck. But – whose neck do I weep into?

At the bottom of the article, a line invites readers to contribute their own letters. Those printed receive £50.

I look up from the screen and notice the other customer is staring over at me. I've clearly been making some sort of sound, although which sound I don't know.

18

Steph

After Rob and I separate at the lights, I don't cross over to the tube. Instead, I turn around and head back up the hill, away from London, the opposite direction to where I belong. I'm striding unnaturally fast, and I'm soon out of breath; by the time I reach the Londis my armpits are damp. Still, I keep on, past the furniture place and the café, as if taking part in a challenge. As I near the prison, I find myself involuntarily slowing right down. Despite my hatred for Luke, I still feel obliged to acknowledge the fact that he's inside there, a couple of hundred metres away.

I ask myself again – is there even the slightest possibility that Luke didn't know what Rob had really done, when he asked me to take part in his scheme?

No. Even if Rob had kept the facts to himself Luke would have googled him, straight away, as soon as they started sharing a cell together.

I wish I could believe Luke didn't know. That he didn't knowingly set me up with Rob, when he was fully aware that I was doing this to escape a man who looked at me like he wanted to kill me, and might well one day act on it .

As I pass the prison, I start to feel calmer, and I realise the fast walking has gone some way to dissolving the anger I felt down there, at the traffic lights. I keep going, at a normal pace now. I've never had any reason to venture this far up the hill. For those of us involved with it, the prison might as well be the end of the road. And I still don't have any reason to pass it, yet here I am now, one foot in front of the other, carrying on into deep, unfamiliar south London. After a few more minutes, I turn off the main road and head into an enclave of residential streets, turning left or right as the feeling takes me. I suppose I'm aimless, although it doesn't feel like it. More that I have an aim but I just can't name it.

I don't usually walk long distances, the shoes I wear don't allow it. Now my heels are rubbing, but still, on I go. The sun is high and the birdsong lively; at mid-morning, it's already one of those summer days when it's impossible to imagine the weather ever being less lovely than this. The streets I walk through are lined with identical small terraced houses, a mix of private and council housing. Fancy wooden shutters in the windows of some; plastic vertical blinds in others. Even the done-up ones are probably worth less than our flat in Driftwood House, but they're perfect to me; all anyone could ever need. I know with absolute certainty that were I to live in one of these houses, just me and Liam, in an anonymous residential area like this, I would be forever happy.

The pavements are populated with young mothers wearing that exhausted, preoccupied look, pushing kids in buggies, cartons of juice and rusks shoved in the bottom, a muslin draped over the hood to shield their kid from the sun. I've never been one to spend much time imagining the lives of others – my own existence seems enough to deal with – but now, as I walk, I wonder about what got them here, to living in these houses and having that baby. Whether they were born into the right families, or chose their partners carefully, or got lucky. Or perhaps they're as miserable as me, and are sticking it out. But there my imagination fails me – I can't imagine they're in as bad a situation as me.

I envy them. Those early months of Liam's life were such a time of innocence. By far the happiest of my life. I remember saying to Mum that I couldn't believe everyone could love their child as much as I loved him – not that I thought either of us were special, but because it just didn't seem possible that the world could accommodate all that strength of feeling. It would just stop operating – nothing would ever get done. I remember thinking that maybe others didn't allow themselves to give in to it, because that love came with the fear of loss. I indulged in dark thoughts of Liam dying, going through every stage from first hearing the news to the aftermath. Imagining the funeral and how I would only get through it with the knowledge that I would be killing myself shortly afterwards. I made the mistake of revealing those fears and fantasies to Tony, because despite my knowledge of him – that he's the least suicidal person on the planet, aside from Luke maybe – I assumed that, as Liam's father, he must understand. But apparently not. He laughed, and said, 'You really are mad.'

And that was in the golden days, before there was any sign of anything wrong with Mouse. Now, I honestly think Tony'd be relieved if our son died.

In that news report I read about Rob, it mentioned the mother of his dead girlfriend telling court reporters that Rob was evil and deserved to rot. Now, as I walk, I idly wonder whether my mum would react like that if Tony killed me. Actually, no need to wonder – she wouldn't. Not even if, unlike Rob, Tony had been aiming directly for me. She'd be sad and upset but still, she would excuse him, somehow. Say he was defending himself; he was provoked; he lost control. *You know what those Winders are like.* There is absolutely no way she would publicly denounce him, and defend me.

Now, I also feel certain that Luke knew exactly what he was doing by not telling me about Rob's crime. He knew I wouldn't have agreed to this, to spending all this time with Rob, if I was aware he'd killed a woman in a rage.

On I walk, deep in thought. Luke. Tony. Rob. Three men. Two officially bad – one not.

After another hour, I have to admit defeat; I can't ignore the pain in my heels any more. And anyway, I've come to a decision. At the next stop, I wait for a bus to take me back down the hill.

It's 2.30 p.m. by the time I reach the shop. The guy with the purple jumper is there, standing behind the till with his fingers pressed against the counter, poised for a sale, although there aren't any customers. His mouth is tight, he looks like he's thinking about something troubling. The Indian woman isn't there. Tina Turner is on the radio.

I browse for a few minutes, so it doesn't look too suspicious, and then pick up an orange top, holding it up and raising my eyebrows at the man to say, 'OK if I try this on?' He nods.

I step into the blue-curtained changing room, inhaling that mix of dust and old detergents that now has an odd charge for me. I can hear someone rustling around in the back.

'Rob,' I whisper. 'It's me.'

There's no reply, but the rustling stops.

'I'm sorry,' I say. 'It wasn't you I was angry with. It was someone else. Please don't take in the stuff.'

Still no reply.

Then I hear a woman's voice – tremulous and faintly excited.

'He's not here.'

Startled, I pull back the curtain. The Indian woman stands there, staring at me. She's in a sea of clothes and I see bin bags have been ripped open, like a family of foxes have been trapped in here all overnight.

'Where is he?' I ask. It's clearly too late to play dumb.

The woman shakes her head. She looks genuinely upset.

'I don't know. He went out for lunch at one, and now it's been two hours and he hasn't come back. And look at this.'

She sweeps her arm across the floor.

'We're all very concerned,' she adds. 'Carl thinks a strip of his hay fever tablets is missing, too.'

19

Rob

Several years ago, I shared a cell with a guy who had once absconded from an open prison on the south coast. He'd slipped away and spent the day sitting in a nearby pub, getting pissed, feeling the buzz of living on borrowed time, just waiting for the police to come and get him. He didn't even try and hide, or arm twist some relative to let him kip in their house, or try his luck on a ferry to Spain. He did it knowing it was only a matter of time before he was caught, and got sent back to closed conditions on an extended sentence.

He did it, he said, because he found it too frightening being in open conditions. It fucked with his head, being surrounded by drugs and living with petty criminals who didn't give a toss, and who would start a fight that meant little to them but could mean a huge setback to the lifer. He wanted to go back to closed, because he felt existence was simpler and safer there.

But the reasons most people shoot off are more basic than that. They've racked up debts for drugs and gambling and not had the means to pay them off, and so they run away to avoid retribution. Or they get in a rage and go off to beat up the man who's replaced them in their girlfriends' beds. I heard of one guy in open who called his missus and heard a man's voice in the background. This new guy taunted the con, saying, 'What are you going to do about it?' Well, what the con did was hang up and then call a mate of his on the outside, who had a motorbike. After roll call that evening, the con snuck out and was picked up outside the gates by his friend on the bike, who drove him eighty miles to his girlfriend's house on the south coast. He got in, pulled the new couple out of bed, beat up the bloke, gave his missus a smack for good measure, and then got on the bike and arrived back at the prison before morning roll call. Were it not for the mashed-up boyfriend calling the police, no one would have known about his night-time flit.

And then some men abscond for gentler motives: to see their mothers. Maybe their mum is having an operation or is on her last legs. Or they just simply have a strong need to go home. Even though it's common knowledge that your mum's is the first place the authorities will look for you, it's doesn't seem to stop men going there. In these situations, the heart usually overrides the head.

One old guy I heard of, a lifer, absconded and went to see his ill mother in her nursing home. He knew this was the first place the authorities would look for him, and he really didn't want to get caught, so he intended on staying just long enough to give her a kiss and say goodbye. When he arrived, his mother was in the middle of watching the Wimbledon final. It was the Federer and Nadal match from a decade ago. I remember watching it myself with Mum; it was just before I met Tania, and one of the last nice times we had together.

Anyway, the lifer's mother, who had dementia and didn't really understand his situation, asked him to stay and watch it with her. So he sat down beside her and held her hand and watched the tennis, even though he knew exactly what was coming to him. And so it did, long before the match was over – five armed officers charging through the care home TV room, probably hastening the deaths of her and the other residents.

It's twenty-five degrees today, according to the electronic sign outside the tube. I'm still pumped with adrenalin from travelling without a ticket, both ways. I thought I'd vault the ticket gates, but it turns out the design doesn't allow that any more, so instead I just squeezed in behind someone else and then melted into the crowd. I kept waiting for the shouts, but none came.

Beside the tube entrance is a busker on steel drums, playing a calypso version of a song I identify, after a moment of listening, as 'Red Red Wine' by UB40. I've always found the steel drums relaxing – one of my best ever neighbours inside, Lee, played calypso music and the tinkly, simple, upbeat tunes had a noticeable effect on the atmosphere of the wing. Men – not me, but others – said they imagined they were in a beach bar in Jamaica, sucking on a can of Red Stripe.

I've never seen the drums actually played before, and I find myself momentarily absorbed by the guy's precise, delicate taps on the dips in the metal bowl. It looks tremendously skilful to me, making music like this – almost like magic – and I feel a pang of regret for not continuing with the guitar at school. Just to add to my list of regrets. I wonder what my skill could be; whether I still have time to have one. I wish

I could give the guy a tip. Instead, I smile at him to signal my appreciation, but his eyes are closed as he sways to the music. I turn and walk away from the tube, back through the crowds.

Farouk is on reception. When I arrive he's staring into space, fiddling with a packet of superking cigarettes, standing the box on its long side then its short side.

'Back early,' he says to me.

'Yeah, I threw up,' I say.

He grimaces as he signs me in.

'Don't come close,' he says. 'My wife will kill me if I get laid down.'

I put my phone in my locker and walk through into the prison. Back at the cell, I find Marko scrubbing at something in the sink. It looks like some sort of clothing. Knowing what I do about his hygiene, I dread to think what would necessitate him washing, so I don't ask.

'Some of your mate's mates were here this morning,' he says, turning to me. His eyes are red and streaming, I assume from his hay fever.

'What?'

'Luke Deller. One of his heavies from down the landing came in, asking for you, banging on about some birthday cards or something. Something Deller left behind. Even started rootling around the cell, the cunt. I told him to fuck off.'

'Really,' I say, but I'm not surprised at the news; only that it's taken this long. I glance over to my bookshelf, which appears undisturbed. I hid the cards inside the pages of my books, dispersing them between the pages of my longest novels. You can't tell; they don't make a dent.

'Thank you,' I say.

Marko squints at me.

'Wha'?'

I shrug.

'Got nothing to thank *you* for, have I,' he says, rubbing his eyes.

'Actually, you do,' I say, pulling a strip of hay fever pills out of my pocket and throwing it over to him. He doesn't react in time and it hits him in the chest. As he bends down to pick it up he glances up and gives me the briefest of nods. Marko's equivalent of a thank you.

He pops two pills from the foil and swallows them without water, and then goes back to his scrubbing.

'Who was it?' I say. 'Which guy came in?'

'Dunno his name. Big. Ugly. Adidas tracksuit.'

I sigh.

'Would you recognise him if you saw him?'

'Yeah, course,' he says, offended. 'I'm not fucking blind.'

'Will you go and find him and tell him I'm here and I have what he wants?'

Marko pauses in his scrubbing. I reckon he's considering what to ask from me, and I'm prepared to give him any of my possessions, but then he drops his cloth in the sink and wipes his hands on his trousers.

'All right.'

Surprised, I watch him slide out of the door. Alone in the cell, I stay standing still, my arms braced at my side. I close my eyes and tune in to the intensity of sounds of the daytime prison. The bellows from the landing and outside; the *Bargain Hunt* theme music from the TV across the landing; further down the landing, competing music from cells: wheedling,

248

nasal R&B and stressful drill; snippets of conversation of those walking past the cell. 'You go gym?' 'My man got dat burn ting innit.' 'Listen, yeah . . .' 'You get me?'

And then, the sound of footsteps stopping outside the cell. My eyes flick open.

The guy is standing there, beside Marko. Marko is right: he is big and ugly. His name is Simpson, and he's one of Deller's old poker buddies.

'Deller needs his birthday cards back,' he says.

'I know he does,' I say. 'But I've got something he wants more.'

Simpson looks at me hard.

'What's that then?'

I shake my head.

'Tell him he needs to come here.'

'He's on B Wing, innit.'

'I'm sure he'll find a way.'

The guy, Simpson, is still staring me down, trying to intimidate me. I just stare back. Then he turns and leaves.

Marko has already switched on the TV and flopped onto his bunk. He couldn't give a toss about what's going on. How simple it must be to be Marko, I think, and not give a shit about anyone or anything that doesn't affect you.

Although what's about to happen will affect him. He just doesn't know it.

'Listen, mate, can you make yourself scarce when Deller arrives?'

He glances over, vaguely interested

'You might want to hide your tech, too,' I continue. 'Is there someone you can leave it with?'

He shakes his head. He doesn't have any friends at all.

'We going to be spun?'

I shrug, *maybe*. Although there's no doubt about it. I watch him as he takes out his two phones and tucks them down the waistband of his tracksuit bottoms before sauntering out of the room. Then I pull myself up onto my bunk to wait.

Twenty minutes later, there's a scratch at the door. Only twenty minutes to find a way to get over from a closed wing – that's pretty good going, even for Deller. I sit up and swing my legs off the bed. He's leaning against the door frame.

'Robbo!' he says, his head cocked to one side, in that way he does. 'What's happening, man?'

I nod and smile, but say nothing, and I see the subtlest shift in his expression as he reads my reaction.

'So how's it going?' he continues, walking into the cell. 'You must be demob happy. How many weeks is it now?'

'Eight,' I say.

'There's this guy on my wing, a Bulgarian, counting down his time in meals,' says Deller jovially. 'So he's on a four stretch, and he's worked out that's, like, three thousand meals. Crosses them off on a piece of paper and everything. At first I thought he was mad but it actually seems a better way than most.'

Again I nod and smile, but don't respond. Deller, ever watchful, changes tack.

'So, these cards,' he says. 'Sorry about all this hassle. I'm a sentimental fool.'

The door is open and the landing seems oddly hushed, as if the whole wing has picked up on the tension.

I move over to my bookshelf and start taking them out one by one from their book hiding places – *Middlemarch, Lonesome*

Dove, Shantaram, A Suitable Boy – then hand them over to him.

'You're a legend, thank you,' he says, as he rifles through them, apparently casually.

'Oh, wait,' I say, reaching for *The Museum of Innocence* and extracting a card from its pages. 'One more. From your sister and Mouse.'

I hand it over, looking at him steadily. This time, there's no ambiguity at all and he knows it. I watch his wonky, handsome face, a face I thought I knew so well. He returns my look, his expression changing; his mouth harder set. Now he knows that I know.

I've thought about this moment for the last few days – ever since I returned to my cell after meeting him in the yard. My suspicion was aroused by a couple of tiny things. He repeated that story about Sturridge, and that he kept going on about those birthday cards. Both of them just felt a bit off – not typical of him. You get attuned to subtle stuff in here. So I got back to the cell and had a look through them, and finally understood why he was keen to get them back.

Then, over the next day, I went through everything in my head and things started to make sense. Steph wearing the same style of dress that Carol wears to do the weather, the kind Deller knows I like. That conveniently smashed phone; asking to use mine. Claiming to have read those books. Using language like *tech*. Just to be sure I'd got it right, I borrowed Marko's iPhone to send that photo of the drawing to Steph, pretending to be Deller, to confirm it really was from her.

'What was her cut, by the way?' I say, now.

Deller opens his mouth to speak, but I realise that, for once, I'm not interested in hearing anything he has to say.

So I cut to the chase, pull back my arm and punch him. I catch him on the side of the head, a good clean hit. I had no idea how strong I am now, after seven years, but he crumples to the ground. I'd planned his fall to an extent - moving the desk and chair out of the way so there was nothing for him to hit his head on. The floor space is only just big enough to accommodate his body. He lies, one arm bent above his head, eyes closed. Then I press the call button, sit down beside him on the floor and wait for the officer, rubbing my hand.

20

Steph

I don't find out exactly what happened until late the following day. That morning, though, it was clear something was wrong. I'd gone to wait at the café, but when a trio of prisoners emerged from the side road, Rob wasn't amongst them. I watched the others run off down the hill, heading for their safety deposit boxes and their girlfriends and their coke deals.

After his disappearing act at the shop yesterday I wasn't entirely surprised that Rob didn't show, but nonetheless I felt gutted. I found myself running after one of his fellow lags, a tall rangy guy with an intricately shaved head, who I'd seen speaking to Rob once, right back at the beginning.

'Excuse me,' I said, drawing up beside him. 'You know Rob, right? Is he OK?'

He stopped to look at me, squinting.

'I seen you before,' he said.

'Yeah,' I replied. 'I'm a friend of Rob's. We – walk together sometimes. I was just . . .'

'No,' he cut me off. 'I've seen you before. In the visit hall, innit. With Luke Deller.'

I stared at him, not knowing how to reply, and found myself just turning and walking away. Maybe if I'd swallowed my shock and asked more, this guy could have told me what happened with Rob and Luke. Instead, I went home to Driftwood House and spent the day cleaning and looking out the window, trying and failing to stop the panic rising, until I broke and texted Luke.

U ok? I first try Luke's most commonly used number, and get no reply. Then I try the other one he uses, but still, after an hour, nothing. Then, I remember that he's got a new number, the one from which he sent me that photo of mine and Liam's birthday card, and so I try that. An hour later, I get a reply.

Rob swagged, followed by a smiley face with its tongue sticking out.

UR dench.

I stare at the screen, and it takes me longer than it should to understand that the sender is not my brother.

Who is this? I type.

Ur nu fella.

For a moment I think it might be Rob, but with a personality transplant. But after a few more texts, it transpires I'm talking to Rob's padmate. I can't think straight enough to speculate about why he's got Luke's phone – maybe they switched SIM cards or something.

Or rather, this guy is Rob's former padmate. Eventually I gather that Rob has been removed and taken to an undisclosed prison after punching an inmate.

I'm still trying to extract more details from this guy when I get a call from a sobbing Roxie, who fills me in on the rest. Luke is concussed, but OK. She knows for certain that it was

Rob who did it. Then my mum calls, and I deal with her hysteria, too. As she doesn't know about the Rob plan, all she's been told is that Luke was decked by someone.

I end the call with Mum, saying I have to collect Liam from school, and hurriedly leave the building. I head towards the Thames path, intending to walk along the river, but after a few minutes I discover that the path has been blocked off because of building work, so I retreat and head down the dusty, noisy main road instead as I try and work out exactly what I'm feeling.

This much I know: about Luke being hurt, I feel nothing. I'm sure both Roxie and Mum could tell that I couldn't begin to match their upset, but I don't have the energy or will to pretend to care.

As I approach Liam's school, I try to rinse my head. I've lumbered Liam with a monstrous father, I've fucked up our one hope of escape; the least I can do is give him my full attention. I'm a few minutes early to school, and as usual I avoid the other parents gathered in the playground. I can't bear their pity, as well as resenting the fact that this pity doesn't extend to inviting Liam to their kids' parties. I look through the window of the classroom to observe the children, watching Liam's classmates swap football cards, wrestle, make their clumsy attempts at connection. Liam, of course, isn't amongst them. He's in the corner, leafing through a book. Who knows if he can read or not? The teacher thinks it's possible, but I think books are just a means to hide and avoid the others, to stay locked into his safe inner world. On the walls are some of his drawings, finely detailed and shaded, in a different league to the immature, splodgy efforts of the others.

As the bell rings and the children are led out, the teacher catches my eye and beckons me over. I can't bring myself to talk to her now, to hear about today's difficulties. I mouth 'Tomorrow?' and put my arm around Liam. He's the only kid wearing a coat in this weather. He always seems to be freezing in the summer yet happy in a T-shirt at minus four.

We walk slowly back to the flat through the hot Vauxhall streets. Usually I natter away to him, asking how his day was, having a one-sided chat. But today, we're both in silence. With his hand in mine I feel stronger; more rational and determined.

I'll just have to find another way to escape. It might take a few years, but perhaps I can save up. Somehow. If I'm extra nice and pliant with Tony, he might start giving me presents again, which I can then sell on without him realising. Or maybe fate will intervene. Maybe Tony will die; have a heart attack at the gym or crash his Audi while texting his mistress.

I wonder if Tony has heard about Luke yet.

As we pass the cranes, Liam lifts up his gaze. For a minute I watch him watching them, and then I tap him on the shoulder and, when he turns to me, I sign *I love you*. In my head, I add *I'm sorry*. His gaze is solemn. His hand stays tight in mine. Maybe he's not so unhappy, I think. Maybe he doesn't notice or mind Tony's attitude towards him. Maybe if I devote myself wholly to him, that'll be enough.

We arrive back at Driftwood House. Abdul is on reception.

'Oi, something came for you when I was on shift yesterday,' he says. He rummages under the desk and heaves up a tatty plastic bag.

'This came in the post?' I say, surprised.

'No, bloke dropped it off,'

'Who?'

Abdul shrugs.

'It's definitely for me?'

'Yeah, man. He wrote the wrong surname but then he described you and it's definitely you, innit.' He points at the package and I see, scrawled directly on the plastic in small, smudged black writing, *Steph Deller, Driftwood House*.

I take the bag; it's heavy. Glancing in, I see a number of brown leather books.

'Did the guy say anything else? Any message?'

Abdul shakes his head, already turned back to his phone.

Liam presses the button for the lift. We step in and head up to our floor, me cradling the bag. Steph *Deller* – it can only be from Rob. My pulse is in my throat. I want to pull out the books and search for a message but I know there are cameras in here, and so Abdul could be watching us on the monitor at his desk.

As soon as we're inside the flat, I set Liam up on the sofa with the iPad and *Octonauts*, and take the bag into the bedroom. Tipping the books onto the bed, I pick up the first one and read the title. *Les Misérables*. I thought that was the name of a musical. Then I'm further confused, because all five books have the same title, but on closer inspection I see that each is a different volume, in French.

I don't speak French, but I can guess that *Les Misérables* isn't a laugh a minute. Is that why Rob sent it to me? Is it an elaborate way of telling me I've made him unhappy, that he wishes we'd never met? There doesn't appear to be a note in the bag, but when I upend it and shake it, a scrappy piece of cardboard falls out. On it is a message: *Google this well. R*

I fetch my laptop from the living room and, returning to sit on the bed, type in the title and the author. It's a famously long book. Could this just be a sarcastic joke? A reference to my supposed love for long novels?

But Rob wouldn't go to all the effort to get over here, just to make a dig. And – *Google this well.* That *well* implies there's something else, something I have yet to find.

It takes me unearthing my reading glasses in order to make out the tiny print on the title page, and another half hour of thinking and googling before I come to what I think must be the answer. *Les Misérables* was published in 1862, and these books were printed in 1862. That makes them first editions. And that makes them valuable. One website gives an estimate of £7,000 for a similar set; another £9,500.

I lean back against the headboard, the books scattered on the bed, and stare out of the window. The bedroom door opens and I jump; Liam enters, headphones on and holding the iPad in both hands, like it's a tray of hot drinks. He climbs onto the bed beside me and continues watching, leaning into me, immersed in his underwater world. I put my arm around him and then look back out of the window, watching those silent planes head up into the clouds, and feeling as if I've pressed my hand against the glass in the winter garden and a window has magically opened up for me.

I don't know how long we sit like that, and I don't hear the door open. Even with his headphones on, it's Liam who notices first. I follow his gaze and freeze.

Tony is standing there in the doorway, in his suit. His eyes are fixed on me; it's as if Liam doesn't register at all, as usual.

'Shame about Luke,' he says, his voice even. 'But you know all about that.'

So he's spoken to Luke, or maybe Roxie called him. In any case, I must assume he knows everything.

I notice that Liam has slid off his headphones, and they're now sitting around his shoulders. He can't understand the content of the conversation, I'm sure, but there's no mistaking Tony's voice, and the look on his face. His skin is stretched taut, a white stripe across his cheekbones, and his eyes are holes. I'm not entirely sure what's going to happen now, but whatever it is I don't want Liam to witness it. My gaze fixed on Tony, I lean down to Liam and whisper,

'Go into your room and I'll come in in a minute.'

And he seems to understand, as he picks up the iPad with both hands and stands up. But he stays like that, not moving towards the door, and then, out of nowhere, he drops the iPad to the floor and opens his mouth. The sound that follows could be described as a screech, a bellow, a scream – all I know is that it's the loudest noise that I've ever heard coming from him. Maybe from anyone.

'What the fuck?' shrieks Tony, face contorted and hands clamped to his ears. 'Stop him. Shut up!'

But Liam doesn't shut up. He continues with the same intensity, pausing only to gulp in air before starting up again. I imagine the sound passing through the triple glazing, making the cleaners in the opposite building stop in their tracks.

Tony backs out of the room.

'Fuck's sake,' he says. I hear him go into the sitting room and slam the door, leaving me and Liam in the bedroom. Still screeching, Liam now looks at me, direct eye contact, and in that instant, I realise why he's doing this and what I must now do. I grab a bag from the cupboard and shove in *Les Misérables* and the iPad, and then we leave the bedroom and head for the front door, Liam continuing to sound the alarm.

Tony will realise we've left in a moment – he may have already – and so we must get downstairs quickly. A five-minute wait for the lift might do for us. But when I jab the button the door opens immediately; the lift that Tony took up here is still waiting for us. We get in, and as soon as the doors slide shut Liam stops screaming, as abruptly as if someone had flicked a switch. Oddly calm, we go down to the basement, where I open my secret locker, collect my phone and what little cash I have, and put them in the bag with the books. Then we go back to the lift, but I put my hand over Liam's, preventing him from pressing the call button, make him look at my face, and put a finger to my lips. We wait quiet and motionless, me clutching his fingers and listening for the sound of the lift making its descent. But there's silence from the lift shaft, too. After some minutes, I'm not sure how many, I dare to press the call button. We listen to the soft clunks as the lift makes its way down and, my hands on his shoulders, I direct Liam to stand behind me and face away, out of direct range should Tony appear.

But when the doors slide apart, the lift is empty. As if this was just a routine call, collecting us from a gym workout. We step in and travel up to the ground floor, and again, as the doors open, I prepare myself for him. And again, the coast appears clear. We walk unsteadily across the marble floor, me holding our getaway bag and Liam his iPad. At the door, I turn back and glance back across the empty lobby, at those orchids, that stupid lump of wood, Abdul. All these things I'll never see again. Abdul is staring at his phone and doesn't look up.

21

Rob

Things are much quieter here. My new padmate is a Sri Lankan guy, in for some sort of smuggling. He's clean enough, and he doesn't watch Russia Today, or much TV at all. He can't speak good English and anyway, he seems to prefer to live almost entirely within himself. We coexist in near silence, communicating with smiles and gestures. At night, when he thinks I'm asleep, he sings to himself, very gently, as if he's cooing to a baby.

The cell is in better nick than the last one – half a foot wider, painted in the past year and the toilet has a screen, not just a ripped curtain. I have the bottom bunk now. My bookshelf and wall are still bare; I didn't get the chance to take my things when I was swagged. Actually, that's not true. After I punched Deller and pressed the call button it took ten minutes for an officer to arrive, and I could have packed up, but I didn't. I just sat and waited. I don't miss much of my stuff but I wish I'd brought my bird book, at least. Every morning I'm woken by a call outside the window, and I can't identify it.

Birds aside, it's quiet outside the prison fence, too. This is one of the modern, high security places, near Aylesbury but essentially in the middle of nowhere. Between us and the nearest A road are fields of luridly bright rape and a couple of small, dead villages. There isn't even a nearby bus service. The scattering of houses just beyond the prison's perimeter fence are apparently mostly occupied by officers, who I hope get some sort of credit for so completely surrendering their lives to this institution.

Inside on the landings, it's the usual chaotic shower. And despite our remoteness, we still attract attention. Just last week, a Sunday tabloid published photos of some of the men sunbathing shirtless, with the usual guff about lags living it up at the taxpayer's expense.

No one outside the authorities knows where I am, though. I'm up for assault, but internal adjudications are not made public. Because I'm on an indeterminate sentence, they're saying it will knock me back an extra three years. Stiff for a punch that didn't seriously hurt anyone, but of course, it wasn't just a normal punch. It was from a man who's been convicted of killing someone in exactly that way, and had been deemed fit to be released back into society.

I'm pleased that no one knows I'm here. One thing I've learned over the past seven years is that it's the hope that kills you – now, I won't expect any visits or letters from Mum. I'll just leave her to caress her pots in whatever bit of the countryside she's landed in now; whatever charmingly dilapidated cottage on the estate of some old school friend of hers she's managed to blag a long-term stay with. What you wouldn't guess from that mournful letter in the paper was at the time it was published she hadn't visited me for four months. And after that, there were only two more visits, before they dried up completely and she stopped answering my calls or letters.

Also, contrary to the impression she gave in that article she was the least sentimental person on the planet. She was good at shrugging off things that weren't helpful to her, that weren't exactly how she wanted them to be or which held her back in some way. I knew she'd done it to other people – she cut off her own parents eventually – but I didn't think she'd do it to me too. Despite all the mounting evidence, I just couldn't accept she'd discarded me: my hope sprang up every time I called her mobile and heard it ring, or the visiting slips were pushed under our doors. In the weird airlock of prison, emotional stuff affects you differently than in the outside world; you either under- or over-react.

I wonder whether my mother really believes what she wrote. Whether she really has blocked out what went on with her and Tania, how much she loathed her, thought she was brash and overconfident, how she made it impossible for me to have a relationship with them both. Whether she remembers that she wasn't that upset about Tania's death – implying, if not actually saying outright, that Tania had it coming for her outrageous and cruel behaviour towards me. That it was she who pressured me to plead not guilty and put Tania's family – and myself – through the trauma of the trial. I bet she doesn't. People rewrite their past, don't they, in their favour. I suppose I did, too, on my various bunks over the years. But at least when I did it, I knew it was fiction.

So, my mother is over. I still harbour a small hope, though, that one day I'll come back to my cell to find a letter from Steph lying on my bed. She'll know, from experience with Luke, that if she writes to me at the old place, it'll get forwarded on here – eventually. I'm not sure she knows my prison number, though, and if she writes without it, there's a good chance her letter will never get to me. Maybe she'll find it out somehow. It's not public knowledge, but I bet if she wanted to, she could. She's wily.

Of course, I could write to Steph at Driftwood House, but something's stopping me. I sense that a letter from me has the potential to get her into trouble. I don't know what was happening at home, but I picked up enough to know that it wasn't a happy place. If she's living with a scumbag, then a letter arriving for her from an unknown man inside, with my name and number and address on the back of the envelope, could stir up all sorts of shit.

Anyway, I hope she's not living there any more; that she figured out how to sell those books and has used the money to escape. I've been mulling over everything that has happened, reassessing every detail, and I feel sure she wouldn't have agreed to this scheme of Deller's if she didn't really have to. For whatever reason, she was desperate; as desperate as she pretended to be to avenge her imaginary child's death. I don't have to know what the real reason is to want to help her. The other night, I was lying in bed thinking about it and I wondered whether maybe this was an attempt to redeem myself for Tania. End one woman's life, but give another one the chance to start again.

Funny that I have Marko to thank for that money – all his unsolicited advice on how to spot a first edition picked up from *Antiques Road Trip* and *Bargain Hunt*. I wonder if the person who dropped those volumes into the shop, unceremonious in their Morrison's bag, knew how much they were worth.

Whether they've been walking around since buzzing with their secret generosity, or were just clearing out their dead grandmother's flat and didn't even read the title of the boring old brown books before dumping them. I suppose that, strictly speaking, I've robbed the shop of a few grand, although I would argue that Steph is a charity case. And of course I've left my own donation in the slot of the VHS. I wonder if Carl has discovered the spice yet. I bet he's delighted to be so decisively proved right about me; it's the only way I could please him.

I'm due to start yet another course next week. Whatever your definition of rehabilitation, it's clear I have some way to go. If being rehabilitated means being completely free of the rage that led to Tania's death, then I was tested, and I failed. Not because of Deller – that punch was calculated, in cold blood. Because of that incident with Steph. That moment outside Londis. I should not have still been capable of such molten rage; the place it sprang from was meant to be dormant, dried up over the past seven years.

I've also been thinking a lot about the earlier incident. No, not the 'incident' – Tania's death. The night I killed Tania. In particular, I've been reliving the things only I know – by which, I don't mean crucial information I held back, rather the things that the lawyers didn't deem important enough for court, or which I didn't think important enough to tell them. Like what I was feeling. The flesh on the bones of the facts.

How, in the weeks before, the collection of off behaviours – a gleam to her cheeks, an air of distraction and secret amusement, slipping her phone into her back pocket whenever she left the room – led me to suspect that she wasn't telling the truth that evening, when she claimed to be going over to Liza's to look at wedding photos. It would have been odd in any case – Tania had so resented being a bridesmaid for Liza, why would she then want to pore over the evidence? Tania rarely did things she didn't want to do. I'd kept quiet about my doubts, worried that voicing them would make them true. But that evening, after she'd left, I realised that because I'd bought and set up her iPhone for her, I could activate its location tracker. And so I did, and saw the phone wasn't at Liza's place in Kentish Town but at a club in Farringdon. At about ten I texted Tania asking how it was going at Liza's, and she replied that all was great, now they were in her garden getting hammered and then she would crash on her sofa. I texted back *Have fun* and told her I loved her. Then I found myself making these odd grunting noises, like I was hauling something heavy up a flight of stairs. I needed to talk to someone to dispel my panic, but I couldn't call Mum, because we hadn't spoken since I left Leeds to move in with Tania. So I tried Tania's old mate James, my colleague at the estate agency and the nearest thing I had to a friend in London. He answered and I could hear music in the background - he was clearly out for the evening but said he could talk. I told him I was worried Tania was with someone else, leaving out the part about tracking her phone. He listened patiently and said, 'Don't worry mate, I'm sure it's nothing, just some misunderstanding. Try and get some sleep.' I could hear that Rihanna song, 'Only Girl', in the background, and it made me think of Tania, as she loved it and sang it around the flat all the time.

I went back to watching the dot on the phone, staring at it like a negative meditation exercise. At 2 a.m., not being able to bear it any more, I took a cab all the way from Clapham to Smithfield. Because it was nearly closing the club wouldn't let me in, so I waited outside, pacing around and around the meat market, which had just started business, past the men in their bloody overalls heaving carcasses and amiably abusing each other, absorbing the iron smell of blood.

Then, finally, it was 3 a.m., and the clubbers began to emerge – high, damp-haired, hanging onto each other, holding scrunched empty water bottles. Waiting for cabs, heading for the bus stop, standing around deciding where to go on to. And then, there was Tania. I was surprised to see she was wearing the same jeans and vest top she had left the flat in; as if this Tania was an entirely different person to the one I thought I knew, and so should be wearing different clothes. And there, beside her, was James. He was attached to her, literally; he had one hand dug right down the back of her jeans, so casually, like they'd been connected like that all evening, his hand in her pants. I could see that she was still wearing the ring I gave her.

When I got closer to them, even before they turned to see me, I could tell they were very high, their pupils huge and skin thickened and flushed. James saw me first, pulling his head back in cartoonish surprise. Even from a few feet away, I could see the crust of coke around his nostrils. It might have been sold to them by Deller's gang.

Then Tania followed his look and screamed in shock when she saw me. That scream aggravated me. It was a habit of hers at home that when I'd open the door to the room she was in, or did anything she wasn't expecting, she would jump and say I'd scared her, making me feel I'd done something wrong when really it was her who was over-

267

reacting to perfectly normal behaviour. And here, in this circumstance, on the cobbles outside the club, I felt that was what she was doing – saying 'Oh my god, you scared me!' Making out it was my fault.

Obviously this was a very different situation, and also she was clearly extremely high, more so than I'd ever seen her before. The coke surging around her system had massively intensified the shock and adrenalin of seeing me. Her eyes were darting all over the place and she couldn't keep still, kept pacing around like a boxer.

Words were exchanged; the unfinished sentences you'd expect, the ones that were repeated in court. 'What the fuck . . .' 'Mate, I can explain . . .' 'Oh shit . . .', and then the words got angrier and angrier as the shock turned into defence. And then something was said that the court didn't hear. Two things, actually. I didn't tell my barrister, and it happened that James didn't bring it up during his evidence. I don't know whether he forgot, although I doubt it. I think he didn't mention it because it looked bad on him.

The first of these things he said to me was, 'Sorry mate, she just needed a proper shag.' And then he turned to Tania – 'Don't you, darling?' And she hadn't replied, just stared at me, wild-eyed, still in shock. And then a little while later, James added, 'Maybe you can marry your mum instead.'

It was after that that I swung at them. I was aiming for James, but that's because it was he who was taunting me. Such was the state I was in, maybe I'd have aimed for Tania if she'd been the one speaking. At that point, I wasn't really differentiating between them – they had fused into one terrible betrayal. But, of course, I hit Tania anyway. Jittery, unable to keep still, she had ducked in front of James.

So, I suppose I did hold something back in court, those two things James said, and they may possibly have helped me in my claim of provocation. I suppose they were embarrassing: if they'd been aired and dissected in court, everyone would know I was a virgin before Tania, and I'd been known as a mummy's boy. But that wasn't why I didn't mention them. The reason was I didn't want to be helped. I didn't want my case to be strengthened.

I know some people believe that if you do something like I did, then you have to spend the rest of your time on earth atoning for it. Not just in prison; I mean, even when you're released. Well, I think I'm with them.

During my time here, staring at the ceiling, I've wondered whether that punch to Deller was the one I meant to deliver to James. Maybe I was replaying the incident as it should have gone. If, in Smithfield, my fist had landed on James, the chances are he wouldn't have fallen and knocked his head on the kerb. He was bigger than Tania, and he was squaring up to me, prepared to get hit. I might have got GBH, but it's also possible that James wouldn't have pressed charges, accepting a scrap was his due for stealing my girlfriend.

But I can admit, too, that my decision to hit Deller also came from another place. During those final months in open, I got a glimpse of what my life would be like on the outside. Not just the practical stuff, like lack of money and jobs and accommodation, but who I am out there. The person I am outside. Someone not even fit to volunteer at a charity shop.

Inside, though, I'm not a bad person. And I can be useful in here, probably more so than I can be outside; especially if I start Listening again. Inside, no one judges me. It turns out I'm actually given a bit of respect for punching Deller; a few people in here have had dealings with him in the past. I haven't told them why I hit him, but they all automatically assumed he'd fucked me over somehow. I wonder if I'll meet anyone over the next three years here who I trust enough to tell them the whole story. They probably wouldn't believe it, they'd think I was just bullshitting or embellishing, as we all do.

I try not to think about Deller too often, though. Despite everything, his betrayal still hurts. I don't want to spend my nights reliving all the nice times we had together, knowing he was plotting this, wondering at which point he decided to do it. It's like trying to work out when exactly Tania lost interest in me and when James made his move, despite them both knowing what I sacrificed for her, and her having just accepted my proposal. It's a certain path to madness.

So whenever I find my thoughts drifting towards Deller, I try and divert them to the safer place of Sturridge. The silent player in it all. I'd call him the innocent party, but that's an inappropriate phrase in our circumstances. Does he have any idea about any of this? My guess is not, and he's still worrying about his BMW's MOT, with no idea how he was used. My best guess is that Deller bumped into him, or heard about this new guy in on a careless driving charge, and then when his plan for me started coming together, decided to use Sturridge as the bait. I wonder if Sturridge was really texting his mistress when he killed the kid, or whether that was a Deller embellishment. I suspect it was Deller. He would have googled me and read the stories about the trial, and knew about James and Tania's affair.

Anyway. Sturridge might be a grade-one arsehole, or he might be a perfectly decent but unlucky man. In any case, he'll be out soon and his comfortable life will start up again, this unfortunate period of his life just a little blip, soon to be converted into an anecdote, and eventually consigned to history.

Obviously I'm pleading guilty to this adjudication. If I get three years, then I'll have been inside for a decade. I'll be thirty when I finally come out. Who knows, maybe life will begin then.

In this place the resident barber is a guy called Nikesh, who lives four cells down. In return for three cans of tuna, he's just given me a nice neat fade. It usually costs two, he explained, but there's always more demand now we're coming up to Christmas.

'Yeah, we all want to look nice for the family,' I replied, which was a statement of the obvious. I realised I'd said it because I wanted him to know that I'm getting a visit too.

Here, there's no dedicated visit hall – visits take place in the canteen. As I stand in line for my bib, I nod hello to a few of the other guys waiting. I wouldn't say I have good friends but now, after six months, I know a lot of them. Here, inmates are taken into the hall before the visitors are brought in, rather than the other way round, so after we head in and sit down, I have time to look around and try to see the room through her eyes. There's a sign on the wall advertising the results of a *Great British Bake Off* -inspired cake competition a few months back. The Christmas decorations have been up since November, and one half of a paperchain has come loose from the ceiling and is dangling free in the middle of the room. The servers are busy preparing the hot food for the visitors – lowering burgers into the fryer, tipping baked beans into the metal dishes – and trying to look nonchalant in their hairnets.

I sit there, my knee jiggling under the table, and watch as the door at the far end of the hall opens and visitors trail in. Mostly women with kids. Some of them barrel headlong towards their men; others skulk in and just nod a greeting before herding the kids to join the food queue. At the table next to me is Philby, a nasty piece of work who lives on my landing. He tells me he's being visited by his missus and points her out as she enters, looking very done up, pushing a buggy. When she spots him she starts half-running towards him, awkward in her heels, and then hugs him for a long moment. When he pulls away, he notices that a smear of her makeup has transferred onto his T-shirt.

'What the fuck,' he says, genuinely pissed off. 'Be careful, eh.'

As her smile drops I look away, back to the door.

The trail of visitors are thinning out now and I'm starting to worry that she's changed her mind, or that she's stuck in a traffic jam on the M40. It really is a long way here from Shropshire. But no – here she is, one of the last in before the officers shut the door. She's wearing a fluffy white fake-fur coat, and her hair is in those Coke-can sized curls. A boy is holding onto her hand, as solemn and silent as a Victorian child. Finally, the famous Mouse. I rise up out of my seat, hands stuffed in my tracksuit pockets, and she returns my smile as they weave around the tables towards me.

Author's note

One of my aims with this novel was to accurately portray the daily life of a prisoner nearing the end of a long sentence. The prison system is opaque, so I was lucky to have a source on hand to answer questions and check for authenticity. However, he had never been at Brixton Prison and regimes vary from place to place, so some details are down to educated guesswork. I have also taken liberties with the geography of the area. Although inspired by Brixton, the story could be set in any urban prison where offenders are allowed out.

Acknowledgements

Huge thanks to those who made this book happen: my editor James Gurbutt and my agent Antony Topping; Olivia Hutchings, Hayley Camis and Celeste Ward-Best at Corsair; Steve Gove; and all at Greene and Heaton.

Chris Atkins gave extensive and invaluable guidance, as did my mother Deborah Moggach. I'm also grateful to Joe Maloney and Marc Conway, and to Mike Paterson of London Historians, who organised the visit to Brixton Prison that sparked the idea.

Love and thanks, as ever, to Sathnam Sanghera, Susannah Price, Alex O'Connell, Tom Moggach and Larushka Ivan-Zadeh. And, of course, to Horatio Mortimer, the person I'd want in my cell.